RL: 5.3

Pts: 10.0

THE CREATURE DEPARTMENT

THE CREATURE DEPARTMENT

By Robert Paul Weston

razOr
bill

An Imprint of Penguin Group (USA)

razOr
bill

A division of Penguin Young Readers Group
Published by the Penguin Group
Penguin Group (USA) LLC
345 Hudson Street
New York, New York 10014

USA / Canada / UK / Ireland / Australia / New Zealand / India / South Africa / China
Penguin.com
A Penguin Random House Company

ISBN: 978-1-59514-685-4

Printed in the United States of America

3 5 7 9 10 8 6 4 2

FOR MACHIKO

CHAPTER 1

In which Elliot doesn't want to go to Foodie School, and Leslie would rather be in Paris

lliot von Doppler, you come down here right now or I swear, I'll boil you in soup and serve you to your father!"

Elliot pulled the covers over his head. This soup ultimatum was the third such threat in the last five minutes (his mother had also promised to flash-fry one of his kidneys and pickle his fingers in vinegar).

Of course, it is important to stress that Elliot von Doppler's parents had never eaten anyone, nor did they intend to. They weren't cannibals. They were food critics.

Peter and Marjorie von Doppler edited the Food section of the *Bickleburgh Bugle*. Together, they wrote a daily column called "Chew on This," offering reviews of local restaurants. Occasionally, they even went on tasting trips across the country and around the world. In short, they had haute cuisine on the brain (even when they were trying to get their son out of bed in the morning).

"I'm not kidding, Elliot. You know how much your father likes a good borscht!"

Elliot groaned.

"I'm going to count to three, young man. After that, I'm coming up there to drown you in hollandaise sauce."

(Don't worry, Elliot's mother would never do this. In fact, she doesn't know how to make hollandaise sauce. In spite of their jobs, both Elliot's parents are terrible chefs.)

"*One!*"

Elliot rolled out of bed and dressed himself. He put on shorts and a T-shirt, topping them off (as always) with a bright green fishing vest.

"*Two!*"

Elliot reached for his most prized possession: an original DENKi-3000 Electric Pencil with Retractable Telescopic Lens. It had been a gift from his uncle Archie, and it was an antique. The electric pencil was the first product DENKi-3000 ever produced.

"*THREE!* That's it, young man. I'm sending your father up there with a garlic press."

"I'm coming!" Elliot called back. He slunk down the stairs to the kitchen and saw breakfast was on the table. Soggy boiled tomatoes and burnt toast.

"We spent a lot of time on this breakfast," his father informed him. He sat at the head of the table, the morning's *Bickleburgh Bugle* in his hands. "So I don't want to hear any complaints."

"Have a seat," said Elliot's mother, eyeing him carefully. "Tell us what you think."

Elliot did his best to moisten the blackened, rock-hard toast with the juice of the tomatoes. It didn't help.

He was halfway through eating (more like forcing down) his breakfast when he noticed an envelope sitting in the middle of the table.

It had his name on it.

"What's that?"

"Your uncle stopped by on the way to work this morning," his mother told him.

"*What?* He was here?" Elliot was astonished.

His mother nodded ruefully. "He vanishes for weeks on end, *as usual*, and then—POOF!—he shows up looking for you."

"*Me?*" Now Elliot was *even more* astonished. Uncle Archie practically lived at DENKi-3000 headquarters. The company's unusual buildings were just on the other side of Bickleburgh Park, but Uncle Archie never "stopped by," not for anything. He was famous for missing birthdays, Christmases, soccer games...all the usual stuff. "Why didn't you wake me up?"

"I have enough trouble getting you up at the *regular* time. Anyway, he left you that note."

Elliot (happily) gave up on his breakfast and tore open the envelope. Inside was a brief, hastily jotted letter.

Dear Elliot,

For years, you've been asking me for a tour of the company, but I've always been too busy. With the way things are going, though, I've decided that now is the time. Why don't you stop by today and I'll show you around.

Yours truly,

Uncle Archie

PS: You'd better bring your friend, Leslie, too.

Elliot squinted at the letter, his mouth hanging open.

"What does it say?" asked his father.

"Uncle Archie wants to give me a tour—*today*."

Perhaps noting his bewildered expression, his mother asked, "Shouldn't you be happy about that?"

"I am, but . . ."

"But what?"

"But *who's* Leslie?"

"I'm not sure I follow," said his mother.

"Look," said Elliot, pointing to the bottom of the letter. "It says, 'PS: You'd better bring your friend, Leslie, too.'"

"Nice of him to invite her as well," said his father from

behind his newspaper.

"But *I don't have* a friend named Leslie." Elliot didn't want to admit it, but he didn't have many friends at all (or any).

"Wait," said his mother. "Isn't that the name of the girl from the science fair?"

"*Leslie Fang?*"

"Of course," said his mother. "That must be who he means."

"It can't be," said Elliot. He hardly knew Leslie Fang. She had arrived only a couple months before school let out for the summer, so there wasn't time for *anyone* to make friends with her. "Why would he want me to bring her along? We're not even in the same class."

It was true. The only reason Elliot knew Leslie was because they had tied for third place in the Bickleburgh City Science Fair. (They had both designed nearly identical model rocket ships, which was kind of embarrassing, even if you ended up tying for third place.)

His mother thought about the question for a moment. "I often see that girl on my way to work, just sitting all by herself in the park. She's been there nearly every day since school let out for summer, and to be honest, she looks quite lonely. Maybe Uncle Archie noticed the same thing."

Elliot slumped in his chair. He didn't much like the idea of sharing his uncle with someone else, but what could he do? Leslie Fang was the only Leslie he knew, and there was *no way* he was going to pass up a once-in-a-lifetime tour of DENKi-3000.

"Fine," he mumbled. "I'll ask her. *If* I see her. Can I go now?"

"Not until you finish your breakfast," said his father.

"*And* give us your review," added his mother.

Elliot looked glumly down at his plate. He pushed some black crumbs across a puddle of tomato juice. Struggling to gulp down the rest of the meal, his eyes wandered to the front page of the newspaper in his father's hands.

There was a large photograph of the DENKi-3000 head-quarters. Spanning across it was a headline:

Technology Giant to Close Its Doors?

Elliot choked on a mouthful of breakfast (which wasn't hard to do at all). "*Close its doors?*" he spluttered. "As in shut down?"

His father nodded. "That's probably why Uncle Archie is finally giving you a tour. It's now or never."

"What does that mean?"

"There's another company," his father explained. "Some big investment firm. They're gonna buy the whole thing. People expect them to move the headquarters overseas."

"But . . ." Elliot couldn't believe what he was hearing. "What will happen to Uncle Archie?"

"Hard to say," said Elliot's mother. "Nobody really knows."

Elliot stared at the newspaper. In the bottom corner of the majestic image of DENKi-3000 was an inset photo of a very old man. He had shaggy gray hair and a thick gray beard and he was dressed in a brown cardigan and circular, gold-rimmed spectacles. The caption below the old man said: *Sir William Sniffledon, DENKi-3000's longtime CEO, admits serious financial difficulty.*

It was odd to think this old man, who looked more like a doddering librarian, was the high-powered CEO of a company as big as DENKi-3000. Elliot's eyes moved to the first few lines of the article:

> The head office of DENKi-3000, the fifth-largest technology producer in the world and one of Bickleburgh's largest employers, could be set to close its doors in a matter of months.
>
> Following a year of less-than-stellar profits, the company seems ripe for acquisition by Quazicom Holdings, a private capital investment firm. DENKi-3000 CEO Sir William Sniffledon said, "It would be a sad day for Bickleburgh if . . .

Elliot returned his eyes to the photograph. The DENKi-3000 buildings were the most interesting things in the city: four glass towers climbing up from a vast oval of land. In spite of having an uncle who was head of the company's Research and Development Department, Elliot had never set foot inside the heavily secured gates.

He pushed his plate away, finally finished. "If Uncle Archie invited me, I'd better not keep him waiting."

"Not so fast, mister." His father pointed to the red-and-black mash drizzling across his plate. "Not until we get our review."

"Do I have to?"

All his parents cared about was *describing* food. Was it really so crazy to just want to eat it?

"How are you going to get into Foodie School if you don't start practicing?" asked his father.

"What if I don't want to go to Foodie School?"

"Don't you want to grow up to be a famous food critic, like your parents?"

"Maybe I'd rather be more like Uncle Archie."

"I'm not sure he's someone you want to emulate." His mother glanced at the newspaper.

Elliot, of course, had no intention of becoming a famous food critic. However, he knew if he wanted to see his uncle, he would first have to appease his parents.

"So?" asked his mother.

"Be as descriptive as possible," said his father.

Both of them leaned anxiously across the table.

"Well . . . it was . . ." Elliot struggled to find the words. "Crunchy. And wet."

His father frowned. "That'll *never* get you into Foodie School."

"Can I go now?"

"I suppose," said his mother, a little reluctantly. "Say hi to your uncle for us."

Whenever her mother moved them to a new city, Leslie Fang sought out the best places to be alone. Here, in this sorry excuse for a *real* city, the best place she had found was a secluded and relatively comfortable wooden bench in Bickleburgh Park. It wasn't that she particularly enjoyed being by herself (she liked making friends as much as anyone), but what was the point when you knew your mom would probably pull up digs and move away at the drop of a hat?

It was the same every time. Her mother would break up with a boyfriend or get bored of her job and—WHAMMO—"*Load up the rusty red Volkswagen, Leslie, 'cuz we're hitting the road!*"

It was better to hang out by yourself, Leslie thought. It just made sense. Fewer people to say goodbye to.

Besides, Bickleburgh wasn't Leslie's kind of town. She preferred the New Yorks, the Londons, the Parises of the world. *Definitely* not the Bickleburghs. The only reason they came was because Leslie's grandfather ran a restaurant in Bickleburgh's Chinatown. He had promised to give Leslie's mother a job as a waitress and he even said there were spare rooms for them in an apartment above the kitchen.

Leslie looked down at her black T-shirt, her black wrist-bands, her poofy black dress, her black tights, and her black saddle shoes. She was proud of the outfit. She had been going for a *leave-me-alone-'cuz-I'm-leaving-any-minute* goth look— and she had nailed it perfectly.

Or so she thought.

If her outfit screamed *leave me alone*, why was that kid from the science fair walking straight toward her?

"Uh, hi. Leslie?" He was speaking more to the ground than to Leslie herself. "What's going on?"

"It's Elliot, right?"

"You know my name?"

"Of course I do. You copied my rocket in the science fair."

Elliot snapped his eyes up at her. "*Hey!* That was just a coincidence."

Leslie sighed. "Yeah, I guess. But it was kind of embar-rassing, don't you think?"

"You're telling me."

Tying for third place, however, wasn't the only reason Leslie knew Elliot's name. What made him *most* memorable was that every day, no matter what outfit he was wearing underneath, he always completed the look with that ridiculous green fishing vest.

At first, Leslie had admired the fashion statement he seemed to be making. *Leave-me-alone-'cuz-I-bob-to-the-beat-of-my-own-fishing-boat.* She respected that. But *every day*?

Leslie leaned forward on the bench. "You ever think one of us might have won? Y'know, if there hadn't been *two* model rockets entered?"

"Maybe."

Elliot was silent for a moment. Leslie thought he might be considering the fact that one of them might have won the science fair if only they hadn't had to share the limelight. But no, Elliot was thinking of something else.

He pointed to the dense forest on the far side of the park. "I'm, uh . . . going to visit my uncle."

"Good for you. Does he live in the woods?"

"*No!* I mean on the *other side*. He works at DENKi-3000."

Leslie's train of thought—which had previously been chugging toward a way to get rid of Elliot—suddenly derailed. "DENKi-3000?" she asked. "Your uncle works there?"

Elliot nodded proudly. "He's head of research and development."

Leslie had wondered what went on in those crazy buildings. They were the only things in Bickleburgh that were remotely interesting (not to mention the only buildings that looked like they belonged in a *real* city).

Her grandfather made regular deliveries to the place, but he never let her come along for the ride, even though she had asked several times. Why had a big company like DENKi-3000 chosen to build its world headquarters in a place like this?

"Anyway," said Elliot, suddenly looking very anxious. "My uncle's going to give me a tour and, well . . ."

"A tour," said Leslie. "That's cool." She was trying very hard not to be jealous *or* to burst out with a bunch of exuberant questions. "Maybe my grandpa knows him."

Again, Elliot's eyes snapped up to meet Leslie's. "Is he an inventor too?"

"Sort of," she said. "He's a chef."

Elliot squinted at her. "Does that count as an inventor?"

"Experiments. Inventions. Steamed rice balls. It's all chemistry, right?"

"I guess."

"He runs a dim sum restaurant. Maybe you've heard of it. Famous Freddy's Dim Sum Emporium?"

Elliot winced. "I don't think he's as famous as he thinks."

Leslie rolled her eyes. "It's just his nickname."

"I'll bet my parents have heard of him. They're all about food."

Leslie wasn't surprised Elliot had never heard of the restaurant. It was empty most of the time. Nearly all the orders were for takeout or delivery. It meant her mother hardly did anything but stand around, reading magazines.

Any day now, Leslie thought, her mother would get bored and the whole thing would start all over again. This was precisely why it was pointless to make friends, even if the potential friend had an uncle who worked at a cool place like DENKi-3000.

Even still, she couldn't help admitting, "It's a pretty cool-looking building, isn't it?"

Elliot smiled. "I can't believe my uncle *finally* invited me for a tour!"

Leslie dug the toe of her saddle shoe into the dirt, twisting it a little. "I've kinda always wondered what it's like in there myself."

"Well, actually . . ." Elliot's smile faded and he was suddenly nervous again. "That's sort of why I came over to talk to you."

"Because . . ." Leslie couldn't see the connection.

"I have no idea why, but my uncle invited us both."

CHAPTER 2

In which the professor reveals "where the magic happens"

From the street, the headquarters of DENKi-3000 looked like four uneven buildings. The impression that they were separate, however, was an illusion. The bases of the four towers swept down to join a single ring-shaped building that formed the perimeter of the company grounds.

Seen from above, the offices resembled an enormous circular compass, with the four cardinal points rising from its edge. The north tower was the tallest. With the addition of a slender white radio antenna sprouting from its roof, it soared above the rest.

When Elliot and Leslie went through the revolving doors at the entrance, glowing letters appeared on the glass, almost as if by magic:

Welcome to DENKi-3000
Inventors of the wireless breath mint!

Leslie gazed around wide-eyed as they came through the doors into the glittering glass lobby. "Wireless breath mints? They invented those?"

"That was my uncle's team! His department was the first to discover information had flavor. It meant you could download freshness direct from the web."

Elliot's uncle was waiting for them at the security desk.

"Elliot, hello!" he greeted his nephew, a broad smile on his face. "So glad you're finally getting your tour!" He turned his attention to Leslie. "And so glad you could bring your friend along."

"You two know each other?" Elliot asked.

"I know Leslie's grandfather, the very famous Famous Freddy."

"Is he really that famous?" asked Elliot.

"Around here he is," said his uncle. "Isn't that right, Leslie?"

"I guess. You guys certainly order a lot of his food."

Leslie thought Professor von Doppler was surprisingly handsome—at least for the uncle of a dorky kid in a green fishing vest. On the other hand, there was something very *Elliot-like* about him. He was tall and thin, his lanky limbs swathed in a rumpled lab coat. On his head was a shock of wild brown hair that swept up and away from sharp, determined features.

"Pleased to meet you, Professor." Leslie put out her arm and the two of them shook hands.

Elliot's uncle asked the security guard at the desk for two visitor's badges. "As long as you have these in your pocket," he said, handing them the identification, "you can come and visit me whenever you like." He glanced at the security guard. "Isn't that right, Carl?"

Carl, the security guard behind the desk, was a plump,

jolly-faced man with a quick smile that was all dimples. "Of course," he said. He turned to Leslie. "If it wasn't for Professor von Doppler and his R&D guys, I doubt DENKi-3000 would exist at all."

"Carl is the company's head of security," Elliot's uncle explained, "but he still comes out here to work the front desk."

Carl shrugged. "I've always been a hands-on kind of guy."

"I could say the same thing about myself," the professor agreed.

Carl chuckled, beaming another one of his bright smiles. "I suppose that's why, even though we're in pretty different lines of work, we still get along so well."

Elliot's uncle nodded thoughtfully. "Maybe so." He turned to Leslie and Elliot. "Now then, I'll bet you two are anxious to see the sights. Let's go." He turned and led them out of the huge lobby.

Leslie grabbed hold of Elliot's arm and whispered, "I can't believe how cool your uncle is!"

Elliot smiled. He wasn't accustomed to being associated with "cool" things.

His uncle led them down a long, curving hallway. It was the inner corridor of the circular building that formed the base of DENKi-3000 headquarters. The glass wall looked in on a huge courtyard, full of pathways and gardens.

Elliot's uncle stopped. "Here we are."

"Here we are—*where*?" asked Elliot. They were standing in the middle of the empty corridor, seemingly with nowhere to go.

"*Right here.*"

Professor von Doppler stepped closer to the glass wall, and sensing his presence, it split into two separate sections, which floated apart as if by magic.

Elliot gasped. "I never would've known that was there."

His uncle winked at him. "Keep an eye out. This place is full of surprises—and I don't mean only the doorways." He stepped outside into the open air. "My department's on the far side of the courtyard."

Glass and steel towers rose up high above them, all connected by shimmering skywalks. Inside each one, important-looking men and women hovered up and down on escalators tilted at all angles.

"This place. Is. Incredible," Leslie breathed. And it was: DENKi-3000 was everything she imagined it would be. Gleaming. Futuristic. *Amazing!*

Similar thoughts were filling Elliot's head. But they were overshadowed by another: *Why why why did my uncle wait so long to invite me?!*

It wasn't just the glittering towers above them that were impressive; it was also the courtyard itself. It resembled a fairy-tale labyrinth. Cobblestone paths wove around fountains and huge topiary sculptures of dragons and rocket ships.

"Amazing!" Leslie cried.

They came around a towering hedge trimmed into the shape of an elephant bathing itself and were faced by a building completely different from everything else. It was so different, neither Elliot nor Leslie noticed it—at least not at first. They were both too busy gaping up at the glass and steel above them.

"This way," said Professor von Doppler, drifting toward

the anomalous building. "This is my department."

Elliot and Leslie lowered their eyes and saw it: a rambling, crumbling, lopsided mansion that bristled with eaves and gables, pillars and porches, turrets and towers. The walls were built from faded red and orange brick, while the cracked gutters and shingles were a pale green color, like aging moss.

Anywhere else, it would have been the largest, most interesting building on the block. But here, compared with the rest of DENKi-3000, it looked like the company's toolshed.

"Are you kidding?" said Leslie, realizing where Elliot's uncle was leading them. "It looks like a haunted house."

"Is that really where you work?" Elliot asked, a bit disappointed.

"Of course," said his uncle. "Just look at the sign."

Elliot stared at the words in disbelief:

DENKi-3000
RESEARCH AND DEVELOPMENT

"Why is it so old?"

"Not just old," said Professor von Doppler, "the *oldest* building in the entire company."

"You'd think they could fix it up a little bit," said Leslie.

"Even if the CEO, Sir William himself, wanted to give this place a makeover, he couldn't change a single brick. It says so in the original DENKi-3000 charter, written when the company was founded: No one can ever alter the Research and Development Department. In fact, the only person who's allowed in and out is the acting chief of R&D—meaning yours truly." The professor took a small bow.

"What about us?" asked Elliot.

His uncle laughed. "Don't worry, you're my guests." He turned toward the building. "Shall we begin the tour?"

"I guess," said Elliot, his eyes scanning the front of the building. "Except for one thing . . ."

Leslie saw it too. "There's no door."

It was true. Everything about the mansion looked normal, everything was in place—the windows, the pillars, the veranda, the gables—but there were no doors. The building had no entrance.

Again, the professor chuckled, leading them up the steps to what appeared to be a solid brick wall. "As I just explained, the one person allowed to come and go"—he approached the wall and, just like the glass in the corridor, the bricks creaked magically open—"is me."

"Amazing!" Leslie whispered.

Stepping through the doors was like falling backward through a time warp. Lying heavily over everything was the musty, dried-out smell of age. Even so, the interior of the old mansion wasn't as dilapidated as it appeared from the outside.

Every surface in the large foyer was hewn from warm, brightly polished wood. The high ceilings were hung with chandeliers that cast flickering light on the walls, over the mantels, and across carpets woven with flowery, interlocking patterns. The inside of the mansion was luxurious, but it was a faded, outmoded luxury. It was like a gorgeous old car just beginning to rust.

"I don't get it," said Elliot. "I mean, it looks nice and every-thing, but it's just a big old house. Where's all the science? All the inventions? All the, y'know—*research and development?*"

The professor frowned. He seemed disappointed he hadn't impressed his nephew. "Perhaps I'd better show you my office," he said hopefully, leading them deeper into the house.

They arrived at a door labeled with a brass plaque:

Professor Archimedes von Doppler
Chief of Research and Development

Elliot expected to see something new in his uncle's office—a large, modern room with banks of flashing computers or tables packed with prototypes for strange inventions—but when the professor opened the door, what greeted them was a small, drab office with a cramped desk and a few wooden cabinets.

Elliot's uncle sat down behind the desk and spread his arms. *"And this,"* he said, "is where the magic happens."

Elliot and Leslie looked at each other.

"I don't get it," said Leslie. She was glaring at the carpet, her eyes darting back and forth, as if she were trying to figure something out. "It doesn't make sense."

Elliot agreed. "It's a huge old house, but it's empty. You're the only one here."

"Are you sure about that?" There was an odd twinkle in his uncle's eye. "The tour isn't over yet, you know."

"Oh, I get it," said Elliot. "There're more secret doors—*and secret passages*—like the one that got us in here." He moved around his uncle's desk to a simple wooden filing cabinet. "I'll bet there's one right behind here. . . ."

Elliot's uncle jumped up from his chair. "Don't touch that!"

Elliot froze and backed away from the cabinet.

"Thank you." His uncle smoothed his lab coat and sank back into his chair. "I understand you're very curious, but you have to be patient. There're a few things I want to explain before we go any further. After all, a private tour of the DENKi-3000 Research and Development Department isn't something that happens every day."

"You're telling me," said Elliot.

"*Ahem.* As I was saying, my decision to give you both a tour today is no coincidence. DENKi-3000 is in trouble and we need to take steps to—"

"Elliot's right," said Leslie. She was still staring at the carpet, still looking confused. "There *has to be* more to this place."

"If you'll just give me a moment to finish, I'll be able to—"

"It's impossible!" Leslie cut in. She was scrutinizing the professor, particularly his stomach.

Elliot had the distinct impression she was talking about something only she understood.

"What do you mean, *impossible*?" The professor squinted at her.

"It can't just be you in here," Leslie answered. "Look at you. You're a stick man! There's *no way* you could eat all that food!"

Now Elliot was even more confused than before. "What are you talking about?"

"The deliveries!" said Leslie. "Remember I told you about my grandpa, Famous Freddy, from Famous Freddy Fang's Dim Sum Emporium?"

"The chef."

"Yes! He makes big deliveries here—*huge deliveries*—almost every day. If it wasn't for the Research and Development Department at DENKi-3000, we'd be completely out of business."

"That's what I've been trying to tell you," said Elliot's uncle. "The reason I brought you here is—"

"Now I remember!" Leslie snapped her fingers. She leaned across the professor's desk, a deeply inquisitive look on her face. "Tell me, Professor von Doppler, what exactly are you keeping behind that door at the end of the hall?"

The professor's face froze. "What?"

"Second-to-last door on the left, I believe."

"Wait. How do you know about that?"

"Famous Freddy told me."

"Do you seriously call him that?" asked Elliot.

Leslie shrugged. "Sometimes."

"Let her finish," said the professor.

"One time we were cooking up all these crates of food and I just couldn't believe it was all for a single order. My grandpa said, 'Oh, sure! You'd *never believe* what they have in that weird old place at DENKi-3000.' By 'weird old place,' he obviously meant *this* weird old place." She glanced around the professor's office. "'It's all behind that door at the end of the hall,' he said, 'Second to last on the left.'"

The professor frowned. "Wonderful. So he completely ruined the surprise."

"What surprise?" asked Elliot. "Could someone please tell me what we're talking about?"

His uncle, however, was too busy stroking his chin thoughtfully. "I think I'll have to have a little chat with the very famous Famous Freddy. He swore he'd never tell anyone the secret of the Research and Development Department."

"What secret?" asked Elliot.

"He didn't tell anyone else, did he?" Suddenly, the professor looked very worried. "Who knows what could happen if word got out."

Leslie shook her head. "I don't think so. It's just that sometimes, when he's working in the kitchen, my grandpa drinks a little too much cooking wine and then he says all sorts of weird stuff, but most of it's nonsense. The only thing he told me about this place is that I'd never believe what's behind the second-to-last door on the left."

"Hm . . ." The professor was still stroking his chin. "So perhaps he *didn't* ruin the surprise after all."

Elliot stomped his foot on the carpet. "WHAT SURPRISE?!"

Finally, his uncle looked at him.

"Maybe it's best if I simply show you." The professor opened a drawer and took out an enormous key ring, jiggling with a hundred keys of different shapes and sizes.

They left the professor's office in silence, and he led them down the corridor to the second-to-last door on the left. Two faint letters were embossed on its brass plaque:

CD

The professor chose the correct key, a small one with a sparkling green emerald on the handle. With one slow revolution, he freed the dead bolt and pushed open the door.

"In here," he whispered, "is where the magic *really* happens."

CHAPTER 3

In which Jean-Remy sees doomed love
where there isn't any and Gügor demonstrates the
fine art of rickum ruckery

The door opened onto a huge room filled with banks of flashing computers and a sea of laboratory tables.

Each one was topped with the strangest of things: elaborate chemistry sets that fizzled and popped with colorful fluids; whirring machinery that reminded Elliot of the most complicated clocks—only ticking much faster than time itself; screens like old, half-assembled televisions, broadcasting images that seemed to come from another world.

This is more like it. That was Elliot's first thought. This was just sort of scene he expected to see in a Research and Development Department.

But it wasn't *the room* that stunned Elliot and Leslie the most. It was the people.

Except that they *weren't* people. They were . . .

Creatures.

Stooped, troll-like creatures with jutting jaws and broken teeth. Tiny winged things, part insect, part pixie, that sparkled as they flew. Huge, hulking, hairy *un*-humans (with horns).

Creatures with too many heads, too many arms, too many tails, or just the right number of tentacles.

There were things that looked like dragons, ogres, gremlins, and—well, things that defied comparison with any storybook beast. Strange, outlandish creatures who pondered down at their strange, outlandish contraptions and strange, outlandish experiments (often through comically tiny spectacles).

"Welcome," said Elliot's uncle, "to the Creature Department."

Leslie and Elliot were too shocked to respond. They could only stand and stare as the activity subsided and, very slowly, every strange, otherworldly eye in the room swiveled to face them.

"Everyone," Professor von Doppler announced. "This is my nephew, Elliot, and his friend, Leslie. They're the ones I told you about!"

There was a variety of reactions. Some of the creatures smiled sheepishly and waved. Others narrowed their eyes suspiciously. Many of them took very little notice at all.

"Is it just me?" asked Leslie. "Or does this laboratory seem . . . I don't know . . . a bit too big?" She looked behind them, out into the corridor that led back toward the entrance.

Elliot agreed. The laboratory was the size of a massive warehouse, big enough to stretch out to the street (or even past it). "I was thinking the same thing. This one room is bigger than the whole mansion. *I think*. How is that—"

"Possible?" asked his uncle. "Simple. This old place was built by creature architects, using creature physics. It's quite different from the math we humans use, so the building has quite a few, let's say, *unusual* features. Laboratories that are bigger on the inside than the outside, for instance. But don't worry, once you get to know the place, it won't seem so topsy-turvy."

Elliot noticed a shiver of movement, up near the scaffolds suspended from the ceiling. The shape appeared to be a bird, a large black raven, perched on one of the railings.

When it spread its wings, however, Elliot saw there was nothing bird-like about it. For one, the wings had no feathers. They were the wings of a bat, yet the skin stretched across them was oddly luminescent, shining with the foggy gleam of a pearl.

The creature—whatever it was—launched itself into the air and swooped straight for them.

Leslie gasped. "What is that?!"

"Not to worry," said the professor, "it's only Jean-Remy, one of my assistants."

It wasn't a raven gliding toward them, it was a tiny man, no taller than the distance from Elliot's elbow to the tips of his fingers. The flying man's skin was ghostly pale and stood out in sharp contrast to the black three-piece suit he wore. Of course, calling him a man—as in "human being"—wasn't quite right (human beings were a lot taller, for one, and very few of them had wings).

"*Bonjour, mon ami,*" the little man greeted the professor in French. "Who is zis? Visitors are so rare in ze Creature Department!"

"This is my nephew, Elliot," said the professor. "And this is Leslie."

"Ah!" cried the little man. "You have a nephew!" He swooped to Elliot's face for a closer look at the boy. "You may call me *Jean-Remy de la grande famille Chevalier*! Or, if you prefer, just 'Jean-Remy.'"

The man's face was deathly white, with dark, mournful eyes, a wild shock of black hair, and an upturned nose that made him appear slightly ghoulish. Yet in spite of all this, Elliot had to admit he was oddly handsome.

"Nice to meet you," said Leslie, raising her hand.

Jean-Remy Chevalier flapped away from Elliot and fluttered down to Leslie's side. He reached out with one hand, as if to shake, but since he was so small, he could only properly grasp the tip of Leslie's thumb. Nevertheless, he held it confidently and gave her fingernail a gentle kiss.

"Enchanté, mademoiselle!"

Leslie giggled in a way Elliot had never heard from her before. He felt himself standing up a little straighter. "She's a friend of mine," he said. "From school."

"You have chosen well, *mon ami*," said Jean-Remy to Elliot. "I believe she will make you very happy."

"Um . . . what are you talking about?"

Jean-Remy waved his tiny hand dismissively. "Please, there is no need to be so coy. I am a Frenchman, after all, and so I know a fiancée when I see one."

"F-f-f-fiancée?!" Elliot stumbled backward as he said the word.

"Hold on there, buddy," said Leslie (she would die before she married someone in a green fishing vest). "In case you hadn't noticed, we're only twelve!"

"Ah! *Bien sûr*. I see zis now. You are much too young for such things."

"You'll have to excuse Jean-Remy," the professor told them. "He's a fairy-bat. Wherever he looks, he sees . . . you know, *doomed love*."

"Hey!" said Leslie, pointing at Jean-Remy. "Are you saying I'm doomed?"

"Oh, *non non non*! It is simply zat I am half ze fairy, half ze *vampire*!" He shrugged. "It is not what zey call a traditional coupling, you see? Ze families of my parents? *Non non non*, zey did not approve. And so, ze doomed love, it is—quite literally—in my blood." He waggled a tiny finger between Elliot and Leslie. "But you two—*non*! You are not doomed. Zat is obvious, *non*? You are made for each other!"

Leslie looked sideways at Elliot's fishing vest. "Maybe it's better to be doomed."

"Um, speaking of blood," said Elliot nervously. "Did you just say *vampire*?"

"Please, do not be alarmed." Jean-Remy swept one arm from his elegant shoulders to his elegant waist. "I inherited only my father's impeccable dress sense and *none* of his unfortunate bloodlust."

"Lucky for us," said Leslie.

"Jean-Remy is one of our best engineers," said the professor, possibly to steer the subject away from vampirism.

"I have ze very tiny hands, you see?" Jean-Remy held them up and wriggled his fingers. "It makes me very good with ze . . . how do you say . . . *ze fiddly bits*!" He proved this by taking a tiny ID badge out of his breast pocket. It featured a dashing photo of his face, along with his job title:

Jean-Remy Chevalier
Chief of Fiddly Bitology

"Come on," said Elliot's uncle. "I'll introduce you to the rest of my team." He turned to a large pink blob of gelatin with three stumpy legs and said, "Have you seen Gügor?"

The blob of jelly quivered and jiggled and made a noise like someone blowing bubbles into a bowl of custard.

"Of course," said the professor. He pointed to a large steel door, all painted bright red, on the far wall. "In the Rickum Ruckem Room?"

The blob burbled some more.

"Thanks," said the professor.

"The *where*?" asked Elliot. What his uncle had said sounded more like a tongue twister than an actual place.

As his uncle led the way to the red door, he tried to explain. "You know when you put your money in a vending machine, but the drink doesn't come out? Sometimes, the only way to get it working properly is to give it a good swift kick. That's what the Rickum Ruckem Room is for."

When they arrived at the red door, Professor von Doppler was just about to swipe his ID card through the reader when he stopped.

"Maybe you guys had better stand back."

Elliot and Leslie each took one giant step backward, while Jean-Remy flapped upward, hovering above their heads.

Professor von Doppler swiped his ID card and the red door opened instantly. They were all greeted by the crashing and banging of metal, combined with what sounded like the snorts and groans of a wild animal going berserk.

"Excuse me, Gügor?" The professor spoke politely into the room. "I was wondering if—"

He ducked suddenly as a huge metal pipe came sailing out of the room, only narrowly missing his head. It crash-landed onto a chemistry experiment being conducted by a pair of gremlin-like creatures over on the far side of the room.

"Gügor! Cut it out!" the professor shouted. "Can't you see the door's open?!"

The growls and screeches of tearing metal halted abruptly.

"Sorry, Professor," came a slow, methodical voice from

within the Rickum Ruckem Room. "Gügor did not realize you were standing there. Is everybody okay?"

The professor nodded. "I came to introduce you to my nephew and his friend. They've come for a visit."

Elliot and Leslie peered into the Rickum Ruckem Room. What they saw was a creature that resembled a muscly eight-foot salamander—if salamanders grew sloppy dreadlocks, walked around on their hind legs, and had enormous knobbly hands.

The creature's skin was a light brown color, sprinkled all over with black and gray freckles. His face wore a slightly empty expression. Some might call it an expression of "child-like innocence," but it could easily have passed for extreme dopeyness. Elliot could just make out the creature's DENKi-3000 ID badge:

Gügor the Knucklecrumpler
Chief of Rickum Ruckery

The creature's face was oddly calm. In fact, with its eyes half closed and its flat, expressionless mouth, it looked half asleep. Elliot had difficulty connecting this tranquil behemoth with the incredible wreckage strewn across the floor. Wires and cables, cogs and chains, transistors and circuitry boards, disembodied levers and smashed buttons—the stuff was lying everywhere!

"Did you get it working this time, Gügor?" asked the professor.

"Almost," said Gügor regretfully. He took a long, slow look around at the electromechanical carnage. "Sorry, Professor, Gügor will try harder next time."

The professor patted Gügor's arm reassuringly. "I just hope we get a next time."

"What was it you were trying to make?" asked Elliot.

"It would have been a great success!" cried Jean-Remy. "It would have provided for ze dematerialization of matter, ze sending of zis matter through space, and at last ze *re*-materialization of ze matter—*in perfect condition*! Amazing, *non?*"

Leslie narrowed her eyes. "Is he saying what I think he's saying?"

The professor nodded. "A teleportation device. Unfortunately, so far we've only got as far as teleporting hair. See?" He pointed to one of the tables. Heaped on top of it was a pile of fur the size of a small car. Some of it was in unnaturally bright colors—pinks and blues and glowing greens.

Elliot wondered if they had been testing the machine on punk rockers, but he realized the source of the hair was the creatures themselves. He noticed several of them had oddly shaped bald patches on their arms and backs.

"Teleportation has always been a very personal project for us," the professor explained. "Because, believe it or not, not all creatures are as nice—or as clever—as the ones we have here in the Creature Department. There are certain creatures out there that are, let us say, *best avoided*. A reliable teleportation unit would help us avoid them entirely."

Elliot couldn't help but shiver. "What sort of creatures?"

"In my experience," said the professor, lowering his voice, "the very worst ones are called—"

"*WAAAAAH!*" cried a nearby creature, one who looked like a chocolate doughnut with arms and legs. He seemed to be covering his ears (or at least where his ears should have been).

"All right, all right," said the professor in a reassuring voice. "We won't mention them. But trust me," he said to Leslie and Elliot, "a teleporter would certainly help my creature colleagues come and go without being found."

"You mean they're hiding?" asked Leslie. "Here in the Creature Department?"

"In a way, yes. In fact, that's how most of the creatures' inventions began, as ways to keep the Creature Department a secret."

"Like a door that doesn't exist," Elliot suggested.

"Precisely!" His uncle looked to Jean-Remy, still perched on Elliot's shoulder. "Now then, why don't you help Gügor clean up the mess? I'll take Elliot and Leslie to meet the others."

Jean-Remy bowed. "Of course. As always, I am at ze service of my fellow creatures." Elliot felt a breath of wind ruffle his hair as the suave fairy-bat flapped toward the Rickum Ruckem Room. Before vanishing through the doorway, he called out, "Do not worry, Professor, ze next time we build a machine such as zis, *it will work*. I am sure of it!"

The professor nodded hopefully. He led Elliot and Leslie up metal stairs to the scaffolds above.

"So let me get this straight," said Leslie as they reached an unmarked office door. "All the crazy things DENKi-3000 has ever produced . . . *were invented by them*?" She pointed down at the creatures below.

"That's right," said the professor, "and nobody knows about it except me."

"And us," Elliot corrected.

"And Grandpa Freddy," Leslie added.

"Mm, yes," Professor von Doppler grumbled. He stopped at a door where one scaffolded platform met another. When he opened it, Leslie and Elliot saw something even weirder than anything else they had seen so far.

CHAPTER 4

In which Harrumphrey has an idea, Patti drips on the floor, and something explodes

The creature standing inside was all head. Well, *mostly* head (and what a head it was!). This was the enlarged noggin of a fairy-tale troll: leathery skin, beady eyes, wild hair sprouting in every direction, a bushy beard streaked black and brown and gray, and a big bulbous nose, upon which was perched a pair of dainty pince-nez glasses.

The head was so big, in fact, it came all the way up to Elliot's waist, and the whole thing (the whole head, that is) was attached directly to the creature's feet. The creature had no arms, only two fat yellow horns. They curved upward on either side of its head, while from behind, stretching out from the base of its enormous cranium, was a long furry tail. It curled up and waved at Elliot's uncle.

Perhaps odder still was the *very peculiar hat* the creature was wearing.

It looked like an umbrella crossed with an accordion: The umbrella-like tip pointed upward, while under the canopy was the zigzagging fabric of an accordion's bellows. The whole apparatus opened and closed of its own accord, as if it were breathing slowly. A thick rubber tube extended from the top to a humming mainframe computer in the corner of the room.

"Leslie, Elliot," said the professor, "I'd like you to meet Harrumphrey Grouseman, our resident genius."

Harrumphrey couldn't resist embellishing on the compliment, speaking in a voice that was raspy and gruff. "I have a degree in abstractional physics from the CCC. That'd be the Continental College of Creaturedom."

Neither Elliot nor Leslie had any clue what that meant, but it sounded impressive enough.

"Pleased to meet you," said Elliot. He didn't put out his hand to shake (of course), but he did notice the ID badge pinned to the creature's beard:

Harrumphrey Grouseman
Right-Hand Head

"Harry," said the professor, "this is my nephew and his friend, Leslie."

"Pleasure's all mine," said Harrumphrey.

"Can I just ask," said Leslie, "what's with the hat?"

(Elliot had wanted to pose the very same question.)

"You've never seen a cerebellows before?"

They shook their heads.

Harrumphrey glanced up at the umbrella-like awning as it flapped open above his ample forehead. "It's a—well, y'know . . . *a cerebellows*."

Elliot shook his head. "That's not helping."

"I thought it'd be obvious from looking at it," said

Harrumphrey. "It's for sucking ideas outta yer noggin. See? They go up through the tube and into that computer over there."

"How is that possible?"

"They're quite common in creaturedom," Elliot's uncle explained.

"You gotta understand," said Harrumphrey. "Things work a bit differently from human science."

"No kidding," said Leslie.

"Hey, Harry! Y'all git anything?"

This latest voice came from an open door on the far side of the room. A woman entered, wearing a gauzy, green-tinted ball gown.

Although the woman was beautiful, it took a moment to see her skin was entirely covered in silvery scales. As she came closer, her sheer fishiness became more apparent: the leaky gills on the sides of her throat, for instance, the severely webbed hands, the dorsal fin that stuck out of her back. There was also something odd about her hair. At first glance it looked like regular hair, but now Elliot saw it was more like . . . *seaweed*.

"Guys," said the professor. "This is Patti Mudmeyer. She's head of design at the Creature Department."

The fishy woman came closer and they saw her dress wasn't actually dyed green. In fact, the dress was white, or at least it *used to be*. Now, however, it was stained all over with greenish-brown blotches.

Patti stopped and put her hands on her hips. "Well, sheer me bald and color me sheepish! Didn't your uncle teach you it ain't polite to stare at a lady?"

"Oh! Sorry!" Elliot felt himself blushing. "I didn't mean to stare, but your dress—what happened to it?"

Patti sighed. "Just a fact of life, I'm afraid, for a bog nymph."

"A what?" asked Leslie.

"Y'all have prob'ly heard of them *river* nymphs and *forest* nymphs. They're the famous ones, but lemme tell ya, once upon a time, way back when, everything was *all swamp*. Rivers?! Forests?! No way! We Mudmeyers were running the show back when them cutesy pond sprites weren't nothing but pupae!"

"Um . . . okay, but how does that explain the stains on your dress?"

"Like I said, I'm a *bog* nymph. It's all 'cuz of my hair." She ran her hands through her strange kelp-like locks. When she brought her fingers out, they were covered with a greenish-gray sludge. "I got this stuff dripping off my hair twenty-four seven. You oughta *see my pillow* in the morning! It's like the worst dandruff problem in the universe. But what can I do? It's just in my nature."

As if on cue, a glob of silt dripped out from behind Patti's ear. It dribbled down the front of her dress and plopped on the floor.

Leslie jumped sideways to avoid the back splash. "So what is this place, the slime room?"

"I'll pretend I didn't hear that," said Patti. "'Cuz obviously, y'all don't know how useful this stuff can be."

Moving lightning quick, the bog nymph began molding the sludge she had just swiped from her hair. In seconds, she had produced a small greenish-gray bust that looked exactly like Leslie.

"It's me," said Leslie.

"That's incredible," said Elliot.

Patti shrugged. "Guess you could say I've got a pretty versatile scalp."

"Enough with the pleasantries already," Harrumphrey harrumphed. "Aren't we supposed to be having a meeting? Where's JR and that big dopey knucklecrumpler?"

"They'll be here soon," said the professor. "Just tidying up the Rickum Ruckem Room."

Harrumphrey groaned. *"Again?"* He reached up with his tail and removed the cerebellows. "Check the computer, Patti. We get anything?"

Patti peered at the monitors. "Same as last time. Six-legged roller skates."

Harrumphrey sighed. "I haven't had a new idea in ages."

"What're six-legged roller skates?" Elliot asked.

"I call 'em the creepy wheelies," said Harrumphrey. "I've got a prototype right here." He waddled around behind the table, and when he came out again, he was wearing a pair of bright white roller skates with bright red wheels—six wheels on each foot. Each wheel was supported by metallic, articulated arms, so Harrumphrey looked like he was riding on the backs of two very odd-looking spiders.

"No wonder you call them creepy," said Elliot.

"What are they for?" asked Leslie.

Harrumphrey smiled, or rather he smirked out of the side of his mouth. (True to his name, Harrumphrey Grouseman was far better at scowls, sneers, grimaces, and other related frown-like facial expressions. He was a master of the harrumph.) "The creepy wheelies," he announced, "finally solve the age-old problem of roller skating up and down stairs."

"Are you serious?" asked Leslie.

"If you'll indulge me—and since the others are late—I'll give you a demonstration." He wheeled around to Patti. "Bring out the testing stairs."

Patti didn't look very enthusiastic. "Y'all sure you wanna do that?"

Harrumphrey nodded and skated back to the rear wall. Patti pushed a set of four simple wooden stairs out of a closet and placed them in Harrumphrey's path.

"Ladies and gentlemen: The creepy wheelies." He skated full-bore at the stairs and when he reached the first step—

CRASH!

Harrumphrey, both creepy wheelies, and even the mock-up stairs themselves went flying. Harrumphrey ended up flat on his back in the corner, while the creepy wheelies rolled under the table.

"Like I said," Harrumphrey explained. "It's still a prototype."

"I'd totally want a pair of those," said Leslie. "If they worked."

"I'm sure you would," the professor agreed, "but articulated roller skates won't save this company. What we need is something truly spectacular."

"And we gotta come up with something quick," said Patti. "The shareholders are gittin' all tetchy on us."

Just then, Jean-Remy flapped in behind the professor, followed by the lumbering Gügor, who stooped deeply to enter the room. Both of them joined the others around the conference table.

"Finally," Harrumphrey harrumphed. "We can start the meeting."

"What about us?" asked Elliot. "Can we come?"

"Aw, let 'em stay," said Patti. "They're adorable!"

"They're more than just adorable," said the professor. "They're going to help us rescue the whole company!"

"They are?" asked the creatures.

"We are?" asked Elliot and Leslie.

"Of course," the professor told them. "Did you really think I'd bring you here just to look around?"

"That's sort of what the word *tour* means."

Elliot's uncle waved his hand. "I put that in the letter so your mom and dad would let you come. If I'd said, 'Please let Elliot and his friend come help a secret department of weird creatures come up with some revolutionary new invention to save all of DENKi-3000 from bankruptcy,' I'm sure your parents would have had a lot of difficult questions."

The professor had a point. "But why us?"

"Leslie's grandfather told me about your success at the city science fair, so—"

"I wouldn't exactly call that success," said Leslie. "We tied for third place."

"It's not the placing," said the professor. "It's *how you competed.*"

"Messily," said Elliot.

"Think y'all better explain what happened."

They did. On the day of the Bickleburgh City Science Fair, both Elliot and Leslie showed up with extremely similar experiments. They had tested how high they could launch a model rocket. The only difference between their approaches appeared to be one of style. While Elliot's rocket was bright red (with orange flames lapping down the sides), Leslie's was entirely black, with a grinning skull painted on the nose cone.

Both of them claimed they had broken the city record for the highest-ever flight using only a high-pressure vinegar and baking soda solution. The judges were impressed, but there was a problem. The two entrants had independently achieved the very same results. In fact, all their data was identical!

This could only mean one thing: Before the judges could settle on the final standings, there would have to be a "blastoff."

Elliot and Leslie took their rockets out to the middle of the running track, and both of them put everything they had into the test. Together, they counted down (*Three . . . Two . . . One . . .*) and then—

PHWOOOSH!

Both rockets drenched every one of the judges in a sour, foaming, high-pressure spray of vinegar and baking soda! At the same time, the launch went perfectly . . . *and* set a brand-new record, beating all the results of their original experiments . . . *and* (once again) both rockets flew to *precisely the same height!*

It was infuriating.

Elliot and Leslie requested a second tiebreaker, but the judges weren't interested. They were furious that they would now have to spend the rest of the day reeking of vinegar, and they had no desire for a second drenching. However, the rocket launch had been so impressive they had no choice but to award both Elliot and Leslie a prize in the competition. (Third was the lowest placing they could award them without looking petty.)

"Basically," said Patti, "y'all created one great, big,

vinegar-flavored explosion."

"That's one way to put it," said Elliot.

"Perfect," Harrumphrey harrumphed. "You'll fit right in around here."

Jean-Remy nodded solemnly. "After hearing ze story, I can certainly see why ze professor wanted you to join us in our time of need."

"Speaking of which," Elliot's uncle began, "I don't need to remind everyone that DENKi-3000 hasn't come up with a single new product since last year's TransMints. If we don't come up with something to impress the shareholders soon . . ."

"Something bad will happen?" suggested Gügor.

"*Very* bad," said the professor. "The whole company will be sold to Quazicom Holdings International, which is why we need to come up with something truly revolutionary, something so amazing it'll convince the shareholders not to sell." He looked around the table at everyone, even Elliot and Leslie. "Any ideas?"

No one said anything, and besides, before they could even open their mouths—

BOOM!

"Was that what it sounded like?" asked Leslie.

All the creatures nodded.

"Yep," they said. "An explosion."

CHAPTER 5

In which Reggie awakes
and Elliot sees something in the woods

They rushed out of the meeting room, thumping back onto the scaffolds. An acrid plume of emerald-green smoke was rising from the laboratory floor.

"Hurry, Jean-Remy," said the professor. "Fly up and open the vents!"

The handsome fairy-bat soared upward. He tapped buttons on a control panel near the ceiling, opening a series of chimney exhausts.

"Is everything okay?" asked Elliot. He came to stand on the scaffold with his uncle.

"Don't worry," said the professor. "It's only Reggie."

"Who's Reggie?" asked Leslie.

"Colonel-Admiral Reginald T. Pusslegut." Patti shook her head in a pitying way. "Poor fella thinks he used to be a bigwig in the military, but who'd ever believe those cockamamie war stories!"

"Colonel-Admiral?" asked Leslie. "Is that even possible? Colonel is a top army guy and admiral is a top navy guy. They're two totally separate branches of the armed forces."

"Y'all would have to take that up with Reggie. I get the impression they do things a little different down in the South Pole."

"Around here," said Harrumphrey, "we let him be a security guard. Or pretend to be one. Here he comes. You can just about see him through the smoke."

On the floor below, a huge, lumpish silhouette emerged from the haze of green. The shape was nearly as big as Gügor but nowhere near as muscular and intimidating. This was the silhouette of something far more soft and blubbery.

At last the huge, woolly, potbellied creature emerged from the smoke, coughing and spluttering and waving its arms. Its face was part walrus, part English bulldog, with flabby jowls and a massive underbite. The jutting lower jaw was rimmed by a row of jagged incisors that curled over its top lip. Those upturned teeth, however, were dwarfed by a pair of huge, faintly yellow tusks, slicing down on either side.

The creature—"Reggie"—wasn't wearing a white lab coat like the others. Instead, he was dressed in elaborate military regalia, complete with frilly epaulettes, a chest full of medals, and a jangling ceremonial saber. On his feet were possibly the largest pair of rubber boots the world had ever known.

"Please, you must all listen!" he was saying. "Something terrible is going to happen! I've seen it in my dreams!"

"Shouldn't you be hibernating this time of year?"

"I *so* wish you would!"

Darting out from behind Reggie's bulk were two small creatures that looked like a pair of calico rats (ones that walked around on their hind legs). They had pointed, conical faces, bristling with whiskers and set with cold, suspicious eyes. The first was a girl: thin, gangly, and possibly molting; the second was shorter and stockier, with thicker hair but far more unkempt. The two of them looked like the creature equivalent of boxcar hobos.

"Preposterous!" cried Reggie. "How do you expect a gentleman to rest with these infernal night visions?! *And worse!*" His eyes rolled deliriously. "They are the dreams of things to come!"

"Oh, sure," mocked the first rat-like creature. "Like the time your 'night visions' predicted Big Ben was turning into cheese?"

"Gouda," said Reggie.

"Or the time you dreamed it was going to rain camels on Chicago?" mocked the second rat-like creature.

"*Bactrian* camels, no less!" cried Reggie. "That's two humps, not one!"

"Ugh! When have *any* of your 'night visions' come true?"

"Merely because my nocturnal auguries have not yet come to pass, it is no reason to discount them as false! Surely you know a hibernating bombastadon is a premonitory creature! And this latest dream—*oh*!"

"*Wah-wah-wah!*" mocked the first rat-like creature. "Whine, whine, whine!"

"Oh, boohoo! I had a baddy-waddy dweamy-weemy," taunted the other.

"Who are those two?" asked Elliot, up on the scaffolds.

"And why are they being so mean?" asked Leslie.

"They're *hobmongrels*," Harrumphrey harrumphed. "It's in their nature."

"The boy's called Bildorf," Patti told them, "and the girl's Pib. As y'all can see, they don't get on so well with Reggie."

"Why must you *torment* me?!" Reggie cried from down below. "Why can't you leave me in peace, you cretinous things!"

He spun in a clumsy circle, as if doing a sort of interpretive dance inspired by his nightmares. With his blubbery arms spinning round like a helicopter, he knocked over a few more chemistry sets and delicate prototypes, causing a series of all-new (but thankfully minor) explosions.

"Colonel-Admiral!" Elliot's uncle called down, cupping his hands to his mouth. "Calm down! It was only a dream!"

Abruptly, Reggie stopped his manic spinning. He looked up and saw Professor von Doppler and the others, standing on the scaffolds.

"Ah! Archimedes, my dear fellow, there you are! Surely, a man of your intellect can perceive the danger besetting us all! You and *I*—Colonel-Admiral Reginald T. Pusslegut of Her Majesty's Royal Antarctic Brigadiers—we are gentlemen not merely of fortitude, but *foresight*!"

"Um, yeah," said the professor. "Sure thing, Reggie."

"Does he always talk like that?" asked Leslie.

"I'm afraid so."

"But *this* dream! Ho! *Teeeerrible!* Oh! The darkness! Oh! The teeming, insidious hoards!" He started spinning again (and knocking things over).

"For obvious reasons," the professor explained in a low voice, "we do our best to keep him out of the laboratory."

"Oh, fer cryin' out loud!" Patti called down to the other creature scientists. "Would someone *please* get the bombastadon some tea and biscuits?"

The small crowd of creatures around Reggie scattered in all directions. They were all murmuring, "Tea and biscuits! Tea and biscuits!"

It was the two hobmongrels, however, Bildorf and Pib, who were already prepared. Giggling like mischievous children, they opened a nearby drawer and took out a silver tray. It featured an enormous tea set and a plate piled high with chocolate biscuits. It was a struggle for them to carry it, but they managed to blunder it over to Reggie, who instantly stopped his melodramatic spinning.

"Is that what I think it is?" Reggie asked disdainfully.

"Quit blabbing and have some," urged Bildorf. "It'll do you good."

"Go on," said Pib in a wheedling voice. "You know you want to."

"You insult me!" cried Reggie. "I am a soldier and a gentleman! Why, I once brought peace to the vast snowy—"

"*Wastes of Antarctica,*" said Pib, finishing the sentence. "We know. We've heard it *aaaalllll* before."

Reggie turned up his nose to the hobmongrels and their silverware. "Then of course you'll know you can never quell the terrifying night visions of a bombastadon with something so *ordinary* as tea and chocolate ... chocolate ... cho—*I say,* are those *chocolate* biscuits?"

"Chocolate-covered *pickled herring* biscuits," said Bildorf. "Your favorite."

Instantly, Reggie attacked the tray, devouring the biscuits and slurping loudly from the enormous teacup. As he did so, the two hobmongrels backed away to the corner of the room. They pulled back a curtain and helped as some of the other creatures pushed out an enormous velvet divan.

As Reggie continued to gorge himself full of tea and biscuits (the more he ate, the more sluggish he became), the closer the divan was pushed up behind him.

"Teeerible . . . teeerible . . . " he muttered, melted chocolate dribbling down his chin. "Such *teeerible* . . ." With one last slurp from the teacup, he toppled backward precisely and perfectly onto the divan. As soon as he was down, the creatures heaved and pushed the slumbering Reggie back behind the curtain.

All the while, he snored like a poorly tuned pipe organ. "What do you put in those biscuits?" Leslie asked the professor.

"Are they drugged or something?" asked Elliot.

"Not at all," said the professor. "Bombastadons merely have a metabolism that makes them quite susceptible to tea and biscuits."

"He certainly made a mess," said Leslie, looking down at the smoking wreckage. "Does he do that a lot?"

"More than we care to admit," Harrumphrey grumbled.

"But," said Jean-Remy, "it is not as if we can send him away. When it comes down to it, even as annoying as he can be, Reggie—he is one of us."

Elliot's uncle sighed. "He certainly is, and it looks like we'll spend the rest of the afternoon cleaning up this mess." He turned to Leslie and Elliot. "So why don't you two head home for today? Come back tomorrow and we'll get you started working with the others."

Leslie wasn't convinced. "Are you sure you want our help? Just because of how we did at the science fair?"

The professor smiled. "You'd be surprised what you can learn from an exploding model rocket—or two. And besides, it takes a young and flexible mind to understand creature technology. What kind of mind is as young and flexible as a twelve-year-old's?"

"I *guess* that makes sense," said Elliot. Like Leslie, he wasn't convinced, but on the other hand, he was happy they would soon be returning to the Creature Department. Just knowing this place existed was a privilege, but being able to help with the experiments was almost too good to be true.

"Come on," said the professor, leading them along the scaffold. "I'll show you the way out."

On the way home, Elliot and Leslie buzzed with excitement. When they reached the park, they lingered on the field, going over and over everything and everyone they had seen: the words written on glass, the secret entrance to the old mansion, Jean-Remy Chevalier, Gügor the knucklecrumpler and the Rickum Ruckem Room, Harrumphrey Grouseman and his creepy wheelies, Patti the bog nymph, Reggie the bombastadon, and even those two mischievous hobmongrels, Bildorf and Pib.

"I can't believe I thought Bickleburgh would be *boring*," said Leslie. "Now that I've met your uncle, it seems like we might live in the most amazing place in the universe!"

Elliot agreed. "I can't believe my uncle knew about all that stuff—and never told me."

"I could say the same about Grandpa Freddy. Although he *did* tell me. Well, sort of. He hinted at it after downing a couple bottles of cooking wine."

Eventually, Leslie realized she would have to be home soon. "My mom's crazy about punctuality. Once, I was half an hour late getting home and she thought I was 'running with a bad crowd.' We moved away a week later."

"You'd better hurry, then," said Elliot, "because according to my uncle, the Creature Department needs us both."

They parted ways, but not before planning how they would return to DENKi-3000 the following day.

"My grandpa will be making a big lunchtime delivery tomorrow," Leslie said. "Now that I know all about it, he'll *have* to take me along—and you too. Meet me at the restaurant around noon, and we'll all go together."

To get home, Elliot had to cut through the dense forest of trees surrounding the sports fields. If anyone had asked him— even that very morning—whether or not he cared if Leslie Fang moved away, he would have said, *Who's Leslie Fang?* But now, after seeing the Creature Department with her, he thought he might have actually made a new friend.

He was surprised by how concerned he was about Leslie returning home on time. Her mother, after all, sounded like quite an unpredictable person.

He was so concerned, in fact, that it wasn't until he was in the middle of the forest, where the trees were densest and the shadows darkest, that he realized something was wrong. Something about the forest was ... different.

It was the shadows.

They were moving.

No, he told himself, *you're being silly. You spent one very enjoyable afternoon with a whole bunch of weird creatures and now (perfectly understandable) you're seeing creatures every-* where.

Following you.

Rustling in the bushes.

Watching you with their giant eyes.

Their giant, angry, bulging ...

Eyes!

Elliot froze.

That was no shadow. Those were *real eyes.* Huge, blood-shot orbs that gazed out through the bushes. Stranger still, they appeared to be wearing a heavy dose of purple mascara.

He stared back at them in disbelief. Surely, they couldn't be real. No one had eyes *that* big, did they?

He kept staring back at them, waiting for them to dissolve back into shadows, waiting for some sign to prove it was all an illusion. But no, the eyes gazing back at him were real.

He knew this because—

They blinked.

Elliot ran.

Stumbling along the path, he heard the rustling get louder. It was *so loud*, in fact, that whatever was following him *must have been huge*!

In spite of its size, whenever Elliot looked back, he never saw anything, at least not all at once. All he saw were flashes of something truly terrifying.

A huge, crooked smile full of gnashing yellow teeth.

A massive nose the color of oatmeal, its gaping nostrils snorting like a horse's.

One single, enormous ear, big as a dinner tray, twitching feverishly around the black hole at its center.

A giant! thought Elliot. *I'm being chased by a giant . . . Creature!*

Just as this terrifying thought entered his head, all his fears were realized. A huge green hand, tipped with jagged claws, swiped out from the bushes and tried to grab him.

"GAAAH!" Elliot screamed, and dove out of the forest. He somersaulted straight into a group of old men playing cricket.

"Oi! Out of the way, boy, you're ruining the game!"

Elliot looked up, bewildered and out of breath. He looked back into the forest and spluttered, *"G-g-g-giant!"*

"We don't have time for foolishness, kid!" an old man shouted.

"This is cricket, and our man's set to bat for a century!"

Elliot had no idea what that meant. All he knew was that he had to get home as quickly as possible.

He turned and ran straight through the game, ignoring the angry shouts of the old men. He didn't stop until his front door was shut tightly behind him.

CHAPTER 6

In which the man from Quazicom recalls his youth

or Chuck Brickweather, the flight to Bickleburgh had been exceedingly smooth. As smooth, he thought, as the pristine runway at Quazicom's private airstrip.

The company boasted the most advanced corporate air fleet in the world. No matter how much turbulence swirled in the air outside, a Quazicom executive jet sliced through it without so much as a quiver. In fact, the plane soared just like the corporation itself.

Smoothly.

Chuck looked out the window. Down below him were mostly empty fields. The plane turned, banking to the left, and Chuck saw Bickleburgh in the distance. It was the only sign of life for miles around.

What a pitiful backwater, he thought. How could they even call this place "a city?" More importantly, why would the world's fifth-largest technology firm choose to erect its headquarters in a place like this? It was so ordinary. No, he thought, not ordinary. *Dull.*

To Chuck, Bickleburgh had all the insipid hallmarks of a town in the middle of nowhere: dreary, uninspired houses, strip malls full of shops he had seen a million times before, and a gray perimeter of factories and warehouses. The only thing that stood out in any way was Chuck Brickweather's destination: DENKi-3000 headquarters. The company's four towers rose up from the center of town, gleaming in the summer sun.

"*Why?*" Chuck wondered aloud. "Why here?"

A moment later, a Quazicom flight attendant came sauntering toward him. "Did you call for me?" she asked. "Is there something I can get you?"

"Just thinking out loud," Chuck muttered, without even looking at the woman. His eyes remained fixed on the city.

Seeing that she wasn't wanted, the flight attendant drifted back to her seat at the rear of the cabin.

Chuck opened his briefcase on the seat beside him. He heard the clink of glass as two bottles of Dr. Heppleworth's Knoo-Yoo-Juice knocked together.

He had been drinking the disgusting stuff since before he took the job with Quazicom's Corporate Takeover Division. Strictly speaking, Knoo-Yoo-Juice was a diet drink (and yes, it certainly kept him slim), but it tasted *terrible*. Nevertheless, it was something he had to contend with. Keeping his size down was crucial. Quazicom was a sleek company, and they preferred to employ sleek people.

There was a time—although you would never know it—when Chuck Brickweather had not been very sleek at all. Quite to the contrary, Chuck had been *the opposite* of sleek. He had been *fat*. Fat and oafish and simply not the sort of sleek, trim corporate consultant a company like Quazicom would ever contemplate hiring.

In Chuck's mind, there were two versions of himself. The new, fit, super-sleek Chuck of today and ... *that other guy.* That big slobbering lummox he used to be. The new Chuck despised that other guy, his former self, which was why, wherever Chuck went, he always carried a minimum of two bottles of Dr. Heppleworth's foul-smelling, even-worse-tasting purplish-red concoction. In fact, besides the two bottles in his briefcase, he was traveling with several crates of the stuff, safely stored in the plane's cargo hold. Just in case.

When he opened his briefcase, however, he wasn't looking for his Knoo-Yoo-Juice. He was after something else. He wanted to check his DENKi-3000 file one last time.

While the majority of technology companies devoted themselves to making smart phone apps and Internet software, DENKi-3000 was still producing *actual inventions.*

Their success, it seemed, rested on the shoulders of one man: Professor Archimedes von Doppler, the company's Chief of Research and Development. Unfortunately, Chuck had been unable to find very much information on the man. He rarely gave interviews and never talked about where his ideas came from.

Chuck looked through what little he had collected on the professor. There wasn't much more than a few articles and a handful of grainy photographs.

"What's your secret?" he asked, speaking aloud to the images. They didn't answer (of course), and Chuck closed the file.

The professor's secret ...

That was why Quazicom had sent him to Bickleburgh: to uncover the company's secrets. They were the most valuable things at any company. After all, he knew from experience that once you understood a company's secrets, you understood its lifeblood—meaning you understood what made it valuable. Or, to borrow a phrase from his boss, "Once you understand the lifeblood of a company, it's simple enough to tear out its heart."

Chuck, however, had his own secrets to keep. He had a hunch that maybe—*just maybe*—he already knew what the professor was hiding. If so, then Chuck had a plan of his own, but it was one he couldn't put into action until he was *absolutely certain.* . . .

Chuck placed the file on the seat beside him and reached deep into the bottom of his briefcase. He drew out a small sky-blue box with dark green letters. On the label, it said:

TransMints
Get your freshness direct from the web!

The DENKi-3000 logo was printed in the corner. The company was famous for these things, but Chuck had never tried one.

He flipped open the box and tapped one of the mints into his palm. It looked like a miniature robin's egg, a pale blue orb, speckled with tiny white dots. While he was staring at it, the airplane's intercom crackled to life.

"Mr. Brickweather?" the pilot said. "Sit back and relax; we'll begin our descent momentarily."

Chuck did as he was told. He sat back in the plush leather seat and relaxed, a thin smile on his face. At the moment, he was only a consultant with Quazicom, but he could certainly get used to this executive lifestyle.

He held up the TransMint between his thumb and forefinger, glancing at it one last time before popping it into his mouth.

At first, it was disappointing. There wasn't any flavor at all. In fact, the taste was somewhat unpleasant, a bit like having a dry pebble in your mouth. But the unpleasantness only lasted a moment.

Suddenly, his tongue was hit with a tiny jolt of static electricity (if static electricity tasted like peppermint) and his whole mouth was flooded with taste.

Chuck had always thought of the TransMint as frivolous candy, aimed mostly at children, but now he understood it was so much more than that. Somehow, the tiny robin's egg in his mouth was collecting all of the Internet's data about freshness and converting it into . . . *flavors*!

First, he tasted the sweetness of a pine forest at dawn, then the quenching refreshment of a midsummer rain, then the sharp crispness of an arctic night. A vivid memory suddenly returned to him, something he had forgotten until all these flavors brought it back.

He recalled himself when he was much younger, chubby and red-faced, rolling in the very first snowfall he could remember. In his mind, he saw himself lying faceup on the ground as snowflakes silently caked around his eyelashes, melting into tears that ran down the sides of his pudgy cheeks.

It was a moment of pure, unadulterated nostalgia—and Chuck couldn't stand it. Who *was* that kid? Not the sleek Chuck of today, no sir! That kid belonged firmly to his former self, the former self Chuck despised with every sleek fiber of his new sleek body. That self had *nothing* to with the Chuck of today, smoothly slicing through the air above Bickleburgh in a private company jet. And yet . . .

The memory was so clear, the nostalgia so intense that Chuck actually shivered with—

WHOMPH!

The plane lurched sickeningly to one side. Chuck was so taken by surprise that he *swallowed* the TransMint.

The pilot's voice returned to the intercom. "Mr. Brickweather? You better buckle up back there." The man sounded just a bit flustered (which was rather disconcerting). "We're having some trouble up here with, uh . . . well, anyway, you better buckle up."

The intercom went dead.

WHOMPH!

WHOMPH!

Two more stomach-churning lurches rocked the plane. It no longer felt like they were flying. More like *bouncing*!

Chuck gripped the plush armrest of his seat. How could this be happening? Turbulence *never* affected a Quazicom private jet!

Suddenly, the plane veered into an aerobatic maneuver so intricate, with so many spins and twists, that Chuck couldn't help but . . .

Vomit.

He spewed his breakfast all over the window and the seat in front of him.

This was incredibly embarrassing, not merely because he had thrown up, but because for months he had consumed almost nothing but Dr. Heppleworth's Knoo-Yoo-Juice. As a result, Chuck Brickweather's vomit was a bright, almost glowing purplish red.

"That is *definitely* going to leave a stain," he muttered to himself.

The plane went on careening through the sky. Chuck noticed that rolling back and forth through his Day-Glo puke was something that looked like a tiny blue robin's egg.

That was when he figured it out.

"Why you little—" he said, stomping on the Trans-Mint. There was a crackle of tiny green sparks as the thing was destroyed. Almost instantly, the plane stabilized.

The intercom came to life once more. "Hope you're all right

back there, Mr. Brickweather," said
the pilot. "Sorry if we gave you a bit
of a scare, but everything appears
to be working normally now. Let's
try that again, shall we? Sit back,
relax. We'll be landing momentarily."

Chuck wasn't sure he could
relax, especially not with the cuffs
of his pants soaked with the bizarre
contents of his stomach. Worse, he
hadn't even brought an extra pair of
shoes. He found the box of TransMints on the seat
beside him. Turning it over, he found a very clear warning:

CAUTION: Not recommended for use during air travel

"What is that *smell*?" asked the flight attendant, calling to
Chuck from the rear of the cabin.

"Uh, sorry," Chuck replied sheepishly. "I was a bit sick
back here."

"What have you been *eating*?"

How could Chuck tell her? It was far too embarrassing to
explain he had hardly eaten anything but Knoo-Yoo-Juice for
weeks on end, so he simply said, "Bit of indigestion."

As the plane began its approach into Bickleburgh City
Airport, Chuck Brickweather had to admit that for the first
time since he started working for Quazicom, things were *not*

running smoothly. But that didn't bother him. In fact, as the plane touched down—*smoothly*, as usual—he even smiled to himself. He felt he knew exactly where DENKi-3000's heart was, and if he had to, he fully intended to tear it out.

CHAPTER 7

In which Elliot has better hair than Albert Einstein

E lliot von Doppler, you come down here this instant or, I swear, you're going straight into a custard tart! Your father and I have worked very hard to prepare a lovely breakfast, so I'm going to count—"

Before his mother could finish, Elliot came bounding down the stairs fully dressed (including the green fishing vest, of course).

"Here I am!" Elliot jumped from the third step to land directly in front of his mother.

In return, she regarded him with suspicion. "What's gotten into *you* this morning?"

Elliot merely shrugged and waltzed past her into the kitchen. He had awoken to a warm, sunny morning, and somehow the bright blue sky convinced him the giant that had chased him through the forest in Bickleburgh Park had almost certainly been a figment of his imagination. This morning, the only thing on his mind was getting back to the Creature Department.

He wolfed down his awful breakfast for a change—dusty cereal topped with over-fried eggs—and finished off by grinning at his parents and giving them a thumbs-up. "Great job, guys!"

His father peered at him over the top of his newspaper. "I hope that's not your full review."

"Okay, how's this? The salty crumble of the yolk was a unique complement to the wheaty bouquet of powdered muesli."

"Impressive," his father said, a bit suspiciously. "Are you feeling all right?"

"I feel great! Just in a good mood, I guess."

Usually, Elliot spent much of his summer vacation quietly lounging around the house or wandering through the yard, examining the world through his DENKi-3000 Electric Pencil with Retractable Telescopic Lens.

On that morning, however, he practically *danced* around the house, humming jaunty tunes with a big, goofy grin on his face. His parents were astonished. It wasn't that Elliot was an unhappy child, but he certainly wasn't into *skipping*.

Just before lunchtime, Elliot found his mother and father in the kitchen. Together, they were struggling to decipher the instructions on a box of boil-in-the-bag rice.

Elliot cleared his throat. "*Ahem!* I'm going to hang out with Leslie this afternoon," he announced.

"I take it you found her yesterday," said his mother. "In the park?"

Elliot nodded. "She invited me for lunch today. Her grand-father runs a restaurant."

The faces of both his parents brightened.

"*Oh?*" asked his father. "What sort of restaurant?"

Elliot had to think. "Dim something. Oh, wait, that's it! *Dim sum.*"

His mother frowned. "You mean Chinese takeout?"

"I guess," Elliot mumbled.

"Couldn't you find a friend with a molecular fusion restaurant?"

"Is that even food?"

"It's the newest thing," said his father. "You'd like it. It's all *science-y.*"

"Can I go now?"

"All right, but if you want our advice, you really ought to tell this girl's grandfather to open a gastropub. Isn't that right, dear?"

His father nodded. "I hear molecular fusion's already on the way out."

"Didn't you just say it was *the newest thing?*"

Elliot's father lifted the newspaper again, hiding his face. "You know how these trends are. They come and go."

Elliot's only response was to sigh, grab his knapsack, and hoof it out the door.

Famous Freddy's Dim Sum Emporium was in the heart of Bickleburgh's minuscule, but always crowded, Chinatown. The neighborhood was a single block of markets and neon taverns that spilled out onto the sidewalks with vegetables, dried fish, and all sorts of toys and cookware laid out on plain tables.

Famous Freddy's, however, was not on the main strip. It was on a side street that wasn't much wider than a back alleyway. There was no sign above the entrance, and the foggy glass doors looked like they belonged more to a struggling bank than a restaurant. The only hint the establishment served food was a wooden sandwich board out front:

Famous Freddy's Dim Sum Emporium
Best pork dumplings this side of Taipei!

Elliot stared at the sandwich board. He wasn't terribly impressed. In fact, if he were completely honest, he might say Famous Freddy's Dim Sum Emporium looked a little sketchy.

Elliot opened the doors and saw two flights of broad marble stairs. Climbing them, he sniffed what smelled like a hundred different scents.

Spicy . . . salty . . . sour . . . sweet . . .

His stomach grumbled.

At the top of the stairs, the entrance was curtained off by strings of dark green beads. It was impossible to see inside.

Elliot hesitated. This wasn't the sort of restaurant he expected to find. It certainly didn't seem very welcoming.

"Anytime you're ready," said a woman's voice on the far side of the beads.

"H-hello?" Elliot answered.

"Are you coming in or not? Right now all you're doing is blocking the entrance." The woman's voice was forceful and brusque.

"I'm looking for . . . Leslie?"

"Elvis Presley? Try the karaoke bar, two doors down."

"Not 'Presley.' *Leslie.*"

"Fresh tea? Of course we serve fresh tea! Get in here and try some. You'll see how fresh it is!"

"I'm just here because I'm looking for *Leslie Fang.* She's my friend."

There was a pause while whoever was on the other side of the beads considered this information.

"Wait a minute," said the voice. *"It's you!"*

A hand burst through the beads and grabbed Elliot by the

strap of his knapsack, yanking him into the restaurant.

The hand was connected to a long, elegant arm, which in turn was connected to a tall, slender woman with long black hair. She wore no makeup and was plainly dressed in a simple black-and-white uniform: black shoes, black pants, and a white button-up shirt. Even still, Elliot thought she was quite pretty—for a grown-up.

"Have you been *smooching* with my daughter?" she asked.

Elliot was so shocked by this question he would have fallen over if it weren't for the woman gripping so fiercely to the strap of his bag.

"W-w-*what*?!" he cried. "I have no idea what you're talking about!"

"Oh, I think you do." She was pointing a finger right in Elliot's face and speaking through gritted teeth. "How do you explain the fact that my Leslie woke up this morning happy and bubbly and skipping—*skipping*—around the house?!" The woman lowered her voice. "My Leslie is *never* bubbly."

"Wait," said Elliot. "You're Leslie's mom?"

The woman nodded slowly. "And *you*, you little Casanova! You must be *Elliot*." She shook her head. "You're all she's been talking about since she got up this morning."

"Me?"

"You and some crazy uncle of yours, the one who works at that weird company."

"DENKi-3000," Elliot said. He stood up a little straighter, which was difficult because Leslie's mother was pulling so hard on his knapsack. "And my uncle is *not* crazy. He's a genius."

"Is that so? Because from what I hear,

even his own company doesn't know what goes on in that research department of his. Or maybe I oughta call it a *mad scientist's lab*!" She pulled Elliot closer until they were almost nose to nose. "Anyone with *that* many secrets can't be right in the head."

"You can't say that about Uncle Archie! You've never even met him!"

Leslie's mother pursed her lips. "Maybe so, but this isn't about him. It's about *you*. And all I have to say *to you* is: My daughter is *much too young for smooching*!"

"No, wait! You've got it all wrong! *I'm twelve!* I *hate* smooching! I would never, *ever* smooch with Leslie in a million years!"

"Don't be so sure." Leslie's mother narrowed her eyes and looked at him sideways. "A million years is a long time."

Elliot didn't know what to say. "Why does everyone think Leslie is like my . . . guh . . . gir . . . g-g-gir . . ." It was ridiculous. He couldn't even say the word.

"Girlfriend? *I knew it!*"

"No!" Elliot protested, but he realized there was little he could do to convince the woman, so he decided to change his strategy. "The thing is, my uncle gave us a tour of his laboratory. He just wanted to teach us about, you know, *science*. And he made it really *interesting* for us, that's all."

Parents loved it when their kids learned anything about science. If you did well in science class, you could practically set fire to the principal's office and no one would care. You would even have a ready-made excuse. *It was for a science project, sir, I swear.*

"Science?" whispered Leslie's mother. There was a sudden

air of reverence in her voice. She relaxed her death grip on Elliot's knapsack. (The plan was working.) "You're interested in science?"

Elliot nodded. "I'm like Einstein, only smaller. And with better hair. Also, no mustache."

Leslie's mother folded her arms. "Wait a second. If you're a scientist, why are you dressed like a fisherman?"

"*Mo-om!*" Leslie called, entering the room through a pair of double doors in the back corner. "I told you not to mention the vest."

Elliot looked at Leslie. "What's wrong with my vest?"

"Nothing," Leslie answered. "It's lovely. Now, come on. You gotta meet my grandpa."

CHAPTER 8

*In which a profound connection is established
between friendship and food*

Elliot had been so busy fending off questions from Leslie's mother, he hadn't had time to appreciate the interior of the restaurant. It was larger than he expected. A low ceiling sagged above an enormous room filled with many, many tables—all empty.

One wall contained a large aquarium floating with enormous goldfish, while the other three were hung with variations on a single painting: misty mountains descending into deep green lakes. Dangling from the ceiling were paper lanterns and multicolored Christmas lights.

"I want you both to know," said Leslie's mother, still standing near the entrance, "the only reason I'm letting you two go today is because you have a chaperone."

"A who?" asked Leslie.

"Grandpa Freddy," said her mother. "I already talked to him. He's there to make sure there's *no smooching.*"

Leslie rolled her eyes. "Trust me, Mom, you have *nothing* to worry about." She led Elliot to the double doors in the corner. When they swung open, a great puff of steam wafted out and Elliot was momentarily blinded.

"So," croaked a voice from within the fog, "this is Archie's nephew, is it?"

Elliot blinked to clear his vision. He faced an enormous but extremely cluttered kitchen. Plates, pots, and pans were piled everywhere.

The croaking voice had come from an old man, stooped and bald and all dressed in white: white shoes, white pants, white apron, and a white triangular hat that clung magically to the man's entirely hairless head.

"Elliot von Doppler," said Leslie, "meet Famous Freddy."

"Nice to meet you," the old man rasped, stepping forward to shake hands. With his bald head and long, wrinkly neck, he reminded Elliot of a smiling old tortoise. "Leslie tells me that uncle of yours finally revealed his secret."

Elliot nodded. "But you've known about them—*about the creatures*," he whispered, "for a long time, haven't you?"

"Not too long," said the old man. He turned away from Elliot, apparently as a way to change the subject. "We'd better start loading the van. They hate it when I'm late."

Famous Freddy's delivery truck was a huge white trailer hitched to the back of a rusty red Volkswagen. It seemed impossible such a puttering old junker could tow something that big, especially when it was packed to the ceiling with so much food.

When they arrived at DENKi-3000, Elliot recognized the man at the security gate as Carl, the friendly guard they had met the day before.

"Hey there, Freddy," said Carl, waving from inside his security booth. "You got something in there for me today?"

Grandpa Freddy leaned across to the glove compartment. He opened it and Elliot caught a whiff of something delicious. It was a small cardboard box, painted to resemble bamboo, just like the ones loaded in the trailer.

"Your favorite," said Grandpa Freddy, passing the box through the window.

Carl (who was quite a large man) giggled like a baby. He opened the box and immediately popped one of the pork dumplings into his mouth. *"Deeeee-lish!"* he said, swallowing the mouthful. "Lemme tell you, Freddy—you are *not* famous enough!"

Having gulped down the first dumpling, Carl leaned out of his booth to peer into the car. "Hello again," he said, giving Elliot and Leslie a small salute. "Back for another visit, huh? You two are a couple of very lucky kids!"

Leslie's grandpa steered them all the way around the building to a steep ramp that went deep under the ground. The ramp soon became a tunnel illuminated with strips of yellow lights.

Eventually, they came to a dead end. A metal wall stood before them, pocked with rivets and mounted with a sign: CAUTION: RESEARCH AND DEVELOPMENT PERSONNEL ONLY!

"Now what?" Leslie asked her grandfather.

"Not to worry," Freddy croaked. "I come here so much they gave me my own ID." He plucked it out of his breast pocket and held it up, showing off a job title as odd as any of the others in the Creature Department:

Alfred Fang
Movable Feastician

He swiped his ID badge and what had been a dead end was dead no more. The wall split and slid away, just like the entrance to the old mansion. From there on there were no yellow strips of light. The only illumination was the old Volkswagen's headlights.

It was so dark, in fact, it was difficult to see the edges of the road. On the driver's side, where Famous Freddy sat, they occasionally saw the wall of what looked more and more like a craggy, underground cave. On the passenger side, however, there was no such wall. Only darkness.

Famous Freddy drove on this way for a while until they came to yet a second dead end, this one even more convincing than the last: It was just an uneven wall of pocked gray stone. The old man opened his door to get out, and following suit, Leslie did the same.

"*No!*" Lightning quick (and surprisingly fast for an old tortoise of a man), her grandfather whipped out his arm to grab her. "We're not there yet!" Then, very gravely, he whispered, "Close the door."

The sudden seriousness of Freddy's voice startled them. Elliot and Leslie couldn't help peering into the darkness below.

A sprinkling of coppery rust had shaken loose when Leslie opened it. The rust, catching the diffuse light from the car, fell . . .

and fell . . .

and fell . . .

until it flickered into nothingness.

There was no bottom!

Leslie slammed the door. They were parked right on the edge of what appeared to be *a bottomless cliff*! She turned to say something to her grandfather, but he was already getting out on the other side.

The old man toddled to the wall, feeling along it with his hands until he found one very particular crag. He twisted a stone and a door opened up ahead of them. It led directly into a large chamber bathed in eerie green light.

"A secret passage!" whispered Elliot. He pointed to the crag in the wall. "With a secret hidden latch!"

Leslie agreed. "*Way* cooler than scanners and ID badges, that's for sure."

Grandpa Freddy climbed back into the car. He eased them through the mysterious doorway and into the glowing green chamber. Once inside, the doors shut behind them, and they heard the whir of machinery. The secret passageway wasn't just a secret passageway; it was an enormous elevator.

The eerie green light slowly faded as they rose and rose and finally emerged on the floor of the Creature Department.

"HOOORAY!"

There were creatures everywhere, whistling and cheering and clapping their hands (or flippers, or tentacles, or . . . whatever).

"Is it always like this?" Elliot asked.

Famous Freddy smiled proudly. "Every time I deliver."

This explained why there were so few customers at Famous Freddy's Dim Sum Emporium. Leslie's grandfather didn't need any. All his customers were creatures.

The old man got out of the car, waving to his friends, who crowded around him as if he were a rock star (for the first time, Famous Freddy Fang *really did* look famous).

Professor von Doppler battled his way through the crowd. "Welcome back, you two." He beamed at Elliot and Leslie. "You can eat with us in the cafetarium and then we'll get started."

"The where?" asked Leslie. "Don't you mean cafeteria?"

"Nope," said Elliot's uncle. "I meant what I said. *The cafetarium*. Probably the best place to eat in the whole universe!"

"Why's that?" asked Elliot.

"You'll understand when we get there."

The food was loaded onto silver trolleys and wheeled through the many corridors of the old mansion—so many, in fact, that they were quickly reminded of the seemingly impossible size of the building's interior. When they finally arrived at their destination, an even more dramatic example of creature physics awaited them in the cafetarium.

It was a massive room full of heavy wooden benches and tables, and in many ways, it looked like a standard, if slightly archaic, cafeteria. But then they looked up and saw what set it apart.

"The roof!" said Elliot. "It's a big white dome."

"Precisely," said his uncle, "and that's why we call it the cafetarium."

The dome was enormous. It seemed almost as big as the sky itself, spanning from one side of the dining room to the other.

Elliot, Leslie, and her grandfather sat with the professor and were hastily joined by Patti, Harrumphrey, Gügor, and Jean-Remy.

A group of fairy-like creatures zipped around the room, bringing packets of Famous Freddy's food. The bamboo baskets were opened to reveal dumplings and spring rolls, bowls of sticky rice, and steamed green vegetables.

It all smelled wonderful, but Elliot had never had dim sum

before, so he hardly knew where to start.

The creatures, however, weren't shy at all. The moment the tables were laid, they tucked in with gusto! The huge room exploded with the sounds of chomping jaws, smacking lips, and soft slithering tongues.

"You'd better hurry there," said Grandpa Freddy, coming to stand behind Elliot. "If they see you're not eating it, they'll be quite happy to take it off your hands."

"Try that one," said Leslie, pointing to a shiny round packet of pastry. "Those are Grandpa's famous pork dumplings."

Fumbling with his chopsticks, Elliot managed to get the dumpling from the bamboo basket to his mouth. He hadn't tasted anything exactly like this before, but he knew instantly why all the creatures were so crazy about Famous Freddy's cooking.

The dumpling was soft, spicy, and bursting with flavorful juices but without being mushy at all. It somehow made him feel good to eat it. No, it wasn't just a good feeling. It was something deeper than that. Something wonderful he couldn't quite describe . . .

He looked around the room. Whatever Elliot felt, the creatures were feeling it too. They poured great loads of dumplings and spring rolls and huge heaps of steamed vegetables into their enormous (or tiny) mouths, grinning all the while.

The sense of pure well-being he had as he ate this food was tremendous. He turned to Leslie. "You get to eat this stuff all the time?" he asked. "You have no idea how jealous I am."

Leslie grinned. "It's good, isn't it? But you know what? It never tastes this good at home."

"It's the miracle of eating among friends," said Leslie's grandfather. "After all, there's that old saying: The more friends at the table, the better the food."

They ate in silence, letting a sense of contentment and friendship wash over them.

"Ah!" said Jean-Remy. "Look there! Even ze children—zey feel it too!"

"Feel what?" asked Elliot. "I just feel good."

"It's more than that," said Elliot's uncle. "It's something all creatures understand. There are some foods so tasty that— even if you've never tasted them before—they take you back to some happier time." His uncle looked up. "And that's what the ceiling is for."

He opened a control panel mounted in the table, and at the touch of a button, the lights dimmed and the domed roof scrolled with images.

They looked like old photographs, many of them in sepia and black-and-white, showing creases and tears.

"It's like a planetarium," the professor explained. "Hence the name, of course. Except instead of looking at the stars, you're looking at—"

"*Memories,*" Gügor intoned. The knucklecrumpler gazed wistfully upward, watching the pictures float past as he ate.

"Gügor's right," said the professor. "They may look like photographs, but they're actually memories. The cafetarium is drawing memories from each of the diners and projecting them on the ceiling. What you're seeing now is the breadth and depth of all creaturedom."

The images (or memories) showed the creatures younger than they were now, usually somewhere in the outside world. There were pictures of creatures bathing on secluded beaches, hiking up mountains, and especially strolling through vast underground caves. The caves in particular were amazing— full of spectacular stalagmites and rock formations, strange, otherworldly vegetation, and eerie, flickering light.

"You say all these places are in creaturedom, but where is that exactly?" asked Elliot.

"An excellent question," his uncle answered. "*Creaturedom* merely refers to any place where creatures live—usually in secret, of course—like here in the Creature Department of DENKi-3000. You only need to look around this room to see there are many different kinds of creatures in the world. We humans live in many different cities and countries, all with different customs, but there are certain elemental aspects of our nature that bind us all together. The very same goes for creatures too."

"So *creaturedom* for creatures," Leslie suggested, "is a bit like *humanity* for humans."

"Precisely," said the professor, raising his head to look toward the ceiling. "You're looking at the collective memories of creaturedom."

The memories of their youth were soon supplanted by new images, showing the old mansion itself, long before it had fallen to ruin. None of the glass and steel of the DENKi-3000 office towers were there. Instead, the mansion was a sprawling old house in the middle of empty fields. Creatures frolicked on the grass out front, something that seemed impossible to imagine now.

"You two beginnin' to get it?" asked Patti. "Them pictures of the past intensify our good sense of friendship, and that intensifies the flavor of the food. Just like ol' Freddy said."

At the other end of the table, Famous Freddy nodded. "If only I could get one of these in my restaurant. Then we'd be

packed every night!"

In an odd way, the cafetarium had a certain logic to it. But even still, with or without the friendship and nostalgia of the cafetarium, Famous Freddy's food was delicious! Elliot would have to convince his parents to review the restaurant for the *Bickleburgh Bugle*.

New photographs appeared on the ceiling. There was Patti, dressed in a fluffy housecoat with a huge towel wrapped around her seaweed hair. She was lounging on a divan in what appeared to be a health spa (if they built health spas outside, in the middle of a swamp).

There was a photograph of Gügor, high in the mountains. He leapt between rocks while a huge gorge yawned below him. There was also a photograph of Jean-Remy, perched on a church spire, overlooking an ancient European city.

"That's Paris, isn't it?" asked Leslie.

"Mais bien sûr!" said Jean-Remy. "My beloved home!"

There was even a picture of Colonel-Admiral Reginald T. Pusslegut, the bombastadon who had caused such pandemonium the day before. When his photograph appeared, a number of the creatures pointed and giggled. But neither Elliot nor Leslie could understand why.

In the photograph, Reggie was standing on the edge of an ice cliff. He had one leg raised on an outcrop of ice, surveying the empty land below him. Everything about him—his uniform, his posture, even the expression on his face—seemed noble and regal and quite commanding.

"Where is Reggie, anyway?" asked Leslie, looking around the cafetarium. "Doesn't he eat with you?"

"He must be nearby," said the professor, "if the cafetarium is picking up his memories."

"Probably hibernating," Harrumphrey grumbled.

Just as he spoke, there was an image of Harrumphrey himself. Even Elliot and Leslie laughed when they saw that one. It clearly came from a time when Harrumphrey was a baby: a big burbling head, swaddled in a plump white diaper.

Harrumphrey blushed. "Aw, why's it gotta go and pick up on *that* one?"

"You know we can't help what it picks up on," said the professor. "You know that on occasion, it even picks up on—"

He stopped.

The chatter in the room stopped too. That's because a new series of images was scrolling silently above them. Images of war, of burning buildings, of creatures running in panic from strange shadowy figures that pursued them in hoards.

As soon as these first dire images appeared, there were instantly more. *And more.* They popped up and multiplied like a terrifying, unstoppable virus.

The professor pressed a button and the ceiling went blank.

"What was that?" asked Elliot.

Professor von Doppler took a deep breath. "That's the problem with the cafetarium," he said. "I was hoping I could present it to the shareholders as our latest invention. Unfortunately, we can't filter out the bad memories."

"Bad memories of *what*?" asked Leslie. She looked to her grandfather, but he only shook his head.

Professor von Doppler pushed out his chair. "Speaking of the shareholders . . ." He rose to his feet and checked his watch, effectively cutting off any more questions. "They've been called in for an emergency meeting—and it starts in just a few minutes, so I'd better get up there." He took a deep breath and turned to Elliot and Leslie. "As soon as I'm back, I have a job for both of you."

With that, he turned and stalked hastily to the exit.

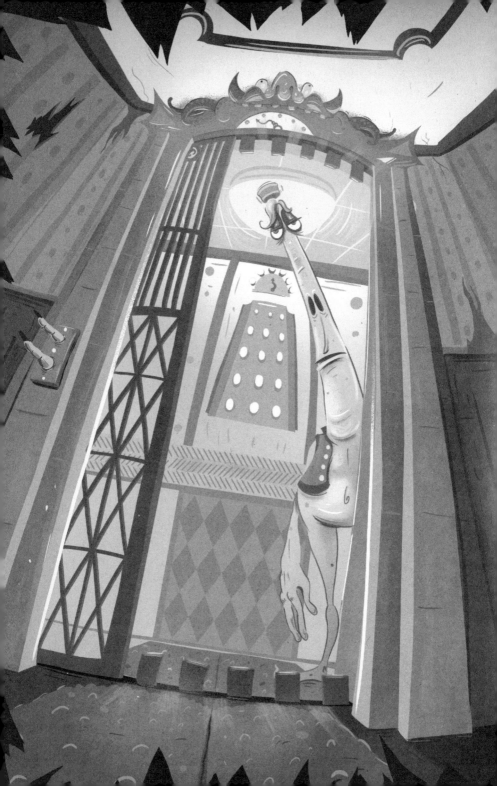

CHAPTER 9

In which expectations aren't what you might expect

"Guess we'd better go watch," Harrumphrey said.

"Be my guest," said Patti. "I can't stomach it. Just hearin' that word—*shareholders*—brings me out in hives. See?" She held out her arm and showed how her scales were shimmering a blotchy red.

"Gügor doesn't want to go either," said Gügor. "Those meetings make Gügor want to live up to Gügor's name." He flexed his enormous fists. "Make Gügor want to *crumple* something."

"What about us?" Elliot asked.

"Can we come with you?" Leslie stood up. "Maybe the professor could use our help."

Harrumphrey shook his head. "We can't *actually* go into the meeting, of course. It's for DENKi-3000 executives and shareholders only. But . . ." A rare smile appeared on his face. "That doesn't mean we can't watch."

Jean-Remy began fluttering away. "Come along, and we will show you."

They followed him down a twisting corridor. Circular

doorways had been carved out of the walls in all different sizes. In many of them, spiraling staircases coiled off in all directions.

Other doorways led to rooms full of cramped bunk beds. Elliot and Leslie realized these were the creatures' sleeping quarters. Some were lumped with slumbering figures, but there was no sign of Reggie.

"Look at them in there," Harrumphrey harrumphed. "Lazy lugs! No wonder this place hasn't produced anything worthwhile in ages!"

"*Non non non*! Zey do not sleep out of laziness," said Jean-Remy. "They sleep because of such a good meal. And zat is because of you, mademoiselle, and your grandfather, with such wonderful cooking."

At the end of the corridor were the silver sliding doors of an elevator. As they got closer, Elliot and Leslie noticed something very peculiar about the buttons. They weren't buttons.

"They're *fingers*," said Elliot.

"But of course," said Jean-Remy. "How else would you call an expectavator?"

"An expecta-what?"

"You'll see when it gets here," said Harrumphrey.

Elliot and Leslie peered at the panel. Instead of the two buttons you might expect on a conventional elevator, the wall panel beside the door featured a pair of fingers. They poked out of two holes in the wall, precisely where the buttons should have been. To make matters worse (or rather *creepier*), both fingers were a sickly green color and tipped with a long, yellow claw.

Leslie pointed at them (they pointed right back at her). "What are *those* supposed to be?" she asked.

"Knottubs," Harrumphrey told her (as if the answer was obvious). "The opposite of buttons."

"Oh, I get it," said Elliot. "*Nottub* is *button*, but spelled backward."

Harrumphrey blinked at him. "Don't be ridiculous. *Knottub* starts with a *K*."

"Um, sure . . ." Elliot responded (there was little else to say when faced with this sort of bizarre creature reasoning).

Leslie leaned closer to the knottubs. They both looked alarmingly real. "So, how do these things work?"

"Are you kidding?" Harrumphrey harrumphed. "Knottubs are the *opposite* of buttons, right? And since you *push* buttons . . ."

Leslie winced. "Oh, no, please don't tell me."

"Yep." With his tail, Harrumphrey pointed to the panel. "Pull the finger."

Leslie reached up and (very reluctantly) gripped the top finger. Disturbingly, it was warm and soft—almost as if it were alive.

She pulled it.

There was a noise like a tiny fart and the doors slid open, making a sound like someone saying *"aaaaaah!"*

Leslie released the finger and leapt backward. "That. Is. *Disgusting!*"

Jean-Remy bowed to her. "Mademoiselle, I quite agree with zis appraisal. Ze mechanism, *it is repellent*! Buuut . . . since it is ze *Creature* Department, I must admit: It also seems a little bit appropriate."

"Excuse me," said a dull, monotonous voice from inside the elevator. "Are you coming in or not?"

Elliot and Leslie peeked into the elevator. They saw a tall, incredibly skinny creature. He resembled a soft brown flagpole (with a potbelly). Two dim, unblinking eyes sat atop the tube-like creature, while its mouth was almost two feet below them, a horizontal opening without lips or any expression whatsoever.

"You may now enter," the creature intoned in a half-dead voice. "Places to go, creatures to see."

"Meet Gabe," said Harrumphrey. "He runs the expectavator."

Indeed, that was precisely what was written on the creature's ID badge:

Gabe
Expectavator Operator

"Sounds like a tongue twister," said Leslie.

"No," droned Gabe. "Just my job."

Elliot leaned in close to Gabe's ID badge. "Anyone want to tell us what an *ex-pec-ta-vator* is?"

"What're you two, blind?" Harrumphrey scoffed, slapping his tail on the floor. "This is it! You're in one!"

"Looks like a plain old elevator to me."

Harrumphrey chuckled to himself. "*An elevator?!* Where are we now, the nineteenth century? You want some steam-powered underpants with that?"

"Actually," said Leslie, "we're in the twenty-first century, and elevators are quite common."

"Not around here they aren't." Harrumphrey waddled through the doors and the others followed him. "All an elevator can do is go up and down, up and down. That's 'cuz it's connected to pulleys and cables and all that stuff. But an expectavator is different. It can go in any direction it wants."

"How does it move?" asked Elliot. "What's powering it?"

"*Hope,*" said Harrumphrey as the doors slid silently shut.

"That's impossible," said Elliot.

"Wait and see."

Gabe, the beanpole of a creature, sat slumped on a stool in the corner. "Where to?" he asked glumly.

Jean-Remy flapped over to the control panel (thankfully equipped with a great many *buttons*, rather than knottubs). Instead of the usual numbers, referring to the floors in a building, however, each button was crammed with tiny words:

Secret Door Behind the Stationary Supplies Closet in the Accounting Department

or

Second-to-Last Ceiling Tile Above the Mezzanine Security Desk

or

Exhaust Vent Beside the Corner Window in Human (AND ONLY HUMAN!) Resources

"Here we are," said Jean-Remy, after a moment of perusing the options. "Ze ventilation shaft on ze west wall of ze North Tower Executive Boardroom."

"Okay," said Gabe. He reached up with a limp arm and pushed the appropriate button.

The moment the button illuminated, speakers mounted in the walls played soothing (but inescapably cheesy) bossa nova music. Everyone waited in silence.

And waited . . .

And waited . . .

Elliot and Leslie looked at each other.

"Are we even moving?" Elliot asked.

"Of course we are," said Harrumphrey, looking a bit offended. "I designed this thing myself."

They listened some more but heard (and felt) nothing.

"No way," said Leslie. "This is silly. We're just standing in a box. You can't run an elevator on hope."

"*Expectavator,*" Harrumphrey corrected. "And *yes*, you can."

Jean-Remy flew to hover in the dead center of the expectavator. "I am afraid what he says is true, mademoiselle. Do you not realize—*hope*, it is a powerful zing, *non*?"

"Well, yes, but—"

"It is one of ze most powerful things in all ze universe! It is something we creatures, we have always understood. But you humans . . . well, not so much."

"My *uncle* understands," said Elliot.

"Well, ze professor—he is very special, you know?"

Meanwhile, Leslie was looking nervously at the ceiling and walls of the expectavator. "So you mean, right now, there's nothing holding us up except for . . ."

"Hope," said Harrumphrey.

"But what does that *mean*?"

"Well, the physics is a bit complicated, of course, but the expectavator adheres to the basic principles of all creature technology—which basically states that all things, even machines, have an essence. If you can isolate that essence and refine it, it becomes not only the machine's power source but—*literally*—the secret ingredient to getting something to work. Get it?"

"Sort of," said Elliot.

"Ditto," said Leslie.

"And the essence of an expectavator is, of course, *hope*. Right now, the components are monitoring how hopeful we are, measuring the weight of our expectations, the strength of our optimism—and using that energy to send us where we need to be."

"You're serious, aren't you?" asked Elliot.

"I would never joke about one of my inventions."

"But that's *amazing*," cried Leslie. If what Harrumphrey was saying was true, the expectavator would be one of the greatest inventions in history. "I don't get it. How come these things aren't all over the world? Why isn't the professor presenting *this* to the shareholders right now? It could save the company."

Harrumphrey tilted his huge head sideways and sucked his teeth. "*Weeell* . . . the truth is, in spite of their name, expectavators don't always work the way you expect them to. They can be a little unpredictable."

To Elliot and Leslie, this sounded extremely ominous.

"Wait," said Elliot. "You mean, like . . . they can fall?"

Harrumphrey shook his head quite emphatically. "Oh, no,

we're completely safe. That's the beauty of an expectavator. It won't ever fall, not completely. There'll always be something to hold us up because, let's face it. No situation is entirely hopeless."

"That's what *you* say," said Gabe, slumping even lower. He looked like a potbellied question mark.

"You'll have to excuse Gabe," Harrumphrey told them. "He has a medical condition: born with overly low expectations."

"Sorry to hear that," said Elliot.

"Meh," said Gabe.

"That's another problem with the expectavator," Harrumphrey went on. "You need to bring along someone like Gabe. Otherwise, there's a chance we'd shoot straight through the roof."

Gabe nodded gloomily. "Just doing my job."

Again, they stood in silence, listening to the lilting tones of Brazilian bossa nova. Leslie and Elliot were beginning (once again) to doubt they were moving when there was the *ding* of a bell and the music stopped.

"We're here," said Harrumphrey.

Elliot shook his head. "It never once felt like we were moving."

"Sure we were! Open up, Gabe, we'll show 'em."

Gabe pressed a button and the doors juddered apart. Leslie saw she was wrong: They *had* moved. Unfortunately, it didn't look like a very hospitable destination. In fact, the doors had opened on a smooth cement wall.

"Is that where we're supposed to be?" asked Elliot.

Harrumphrey shook his head. "See what I mean? *Unpredictable.*"

Leslie tapped on the cement. It was perfectly solid. "Now what?"

"We've come a bit too far," Harrumphrey explained. "We'll have to lower our expectations. Gabe?"

"All right," said Gabe, slumping a bit lower on his stool. "I'll try to think about my divorce. That usually helps." He shut his eyes and sighed deeply. As he did this, the expectavator dropped a few inches.

"It's working," said Elliot. He pointed to a gap of space that had appeared at the bottom of the doorway.

Gabe sighed again and again, but it was no use. They were still trapped inside.

"Sorry," said Gabe. "That's the best I've got. You're obviously quite an optimistic bunch."

"Yes, it is ze children," said Jean-Remy. "In my experience, zey are quite optimistic."

"Okay, you two," Harrumphrey said to them. "Looks like we're gonna need to get about twelve feet lower, so I'd say if there's anything you guys worry about, now's the time to worry about it."

Elliot and Leslie looked at each other.

"Well," said Elliot hesitantly, "I guess I worry that I'm not as smart as Uncle Archie. I want to grow up to be like him, but I worry that my parents have other plans. I'm sure they wouldn't like the idea of me working with a bunch of crazy creatures all day long."

"'*Crazy*'?" asked Harrumphrey.

"I mean cool. *Cool* creatures. But I really don't know if I'm smart enough, and besides, now it seems like the whole company might shut down and then . . . and then . . ."

He couldn't even finish, but it was okay. Saying all of that out loud had certainly thrown a sucker punch into his hopes for the future. Accordingly, the expectavator had descended a few feet. It wasn't enough for them to squeeze through, but it was something.

Harrumphrey turned to Leslie. "Now you."

At first, Leslie wasn't sure what to say, but then it occurred to her. It was so obvious.

"My mom," she said. "She's not great at staying in the same job for very long. She's always quitting or getting fired, moving us to some new town. That's how we ended up here. My grandpa said he'd do her a favor and give her a job in his restaurant. But there are hardly any customers and I don't think she likes it." She hung her head. "I'm worried we're going to move again. Usually, I don't mind so much, because most of the places we go are kind of dull, but Bickleburgh is different. It seemed boring at first, but . . ." Leslie looked up at the others. Her eyes jumped from creature to creature, finally landing on Elliot. "Now it seems like the most incredible place in the whole world. I've made friends with people and creatures I never thought I would have before and what if—"

"*STOP!*" Harrumphrey said. "That's perfect."

Leslie turned around and saw the doors had aligned with a grated platform similar to the scaffolds in the Creature Department. Pipes and wiring ran up and down the walls and the only light was dim and red.

"This is where we get off," Harrumphrey told her, leading everyone but Gabe out onto the platform.

Elliot took one look back as the doors were closing. Gabe, the expectavator operator, was peering dully out at them from his stool in the corner. He had one hand raised as if to wave, only it wasn't moving. He was merely holding it up in a silent farewell. As he did, the expectavator began, inexorably, to sink.

When the doors came together, Elliot was astonished to see how perfectly they disguised themselves. What remained looked like smooth, ordinary concrete.

"Zere are some who say," Jean-Remy began, hovering above the platform, "that to be as young as yourselves is to be free of trouble. But of course, as we have just seen in ze expectavator, it is not true at all. All of us, no matter who we are—or how old we may be—we all have a bit of ze troubles from time to time. *But please*, you should not worry! Ze troubles, zey come and zey go, but among ze creatures of creaturedom, I tell you zis: We believe ze troubles, more than anything else, zey make you who you are. It is true, *non*?"

Elliot and Leslie could see how, in a way, Jean-Remy was right. The things that worried them had a very clear effect on everything they did.

"It's true," said Elliot. He took the electric pencil out of his fishing vest. "If I didn't admire my uncle so much, I probably wouldn't carry this around with me everywhere."

Leslie nodded. "When you stop to think about your troubles that way, it kind of gives you a new appreciation for them."

Jean-Remy nodded, smiling at them both. "Among ze fairy-bats, we are known to even give names to our troubles."

"You *name* them?" asked Elliot.

"Let me give you an example. Once, a long time ago, I was in love with a beautiful fairy princess, but . . ." Jean-Remy sighed deeply. "Well, let us say it did not work out. Now ze fairy princess, she is gone and I am only left with a terrible heartbreak, whom I call Bernard."

Leslie snorted. "You were in love with a fairy princess called *Bernard*?"

"*Non non non!* You misunderstand!" Jean-Remy flapped his arms (along with his wings). "I told you, ze fairy princess—she is gone. Probably I will never see her again. But *ze pain*! Ze pain, it is still here." He tapped his chest with one tiny finger. "And it is *ze pain* whom I call Bernard."

"And you don't think that's kind of weird?"

"*Mais non!* It is quite sensible! Now, you see, ze pain—it becomes like a companion. A strange one, perhaps, but a companion none-ze-less. Now, whenever I feel ze pain, I do not feel sad or frightened. Instead, I say, 'Ah! Bernard, my old friend! You have come to visit me, once again, you little *coquin*, you!'"

Elliot and Leslie weren't sure they were ready to start naming their troubles, but like a lot of things in creaturedom, the practice made an odd sort of sense.

"Forgive me," said Jean-Remy, flying ahead. "I should not waste any more time with such silly stories."

"No kidding," Harrumphrey grumbled. "The meeting'll be starting any minute now."

At the end of the platform, there wasn't a door but instead

a large ventilation shaft. They climbed inside and continued on until they reached a series of slated grates, where taut ribbons of light streamed through from the other side.

Elliot, Leslie, Harrumphrey, and Jean-Remy stood perfectly still and peered out into an enormous board room. . . .

CHAPTER 10

In which Sir William forgets something, Carl has a shock,
and the professor is given one last chance

Sir William Sniffledon was so old, he had forgotten his birthday. Not merely the month and the day, but the *year*.

How old am I really? he wondered, limping down the corridor to DENKi-3000's main conference room. *Eighty-one? Eighty-seven? Ninety?* He had always liked the sound of the number ninety-nine, but surely he wasn't *that* old.

It wasn't just forgetting his age that bothered him. There was something else—something even more important—that he had forgotten.

But what is it?

Every morning, Sir William awoke wondering if this would be the day he would finally recall whatever important thing had niggled at him for so long. Every evening, however, he climbed into bed disappointed.

At last, he approached the doors at the end of the hallway. This might be his very last meeting at his beloved DENKi-3000. It was certainly possible. The shareholders were scheduled to have their final vote on the Quazicom takeover.

If they voted *yes*, DENKi-3000 would cease to exist. The company would be swallowed up by Quazicom and the first thing they would do was spit out the bones (old bones like Sir William himself). Indeed, these were dark times for the company, and not merely because of the takeover bid. The very age they lived in was changing. When Sir William thought of inventing something, he thought of creating things, actual, physical, mechanical things that no one had ever made before.

The electric pencil, for instance. Now *there* was an invention! It never grew dull because tiny servos were constantly extending the graphite tip. Amazing! These days, however, people weren't interested in what Sir William considered *true* inventions. Nowadays everything was *virtual*. Nothing seemed real anymore.

In spite of these rather discouraging thoughts, Sir William did his best to stand up a little straighter as he opened the door.

The shareholders were waiting, a large crowd of men and women in sharp, well-tailored suits. Nearly every one of the suits was either dark gray or navy blue. *I must look like an old hermit to them*, Sir William thought as he limped past, *what with my corduroy slacks and ragged old cardigan*.

The shareholders nodded politely, but most remained facing the stage up front, where the executives of the various departments were seated behind a long table. Sir William's seat was in the middle, beside that of the vice president, Monica Burkenkrantz.

Monica, Monica, Monica, thought Sir William.

When he had hired her two years ago, she had already been the vice president of a toothpick company, a button manufacturer, and some sort of newfangled firm that produced vitamins and dietary supplements. Sir William hadn't cared much for the third in the chain, but toothpicks and buttons—those were solid, useful products. As solid and useful as anything DENKi-3000 produced.

At the start, Monica had been wonderful—so enthusiastic, so full of ideas for improving the company. Lately, however, her enthusiasm had vanished. She was cynical, disappointed, angry.

Sir William had begun to suspect the source of her initial enthusiasm might have had something to do with his own advanced age. Was it possible Monica Burkenkrantz was merely waiting for him to *die*? After all, if anything were to happen to him, Monica Burkenkrantz would become the company's new CEO.

Perhaps, he thought darkly, her wish would soon be granted.

"Ah, Sir William!" said Monica, rising to her feet. She smiled and her teeth gleamed as artificially as her orange suit, which stood out sharply against the conservative colors of the shareholders. "I'm sure you'd like to kick off the meeting by addressing the audience."

Sir William stopped and leaned on his cane. "I will, Ms. Burkenkrantz, just as soon as I make it to my seat."

Monica let out an embarrassed laugh. "Of course, of course!"

One of the shareholders rose to help him up the stairs, but Sir William waved the man off. He wasn't yet so old that he couldn't climb four puny steps.

"In our last meeting," Sir William said, once he had lowered himself into his chair. "You, the shareholders, recommended it would be in the best interests of the company if . . ." He had to pause before the next part. "If we were to accept the current buyout offer from Quazicom Holdings Incorporated. And now here we are, preparing to vote on the matter." He swept his gaze indignantly across the crowd. "As you know, I was—and I remain—*not* in favor of selling."

A shareholder in the front row stood up. He was the appointed spokesperson for the meeting. "With all due respect, Sir William," he said. "I think you're only focusing on the negatives of the takeover."

"Enlighten me, then. What are the positives?"

"It's a very reasonable offer. DENKi-3000's stock price has been falling for nearly a year. In all that time, we haven't brought out a single new product. In light of this, we believe the offer from Quazicom is quite generous."

"There's more to this company than money." Sir William honestly believed that. He didn't know why (perhaps he had forgotten that too) but he felt it, deep down in his old bones.

"Gentlemen," said Monica, "there's no need for animosity. The buyout isn't written in stone quite yet. In fact, Quazicom sent a representative—"

"*A spy*, you mean," grumbled Sir William.

Monica laughed nervously. "Oh, Sir William! What a joker you are! No, no," she added hastily. "Mr. Brickweather is no spy. He's merely here to look over the company. Kick our proverbial tires, so to speak, before anything is finalized."

"If it sounds like a spy and it looks like a spy . . ." said Sir William.

"*Ahem!*" Monica cleared her throat to interrupt. "In fact, Mr. Brickweather *is here with us today.*"

Sir William raised his wiry eyebrows. "Here? Now? Today?"

"Yes. Right over there." Monica put out her arm, palm up, in something of a welcoming gesture. "Ladies and gentlemen, Mr. Chuck Brickweather."

A very tall man rose from the middle of the crowd.

He wasn't dressed in somber blue or gray. Instead, he wore a black-and-white pin-striped suit, with stripes so thick and stark they were almost dizzying to look at.

He had blond hair, a sparkling smile, and an angular face (although, Sir William noted, it was tinged a bit pink, either the result of embarrassment or sunburn—impossible to tell which). Overall, the man was quite handsome, but in a generic sort of way. At the same time, there was something odd about Mr. Chuck Brickweather.

It was his eyes, thought Sir William. There were just *a little* too close together.

"Mr. Brickweather works for Quazicom's Corporate Takeover Division. They have requested that he be granted full access to *all areas* of DENKi-3000." Monica looked down the table at the heads of each department. Her eyes came to rest on Elliot's uncle, who sat at the far end, near the windows. "*Full* access. Isn't that right, Professor?"

Professor von Doppler shook his head. "I'm sorry. As long as this company is called DENKi-3000, it's my duty to uphold the company charter."

"Come now, Professor, I'm sure you won't mind letting Mr. Brickweather have a just an eensy-weensy peek into our R&D Department."

"*Impossible,*" Sir William said. This was something he *did* remember. "The DENKi-3000 charter clearly states that only the head of Research and Development knows what goes on in that department. Right, Professor?"

"I realize it's an unusual stance," the professor conceded, "but our products are simply too revolutionary to risk a leak."

"Besides," said Sir William, "those rules have been in place since the very beginning, and it's made us the fifth-largest technology company in the world!"

"Perhaps if we weren't so secretive," suggested the shareholder spokesman, "we'd be ranked even higher—and not under threat of a takeover." Before the man could say anything more, the conference room doors burst open.

A crowd of people came marching in, carrying signs and banners emblazoned with forthright (if somewhat simplistic) messages:

And so on.

Leading the march of protesters was Carl, the security guard Elliot and Leslie had met earlier.

Sir William wasn't sure what to make of the disturbance. "What's going on here?" he cried.

"You can't be in here!" Monica Burkenkrantz shouted at the protestors. "This is a shareholders' meeting!"

"And what about *our* share?" Carl shouted back at her. "We're the ones who really run this place. Not them!" He pointed to the crowd.

Carl glared at Chuck Brickweather. "Scram, mister!" Carl said to him. "We know all about what happens when Quazicom buys a company. You pick it apart and shut it down!"

Chuck Brickweather opened his mouth to defend himself, but Monica spoke before him.

"Allow me to apologize for the interruption, Mr. Brickweather." She picked her phone up off the desk. "I'll just call security."

"We *are* security," said Carl.

There was a triumphant cheer from the protesters.

Monica moved the phone away from her ear. "That's fine," she said. "I wasn't talking about DENKi-3000 security."

"Huh?" Carl was clearly baffled.

"Didn't you know? Mr. Brickweather isn't the only thing Quazicom sent us today. They were also kind enough to lend us *their own* security team."

"They did?" asked Sir William. (Could *this* be the thing he had forgotten?)

Bringing the phone back to her mouth, Monica said, "Send them in."

Behind the stage, a huge automated door slid open, revealing an army of . . . *robots*.

They were all identical, all round, black droids the size of
large beach balls. Each one was set on three spherical wheels,
making them fast and agile. Their only appendage was a single
metal claw, rising from the top of their . . . *heads?*

They fanned out down the aisles on either side of the shareholders, whirring to the back of the room to surround the
protestors.

"What are these things?" asked Carl.

"These," Monica retorted dryly, "are the sorts of employees who won't interrupt shareholders' meetings."

Carl scoffed. "We're not scared of your little toy soldiers,
are we, guys?"

There were shouts of support from the others behind him.

The robot directly in front of Carl glowed an eerie red
color, and a soothing, perfectly calm voice oozed from its invisible speakers.

"Sir, I am awfully sorry to inform you of this, but I believe
you may be distressing our valued shareholders."

"Can it, dumpy. You don't work here, but *we* do." Carl
jabbed one of the robots with the toe of his boot. "So speaking as a *real* security guard, I hereby request that you take your
little round friends and—"

ZAP!

From behind him, a sizzling arc of blue electricity leapt out
of one of the robots' claws, zapping Carl's butt.

"YOOOWW! Hey, you can't do tha—"

ZZZAP!

"AIEEGH!"

"BWAAAH!"

"MEEEEH!"

Suddenly, there were blue arcs of electricity flying everywhere, zapping butt after butt of the DENKi-3000 protesters.

"We are awfully sorry for any inconvenience that may arise from these minor electrical shocks," said the robotic (but incredibly polite) voice, "but a certain degree of coercion has been deemed necessary."

ZAP!

"OWW!" screamed Carl. "Call that *minor*?! You gotta be kidding!"

"No," the robot replied. "We are not programmed for humor."

ZAP!

"YAAAAH!"

"Kindly accompany us downstairs—"

ZAP!!

"YOOOWW!"

"—and we will be happy to escort you back to your respective stations."

ZAP!

ZZZAP!

ZZZZZZAP!

"EEEAAAAAGH!"

It took less than a minute of "coercion" for Carl and the protestors to be chased from the room. After a moment of reflective silence, Sir William spoke.

"Mr. Brickweather," he said. "Is this how Quazicom deals with employee grievances? With *shock treatment*?"

The man from Quazicom held up his hands, as if in

self-defense. He smiled a shining, thousand-watt smile (one that seemed to feature a few too many teeth). "As Ms. Burkenkrantz mentioned, I don't work directly for Quazicom. It's not *my* company at all. I was merely sent to gather information." Perhaps to demonstrate, he held up an electronic notepad, where he would record his research.

"Nevertheless," said Sir William. "You *do* represent the company responsible for those electric menaces." He pointed to the remaining security bots, standing silently around the room.

"Why don't we set aside a discussion about our security bots for now," said Chuck, "and focus on the task at hand. It really would be ideal if I were granted full access to all areas of DENKi-3000."

"I'm afraid that's not possible," said Sir William. "As long as the company's in my hands, we uphold the charter."

"I should inform you," said Chuck, speaking in a surprisingly sympathetic tone, "you may be jeopardizing the takeover."

"What about a compromise?" said a voice at the back of the room. It was an old woman in a light gray suit that matched her hair.

Not as old as me, thought Sir William . . . *at least I* think *she's not as old as me.* "Yes?" he said. "What sort of compromise?"

"Let me just say," the woman began, "that not all the shareholders are in favor of the takeover. I represent the small minority who, like Sir William, are against it." She put one hand in her pocket and took out a first-generation DENKi-3000 Electric Pencil with Retractable Telescopic Lens. "I've had this ever since I was a little girl."

Sir William nodded proudly. "An excellent product,

madam. Now, what's this compromise you mentioned?"

"It's really a question for Professor von Doppler." She turned her attention to him. "Are you working on something, Professor? We know that if we just could announce a new product—even just a prototype—we wouldn't even need to have this meeting."

Elliot's uncle opened his mouth as if to answer, but it was Monica Burkenkrantz who spoke first. "I'm sure we can all agree the professor has had ample time to produce something new for this company."

"Let's not be too hasty, Monica," said Sir William. "Professor, why don't you answer the lady's question? Have you got some fabulous new invention to unveil for us?"

Professor von Doppler took a deep breath. "We've been working very hard in my department, trying to come up with something truly revolutionary, but I'm afraid—"

"You don't have anything," Monica cut in. "We know."

"That's not true," answered the professor. "There is something."

A murmur of astonishment bubbled through the crowd.

"*There is?!*" Monica Burkenkrantz was as shocked as anyone. "Why weren't we notified?"

"I haven't told anyone," said the professor. "It's something I've been working on privately. A personal project."

Sir William smiled. *Good old Professor von Doppler*, he thought, *I can always count on him to come through in the end.* "Well, Professor," he said, "why don't you tell us all about it?"

But that's not what the professor did. He ignored everyone on the stage and even everyone in the crowd. All his attention was on the old lady at the back of the room.

"When I was young," he said to her, "I was like you. I loved strange inventions. There was one in particular I dreamed of more than any other. In fact, it was the reason I became an inventor and took a job here at DENKi-3000. It seemed like the one place where I might have a chance of realizing my dream!"

"*What* invention?" Monica demanded, slapping the table. "Surely, you can tell us what it is!"

"You'd never believe me," said the professor. "Or you'd think it was silly." He hung his head. "Besides, it's not ready."

The audience sighed in disappointment (even the shareholder spokesman).

"You see? More secrets. If it were up to me, and of course it's not . . ." Monica glanced at Sir William. "I'd hurry up and let Mr. Brickweather do his job and proceed right away with the takeover."

"Be careful, Ms. Burkenkrantz," warned Sir William. "You were correct in saying it isn't up to you."

"That's right," she replied. "It's up to *them*." Monica spread her arms, indicating the shareholders.

Sir William knew she was right. "Yes, I suppose. . . ."

"*Excellent,*" said Monica, rising from her seat. "Since it seems the professor has nothing to show for all his work, and since he is *demonstrably* the person offering the strongest resistance to Quazicom, *and* since we're all here for a vote, I say we put *this* to a vote too."

"Put what to a vote?" asked the professor.

"By a show of hands," Monica went on, "how many people here think Professor Archimedes von Doppler *should be fired*?"

"*NO!*"

Sir William jerked in his seat. So did everyone else. The voice had come from a large ventilation grate on the wall.

"*You can't!*"

There was a loud CRACK and the grating tore away. It fell forward onto the carpet, bringing along a pair of children with it. The boy was dressed in a green fishing vest (a rather dashing accoutrement, thought Sir William), while the girl was dressed entirely in black.

Professor von Doppler leapt to his feet. "Elliot? Leslie? What are you—?"

"*SPIES!*" screeched Monica Burkenkrantz. She paused, a little confused, and leaned across the table to get a closer look at them. "Very. Tiny. Spies."

The two children climbed to their feet and were instantly surrounded by a troop of the extremely polite Quazicom security robots.

"You'll have to pardon us for blocking your way," said one of the robots, "but according to our data, children are not supposed to be in the walls. Mice, perhaps, on occasion, but children?" The robot's claw fizzled with blue electricity. "We're afraid that's highly peculiar, and so we have no choice but to—"

"N-no! Wait! They're with me!"

Everyone looked to the professor.

The shareholder spokesman in the front row frowned. "With you, Professor? Are we to believe the R&D Department is staffed *by children*?!"

"You don't understand," said the professor. "That boy is my nephew, Elliot. He and his friend, Leslie, came to visit me today."

"A visit to *where*?" asked Monica Burkenkrantz. "The ventilation shaft?"

"I must admit that I have *no idea* what they were doing crawling around in the walls." The professor glared at the boy in the green fishing vest. "And I have *no idea* how they could *possibly* find their way in there."

Sir William detected something odd in the sudden graveness of the professor's voice. Sir William wondered if this had something to do with the important thing he had forgotten. Was it something about children living in the walls?

"I wonder," said Monica suddenly, squinting into the hole where the grating had been. "Are those two the only ones in there? Why don't we have a look?"

Professor von Doppler went pale. "You don't have to—"

Before he could finish, one of the robots broke away from the rest and zipped over to the hole in the wall. It jabbed its claw into the ventilation shaft and made a series of *bleep*s and *bloop*s.

"I'm afraid," said the robot at last, "my monitors show no sign of other children."

Sir William beckoned to the professor's nephew and the other child. "Come up here to the stage, please."

They did, looking very nervous.

"Are you having a good visit?" Sir William asked them.

They nodded.

"Would you mind telling us what you were doing inside the wall of our conference room?"

"You can't fire my uncle," the boy spluttered.

"If he's working on something," said the girl, "trust me, it'll be *awesome*."

"I'm afraid it's too late for that," said Monica Burkenkrantz. "And this is a corporate shareholders' meeting. It's no place for children. So can we *please* finish voting on—"

"*NO!*" The boy turned to face the audience. "You just have to believe me. Give Uncle Archie a bit more time. If he tells his, uh—well, *his staff* about this secret project of his, I'll bet they'll have something ready by . . . by . . . *by the end of the week*. I promise!"

"That's quite soon," said Sir William. "What would you know about it?"

"We just do," said the girl. "If anyone can get it done, it's the professor and his team."

There was something oddly convincing about a couple of kids presenting to a roomful of executives. Sir William was pleased to see the expressions of many of the shareholders soften.

"The end of the week, you say?" Sir William looked at the professor. "That only leaves you a few days. If you don't have anything now, what will change by Friday?"

"Well . . ." Professor von Doppler pondered the question for a long time. "*Everything,*" he said at last. "Everything can change by Friday." He seemed to be drawing sudden energy and confidence from the children. "Somehow," he said, "I'll find a way!"

"Good," said Sir William. "That's what I hoped you would say."

"It is?" asked Elliot.

Sir William nodded, his wrinkly face cracking into a huge smile. "Professor, you have until Friday."

"*What?!*" Monica's face burned red with frustration.

"I still have a modicum of clout left in this company, Ms. Burkenkrantz, and I'm going to use it." Sir William leaned heavily on his cane and rose from his chair. "We'll all leave

Professor von Doppler alone until Friday or else . . . or else . . .”

The professor nodded grimly. “Or else we sell to Quazicom.”

Sir William was glad the professor had cut in. Those words were simply too difficult to say. “We’ll reconvene once again on casual Friday—possibly for the very last time,” Sir William announced, an undisguised note of sadness quivering in his old voice. “Professor, you have until then to wow us, and in the meantime . . .” He looked to the consultant from Quazicom. “Mr. Brickweather, you have free rein to go wherever you like *except* to the professor’s department. Until Friday, leave him to his work. Is that fair?”

“For now,” said Chuck.

Finally, Sir William returned his attention to the children. “As for you two, we’d better have—”

“The security robots will escort them out,” said Monica Burkenkrantz. “Quite frankly, I don’t think they should be allowed to return here.”

“*No!*” cried the children.

Monica pursed her lips. “We can’t have kids running around in the ventilation shafts. It’s unsanitary! Not to mention *trespassing.*”

The children and the professor voiced complaints, but in the end, Monica won out. (In a way, she was right. Having children in the ventilation shafts was probably a violation of health and safety standards.) The robots led the two youngsters away.

“And remember,” the vice president called after the robots. “If those kids give you any trouble, *zap ’em*!”

Once they were gone, Chuck Brickweather raised his hand. “Sir William, could I ask you a question?”

“Yes, Mr. Brickweather?”

"Are *all* your shareholder meetings like this?"

Sir William shook his head. "So far, just this one."

"I see."

"Of course, that's not saying much," said Sir William. "We hardly ever have shareholder meetings. In fact, this is the first one we've had since . . . since . . . I'm sorry," he muttered. "I can't remember."

Chuck Brickweather narrowed his eyes, dutifully tapping this information into his electronic notepad.

CHAPTER 11

In which a lullaby for Leslie doesn't work
(and neither do tea and biscuits)

eslie Fang's bedroom was directly above the kitchen at
Famous Freddy's Dim Sum Emporium. It was small,
dimly lit, and reeked of sesame oil.

Apart from the smell, it was the typical room of a twelve-
year-old girl. The narrow bed was covered in a frilly white
duvet, the mirror above the armoire was hung with hair elastics,
multicolored necklaces, and clippings from music magazines,
and on the bottom shelf of the bookcase was a menagerie of
stuffed animals Leslie wasn't quite ready to throw away.

Some aspects of the decor, however, looked like they
belonged more to a brooding teenager. The color of the cur-
tains, for instance (black), or the plush armchair in the corner
(deep red with hypnotic silver spirals). Similarly, several of the
necklaces hanging around the mirror featured tiny silver skel-
etons instead of jewels and pendants.

Oddest of all were her posters of Boris Minor and the
Karloffs, a goth-pop band that had enjoyed its heyday about
twenty years before Leslie was born.

This was what happened when your mother dragged you

from city to city in pursuit of a dream job that never material-
ized. You became interested in things that weren't really aimed
at your demographic.

Three towns ago, Leslie and her mother lived above a used
record shop. The only person Leslie saw on a regular basis
(besides her mother) was the manager of the shop, a pleasingly
plump woman who always dressed in taffeta hoop skirts and
a felt top hat.

"Try this," the woman told her one day, handing her the first
album by Boris Minor and the Karloffs. "I think you'll like it."

Leslie *did* like it, and it was around this time her entire
wardrobe turned black.

Leslie's mother had been so appalled by the monster-movie
imagery of the albums that she blamed the bad influence of the
music for their subsequent move.

Unfortunately (at least for Leslie's mother), by the time
they packed up the car and set off for a new town, Leslie was
already hooked on the band's catchy three-chord melodies. Not
to mention the deep, almost-bottomless voice of the lead singer,
Boris Minor, whose gaunt face glowered out of the poster above
Leslie's bed.

Leslie stared up at him. She couldn't sleep. Ever since she
had visited DENKi-3000, her mind had been racing, repeating
the same three words over and over.

Creatures are real! Creatures are real! Creatures . . .

On the album covers of Boris Minor and the Karloffs,
the band members often dressed in silly costumes, pre-
tending to be zombies or werewolves. It had all been
part of the band's theatrical image. Judging by the way they
capered through the pictures, none of them—not even Boris

Minor himself—took it very seriously. But it *was* serious.

Creatures were real!

They didn't look anything like the cheap costumes and makeup of an old B movie. *Real* creatures were incredible!

Just thinking about them made her lightheaded (not to mention lighthearted). In fact, every time she thought the words—*creatures are real*—her entire body felt lighter than air. She felt as if she were rising up, weightless, hovering above the blankets of her bed! Yet it wasn't merely high-spirited giddiness that kept Leslie awake. It was the basic mystery of it all. She had so many questions. . . .

Where had the creatures come from? How had they gotten there? And what was it in those photographs—*those memories*—that frightened them? Then there was Elliot's uncle. What was the secret invention he was working on, the one he had dreamed of all his life?

She and Elliot would just have to go back. No matter what that Monica woman said, they had to get answers to all these questions. After all, once you had found the most amazing place in the world, how could you resist returning?

There was a soft knock on Leslie's door. "Shouldn't you be asleep?"

"I'm not tired."

"Well, *I* am." Her mother came into the room and plonked heavily down on the edge of the bed. "*I'm bored.* I just stand around all day. Nobody ever comes in here. It's a waste of time, if you ask me."

Leslie recognized her mother's tone. There were always complaints about how dull or difficult a job was just before her mother quit.

Leslie closed her eyes. "I like it here," she said.

Her mother seemed startled. "I thought you told me Bickleburgh was the most boring place we'd ever moved."

Leslie opened her eyes just in time to see her mother slumping forward, elbows on her knees. "It's great to see your grandpa and it's nice that the job comes with a place to live, but I'm really not sure it's worth it."

"If waiting the tables is boring," Leslie suggested, "why don't you let Grandpa Freddy teach you how to cook?"

Her mother shrugged. "Maybe."

"Please, Mom, for once let's stay somewhere longer than six months."

"*Here?*"

"Why not?"

"You honestly like it here? Bickleburgh?"

"I do."

"Is this because of that boy?"

"*Elliot?*"

"Just what I need! Your first crush."

"Mom, trust me. It's *definitely not* because of him." Except, of course, that it was—just not in the way her mother suspected.

"I don't know, Les, maybe I'm just feeling the wanderlust again."

The wanderlust. It was always the reason her mother needed to suddenly leave a place.

"All you ever think about is the next big thing, but when we get there, it's never like you thought it would be. Have you ever thought that maybe the only reason nowhere seems satisfying is because we never stay anywhere long enough to figure a place out?"

Leslie's mother thought about this. "You're smarter than you look, you know."

Leslie nodded happily. "I know."

"Is that what you want? To stay in the same place? Even if it's Bickleburgh?"

Leslie nodded again. "It's the same thing I always wanted. And yes, *definitely* here. Trust me, Bickleburgh is a *way* cooler place than it looks. Maybe you'll see that too . . . if we stay."

Leslie's mother remained silent for a long time. It was one of those moments Leslie wished she could read her mother's thoughts. Or better yet, *influence them*. Of course, that was impossible. All Leslie could do was wait.

"Okay," her mother said at last. "We'll stick it out a bit longer, see how it goes." She leaned down to kiss Leslie's forehead. "Now go to sleep."

Leslie couldn't, of course, and after her mother was gone, she went on lying awake. She started playing one of her Boris Minor albums, the volume turned low. The gentle rhythm of their one big hit, "Monster Gnash," made for a decent lullaby.

It was funny that her mother had assumed Elliot was the reason Leslie wanted to remain in Bickleburgh. Leslie almost laughed, thinking about that vest of his. It looked like something Grandpa Freddy would wear—*on vacation*.

Unfortunately, she felt even more awake than before, so she turned off the music and climbed out of bed. *Tea and biscuits,* she thought. Perhaps what worked for an excitable bombastadon would also work for her. She tiptoed to the door and peeked into the hallway.

Her mother's door was closed, but dim light seeped out around the edges; she was still awake. Leslie would have to be very quiet.

Downstairs, the kitchen was spotless. The surfaces were clean and polished, and all the pots and steamers were stored away on their rightful shelves. The only thing that seemed messy and out of place was Grandpa Freddy himself.

He was slumped in the corner on a metal chair, his eyes closed and his mouth hanging slack. He was snoring like a saw.

One of Grandpa Freddy's arms was slung out onto the counter, fingers wrapped limply around a bottle of his home-made cooking wine.

Leslie tiptoed over to the bottle. It was still open, the cork lying on the counter. The clear liquid inside had a slight pink tinge, the result of a pickled plum floating down at the bottom. Grandpa Freddy put one of those in every bottle. It gave the alcohol a sweet tang that made it easier to swallow—at least that's what Grandpa Freddy said.

Leslie leaned over to take a sniff but pulled away quickly. The smell was *awful*, a bizarre mixture of honey, vinegar, over-ripe fruit, and Worcestershire sauce.

Wincing a little, Leslie gently pried the bottle out of her grandfather's hand and jammed it shut with the cork. She took the bottle to a small alcove off the main kitchen, where he kept his ingredients. On one set of shelves, there must have been twenty or thirty bottles of his pinkish cooking wine. Leslie clinked the half-empty bottle in with the rest.

Many times, Leslie's mother had asked Grandpa Freddy to stop brewing so much of the wine. Grandpa Freddy always responded with a mischievous grin, telling Leslie's mother it was his secret ingredient. Maybe so, thought Leslie, but ever since she and her mother had moved in above the restaurant,

Leslie had never seen Grandpa Freddy *actually cook* with his secret ingredient.

Leslie threw an herbal tea bag into a cup and put the kettle to boil. She wasn't sure if there were any biscuits, but it was worth rummaging through a few of the cupboards to find out.

Leslie didn't find any. She simply leaned on the counter, waiting for the water to boil. As she stood there, something caught her eye. It was out the window, over the building on the other side of the alley. Maybe just a flash of neon in the treetops.

No, something was *moving* through the branches. A big, loose shape. The neon light flashed and something glinted. Shiny and wet.

An eye.

It was staring right at her—and it was *huge.*

Leslie ducked down. What was out there? What had an eyeball *that big*?

She crawled across the room to the light switch and, reaching up with one hand, flicked off the lights. If the kitchen was dark, whatever was out there wouldn't be able to see in.

"*Grandpa!*" she whispered. "Grandpa, wake up!"

He didn't. He just snored. Leslie crawled back to the window.

The trees looked empty. The eye was gone. Leslie squinted into the darkness. A garish rainbow of neon light washed across the building and the trees.

She saw something.

A green that wasn't the green of leaves. It was the soft, mottled green of skin—but not human skin. Leslie tried to follow the shape of it, but it was impossible to make out where the trees ended and the body of the thing began. All she saw was . . .

The eye!

It blinked at her again, and there was more. An ear. A nose. A huge hand, wrapped all the way round a thick branch. Finally, she saw a mouth, an enormous toothy grin, full of crooked, yellow fangs.

She whispered the only word she could think of. *"Huge."*

Her brain screamed that it must be a creature. It must be something from DENKi-3000. And yet, even though she could only see bits and pieces, she knew it looked nothing like anything she had seen in the Creature Department. Nothing she and Elliot had met had been this . . . *frightening.*

"Grandpa, please!" She backed away from the window and tugged on his arm. *"Wake up!"*

She shook him harder and he let out a loud belch. His eyes popped open.

"Wha—? What's going on?!"

"Shh!" Leslie put one finger to her lips. "There's something outside." She pointed to the window.

"What something?"

"It's a creature. I think."

Grandpa Freddy blinked to gather his bearings. He pulled himself out of the chair and hobbled stiffly toward the window.

"Wait," said Leslie, "be careful. Whatever it is, it's really big."

Her grandfather opened the window and craned his bald head out into the night.

"What was it you saw?"

"In the trees." Leslie came to join him at the window. "On the other side of the building."

They both stared into the branches.

"Where?"

"It was there. I just saw it." Now, however, Leslie saw

nothing. "Just wait," she whispered. "It'll be back."

They stood in the darkness of the kitchen and stared. But they saw nothing. Not the eye, not the nose or the ear, not the hand, and definitely not the mouth, with its sinister grin.

What she *did* see, however, was the skin. A small patch of mottled gray-green flesh, dissolving into the darkness.

"There!" She pointed urgently into the trees, but whatever she had seen had vanished completely. "You saw it, didn't you?"

Her grandfather didn't answer.

"Didn't you?"

Again, he didn't respond.

"Grandpa, you saw that, right?"

For a second, Leslie thought he might have fallen asleep again, but when she turned and looked at him, she saw he was wide-eyed and awake. It was the wideness of his eyes that surprised her.

"You *did* see it," she said.

"See what?" Her grandfather shut the window completely and stood up as straight as he could. "Sorry, my eyesight isn't what it used to be."

Leslie sighed. "There was really something there, Grandpa. I saw it."

"Isn't it past your bedtime? Maybe you were dreaming."

Leslie shook her head. "I couldn't sleep. See?" She pointed to the stove top, where the kettle was trembling, the water inside just beginning to boil. Unfortunately, Leslie knew it wasn't going to help her sleep. After seeing whatever it was she had just seen, all the tea and biscuits in the world would be no help at all.

CHAPTER 12

In which Chuck gets a call from the Chief

huck Brickweather liked the office the people at DENKi-3000 had provided him. It was twice as big as his office at Quazicom, and it was located on the top floor of DENKi-3000's North Tower.

However, in spite of his cushy chair, his expansive office, and his beautiful view, Chuck Brickweather was stressed out.

He was two minutes away from a telephone meeting with the Quazicom CEO, a man known only as "the Chief." Unlike Sir William Sniffledon, the kindly old geezer who ran DENKi-3000, the true identity of "the Chief" was a closely guarded secret.

Even on the day Chuck had interviewed for the position, the Chief had only appeared as a gravelly voice on a dull gray intercom in the middle of the table. A tiny digital camera, mounted on an insect-like tripod, had transmitted a live stream of Chuck's answers to some distant monitor in the Chief's secret office.

All that secrecy made Chuck nervous. *And stressed.*

He recalled how he had prepared for the job, going online and ordering every self-improvement book he could find.

Interviews for Dummies, Interviews for Idiots, Interviews for People Who Can't Tell Their Elbow from Their Butt. They all said the same thing: Look your best on the big day! People who were slim, fit, and handsome were more likely to be hired! There were even series of helpful (and depressing) drawings of what the ideal interviewee ought to look like.

Chuck had *definitely not* looked like the ideal interviewee.

That was why he turned to Dr. Heppleworth's Knoo-Yoo-Juice. But the more he drank it, the more he hated talking to the Chief. It was all because of the warning. On the side of every bottle it said:

> **CAUTION: Try not to get too stressed
> while consuming our products.
> UNDUE stress can UNDO weeks of Knoo-Yooness!**

It seemed to be true. As he sat in his DENKi-3000 office, getting more and more nervous waiting for the call, Chuck could almost feel his stressed-out body swelling beneath his skin.

BRRRRING!

"H-hello? This is Chuck Brickweather speaking."

"I trust you know who's calling," said the Chief in his loose, gravelly voice.

"I do, sir."

"Good. Now, Chuck, I'm calling to check on what you've managed to dig up on the DENKi-3000 issue."

"Well, the thing is sir. . . ." Chuck hesitated. The peculiar tang of a recently guzzled bottle of Dr. Heppleworth's Knoo-Yoo-Juice clung to the back of throat. "I haven't quite—"

"Listen, Chuck, before we can start with the takeover, we're going to need to know more about the jewels in the DENKi-3000 crown, if you catch my drift."

"You mean the R&D Department."

"You see, Chuck? I knew you were the right guy for the job. Now, I want you to get in there and find out where they come up with all those amazing ideas. Like that last one of theirs. What was it again?"

"Wireless breath mints," said Chuck. They really were amazing. Chuck genuinely wished to meet the people who made those first prototypes. "They call them TransMints."

"Ha! *TransMints*. Lemme tell you one thing, Chuck, our people at Quazicom would've come up with a much better name." The Chief paused for a moment. "What about this von

Doppler character? He must know something."

"I think he might be avoiding me. He came to a meeting on the day I arrived, but I haven't seen him since."

"Did he call in sick? Take off on a vacation? People don't just vanish."

"I've asked around and no one's—"

"Then again . . . " said the Chief thoughtfully, "if he *has* vanished, it might be to our advantage."

"Sir?"

"All I'm saying is if the top dog in R&D has gone AWOL, it might be the perfect time to go down there and bust your way in. Have a poke around." The Chief lowered his voice. "Make sure you take pictures."

"When you say bust in, sir? Do you mean *break in*?"

There was another pause. All Chuck heard was the crackle of static.

"Chuck," said the Chief at last. "Do you know why I hired you?"

"Because I had good credentials?"

"Credentials! My decisions are based on something far more profound than *credentials*. Can you guess what it was in your case?"

"I haven't the foggiest, sir."

"Your name," said the Chief. "*Chuck*. One syllable. Short and sweet. *Chuck*, I thought, now there's a man of *action*. Do you see what I'm getting at? Chuck."

"I'm not sure I can just—"

WHAM!

Chuck heard a loud thump on the other end of the line. It sounded like the Chief had pounded his desk with a fist.

"*Action*, Chuck, that's what I'm after. I need that report!"

"I understand that, sir. I'm extremely curious myself, but you can't expect me to break into—I mean, *bust* into—"

"Bust in, break in. To*may*to, to*mah*to. What's important here is that you do your job."

"I'm not sure my job description included—"

"Chuck, Chuck, Chuck, don't worry. You take a few of those security robots I sent along. They'll take care of anyone who stands in your way."

"Is this how Quazicom always does business? It sounds quite unorthodox to me."

The Chief sighed deeply. It sounded like a hurricane blowing through the phone. "Listen, Chuck. Do I have to come down there myself? Because lemme tell you, if I do, I'll bring a whole army with me. I'll bust in there personally. Is that what you want?"

"Uh, sir, is that even legal?"

"Legal, illegal. To*may*to, to*mah*to. Yadda-yadda-yadda. You get the picture."

Chuck wondered if the Chief was serious. An army? No, that was impossible. Still, it made Chuck feel even more stressed than before. He could almost feel his gut bulging forward as the stress hormones interfered with Dr. Heppleworth's diet juice. He was beginning to consider the possibility that his employer was a lunatic. "N-no, it's okay," he stammered. "There's no reason for you to come to Bickleburgh. Honestly, sir, I've got everything under control."

"Do you? Because if you're all out of leads, I'd be happy to fly down there with some of my best robots and—"

"*No!* I'm not out of leads."

"You're not?" The Chief sounded surprised (and perhaps a little disappointed).

"I've got one lead left," said Chuck.

"Then what're you doing on the phone to me?"

"You called me, sir. You said you wanted to check up on—"

"Listen, Chuck, I want that report on my desk by . . . when's our next casual Friday?"

"On Friday, sir?"

"Don't give me lip, Chuck. I don't like it."

"No, sir."

"Back to work, Chuck. Look forward to reading that report."

The Chief of Quazicom hung up.

Chuck replaced the receiver and hastily guzzled down the last of his Dr. Heppleworth's. Doing so only served to intensify the sour taste in his mouth.

Luckily, since he was nowhere near an airplane, he reached into his pocket for his packet of TransMints. He tapped two of the small blue candies into his palm and tossed both into his mouth. In seconds, the miraculous, ever-changing freshness had washed away the medicinal tartness of the diet drink.

One lead, he thought.

He had interviewed nearly every employee at DENKi-3000, from Sir William all the way down to a rather nice security guard named Carl. Chuck was astonished to find that throughout the entire company, no one knew what went on inside Professor von Doppler's department.

In the course of his interviews, however, Chuck noticed that every now and again, someone mentioned that there was one person (besides the professor) who was allowed inside. Oddly, this person was a chef.

On his desk, Chuck opened the file containing the scant information he had collected about this unusual person. The only thing inside was a restaurant flyer. It said:

CHAPTER 13

In which Jean-Remy opines on the subject of puff pastry and Elliot gives an honest review

lliot von Doppler, I want you down here in five minutes or, I swear, I'll . . . I'll . . . hold on, lemme see if I can find a cookbook."

Apparently, Elliot's mother had run out of novel ideas for baking, frying, or parboiling her son.

Upstairs, Elliot could already smell the toast burning. He pulled the covers over his nose and mouth, wishing he could turn himself invisible. Then he could simply wander down to the Creature Department undetected.

Now it was Tuesday morning and his uncle only had until Friday to come up with something amazing that would save the company. Worst of all, thanks to the company vice president, Monica Burkenkrantz, he and Leslie were banned from ever going back to DENKi-3000.

Elliot rolled despondently on his side, trying to think of what to do. He wanted to help his uncle, and he *definitely* wanted to go back to the Creature Department. But how?

Out the window, the air was filled with squabbling seagulls. They screeched and cawed (as seagulls always do), but today they seemed particularly aggressive. There was one bird, in fact, slightly bigger than the rest, who seemed to be having an even worse morning than Elliot. The other birds were clearly picking on him, bumping and jostling his large body through the air. Suddenly, perhaps because he had had enough bullying for one day, the large seagull broke away from the flock, plunging straight for the window.

Elliot gasped. He pulled the covers tighter and watched in horror as this big, sloppy, loose-skinned ball of gray and white feathers came swooping straight for him.

BAM!

The seagull crashed flat into the thick glass of his window. Feathers exploded everywhere and the bird slid down the pane to lie limp on the sill.

Two of the seagulls from the flock dove out of the sky and landed on the larger seagull's belly.

"OOF!" said the larger seagull.

They pecked at his head, one final insult before the two smaller birds took off to rejoin their flock.

"After all we have invented," the large seagull muttered (in a distinctly French accent), "I would have hoped zey could have made me a better disguise."

"Jean-Remy? Is that you?" Elliot climbed out of bed and pushed his window open all the way.

"You see?" the seagull muttered to himself, staring blankly at the clouds. "If I cannot fool ze child, how do you expect me to fool ze *actual* seagulls?"

The seagull reached up and unzipped his head, removing it like a helmet. The second head underneath, of course, belonged to the fairy-bat, Jean-Remy Chevalier.

"The disguise isn't that bad," said Elliot. "You had me fooled until you started talking."

Jean-Remy sighed heavily and climbed to his feet, dusting himself off. A few loose feathers wafted in through the window. He raised up the disembodied seagull head, holding it sideways to examine the profile. "Patti made zis for me with her, you know . . ." He waved one wing around his head. "It may look good to you, certainly. Patti, she is very talented, but ze seagulls—*ugh*!" He glanced up at the receding flock. "Zey are very judgmental."

"*Five minutes to breakfast!*" Elliot's mother called from the bottom of the stairs. "If you're late, both your ears are going into a puff pastry!"

Jean-Remy raised his thick black eyebrows. "Who was zat?"

"My mom."

"She sounds quite violent."

"Don't worry. She doesn't know how to make puff pastry."

A wistful expression passed over Jean-Remy's face. "Ah! Puff pastry!" He sighed. "But never with ze ears."

By way of explanation, Elliot said, "My parents are food critics for the *Bickleburgh Bugle*."

"Critics? Bah!" Jean-Remy waved his hands. "In ze world of creatures, we have no critics."

"You don't?"

"*Non!* We believe ze opinion, it must be *earned*. So how do you earn it? By doing ze thing you want to have an opinion about. Let us say you want to be ze movie critic, eh? First, you must make ze movie. It makes sense, *non*? Of course, once you have made ze movie, you have so much fun, you no longer want to be ze critic—*et voilà*! No critics!"

"Sounds like a good system," said Elliot. "But wait. What are you doing here? And why are you dressed like a seagull?"

"*Now*, Elliot!" screamed his mother.

Elliot turned toward the door. It sounded like his mother was coming up the stairs.

"No, wait—"

"All right, young man," called his mother. "I'm on my way up there right now—and I've got an electric whisk!"

"*Ta mère! Elle arrive!*"

"Quick, you have to hide!"

Jean-Remy pressed himself against the window frame. "Okay, you go! Have your *petit déjeuner*, but hurry back. I have something very, *very* important to tell you!"

Elliot rushed into the hall. His mother was indeed on her way up (but thankfully with no electric whisk).

Downstairs, Elliot joined his parents at the table, but he could hardly look at his breakfast. How could he eat burnt toast and cold porridge now that he had tasted Famous Freddy's cooking?

"Listen," he said as soon as he sat down. "You guys *really* have to review Leslie's family's restaurant. Her grandpa's a genius!"

"The Chinese takeout place?" asked his father. "Sorry, son, you have to understand. It's not really our style."

"That's not what our readers are looking for," said his mother. "They want to know about the top bistros in Paris and New York!"

"But they live in Bickleburgh."

"*Precisely*. That's why they want to read about Paris and New York. Now, eat your breakfast and tell us what you think."

It took almost superhuman effort for Elliot to force down the blackened toast and hideous porridge.

"Well?" asked his father.

Elliot was angry about how quickly his parents dismissed his friend's restaurant—without even tasting the food. *Fine*, he thought, *if they want a review, let's see how they deal with the truth.*

"The toast," he said. He paused dramatically and collected his thoughts. "It was like someone had freeze-dried all the world's pain and hit it with a hammer so it split into a million shards of bitterness that shredded the insides of my throat from the very first gulp. As for the porridge? An exquisitely perfect bowl of disappointment." He smiled politely. "Satisfied?"

For a moment, his parents gaped at him.

"Brilliant!" cried his father.

"Bravo!" cried his mother.

They were actually happy.

His father slapped him heartily on the back. "Son, you have a bright future ahead of you."

His mother hugged him. "You're finally learning!"

"Can I go now? I want to get dressed."

"Of course, of course!"

"What a wonderfully descriptive review! I might even use some of that in my piece on Sunday!"

Elliot rolled his eyes and went back up to his room. Jean-Remy was waiting on the windowsill, seagull head in his fairy-bat hands.

"So," Elliot said. "What was it you wanted to tell me?"

Jean-Remy looked up at him, a grave expression on his face. "Ze Creature Department needs you!"

"*Me?* Why me?"

"It is now up to you and your friend to complete your uncle's work in time for ze shareholders' meeting!"

"Complete his—? Wait, why can't he complete *his own* work?"

Jean-Remy's already dark eyes went even darker. "Because your uncle has abandoned us."

"He did what?!"

"Do not be alarmed," Jean-Remy explained. "It has been known to happen from time to time, but never in such dire circumstances. Zere are *some* of ze creatures who worry that perhaps—just perhaps—he has cracked under ze pressure."

"My uncle would never do that."

Jean-Remy shrugged. "Yes, yes, I agree. I hope he will return in time, but we cannot be *absolument* certain zat he will, and so we must continue our work without him. Which is why we need you."

"But why me?"

"Because you too," Jean-Remy cried with great flourish, "have *ze blood* of a von Doppler!" He reached inside his costume and took out a tightly bound scroll of paper. "Also, it is what it says in ze note."

"What note?"

"Ze one your uncle left for us on ze weekend." Jean-Remy handed the paper to Elliot.

I've gone to fetch supplies for my new invention. Sorry for keeping everyone in the dark, but I promise to tell you all about it as soon as I'm back. (I might even have a prototype to show you, and trust me, you won't be disappointed!) While I'm away, please make sure you find a way to put Elliot and Leslie to work in the lab. I've got a hunch about those two, and if anything happens to me, they may be our only hope to save the company!!

Archie

CHAPTER 14

In which Elliot experiences one of his mother's punishments, Reggie mentions something he shouldn't, and the professor's secret (well, one of them) is revealed

 etting folded inside the pastry of a giant dumpling had seemed like a good idea at the time (in fact, it was their only idea at the time).

"Is this really necessary?" Elliot had asked. "What about all the secret passages we've seen? There's gotta be one that'll get us into the Creature Department undetected."

For a moment, Jean-Remy paused thoughtfully in his seagull suit. "I am sorry, but no," he said at last. "Leslie's idea—it is ze best way."

As a result, Elliot found himself (quite literally) experiencing one of his parents' imaginary punishments. He and Leslie had been steamed inside two of the biggest dumplings Famous Freddy had ever made.

Curling up inside a gigantic blanket of dumpling pastry, however, wasn't exactly comfortable.

"This is never going to work," said Elliot, his voice muffled by the pastry.

Leslie elbowed him from inside her own dumpling. "*Shh!*

We're almost there!"

As they drove, Elliot began to worry about his uncle. What did he mean when he said, *If anything happens to me . . . ?* He had only gone to fetch supplies for his new invention, so what could happen? Could it be that simply fetching supplies was dangerous? It all depended, Elliot supposed, on what you were making.

Famous Freddy's trailer slowed as Leslie's grandfather pulled into the security gates. A moment later, the back of the trailer was unlatched.

Through the breathing holes in his dumpling, Elliot saw it was Carl, the friendly security guard who had opened the trailer, only he wasn't looking very friendly. Instead, he looked angry. This was probably because his only duty was opening the back. It was two Quazicom security robots who scanned the interior.

"That is a lot of dumplings," said the first robot. "I had heard those mysterious Research and Development workers enjoy them, but I had no idea how much."

"Those two in the middle," said the second robot, "are the biggest dumplings I have ever scanned."

"Ho ho, yes," the first robot replied. "If I had a mouth, I would be sorely tempted to give those dumplings a hearty nibble."

Hearing this exchange, Elliot assumed that he and Leslie had been caught, that the robots were merely poking fun at the enormous dumplings to taunt them.

However, it seemed the robots were speaking in earnest because the first robot said, "All right, send them in. Let them get it while it's still hot."

"Yes," agreed the second robot. "I've heard that makes a

difference when you have a mouth."

Carl shut the back of the trailer, glowering at the robots the whole time.

When the truck door opened again, it was Gügor who opened the latch. A great cheer rose from all the creatures as Famous Freddy peeled away the dumpling pastry to reveal two soggy children.

As before, everyone ate together in the cafetarium. Nostalgic images of the creatures' past scrolled across the ceiling.

As they came to the end of the meal, it happened again. The imagery turned ominous and sinister. There were scenes of chaos: creatures running for their lives, creatures pursued by hoards of weird, shadowy shapes, creatures dragged away in huge nets, vanishing into darkness.

In the images, the shadowy things were coming closer, coming into focus. Elliot saw patches of mottled green skin, just like the skin he had seen when—

Patti Mudmeyer switched off the ceiling.

"Wait," said Elliot. "What *are* those things?"

The creatures looked around the table at one another, but none of them spoke.

"If you want us to help you," said Leslie, "you need to tell us."

"I believe we owe our young friends an explanation," said a voice behind them.

It was Reggie, the bombastadon.

"You'll only give them nightmares," Harrumphrey grunted. "Nobody needs to know anything about—"

"*The Ghorkolians,*" said Reggie.

"Reggie!"

Several of the more timid creatures whimpered and covered

their ears. Reggie pressed on nevertheless.

"Ghorks!" cried Reggie. "*Ugh!* Despicable creatures! A particularly nasty kind of subterranean ogre. Or perhaps trolls. Perhaps extremely large gremlins. Difficult to say in light of their unusual features. *But oh!* The *teeeerible* dreams I've had about those insufferable ghorks!"

Reggie looked just about ready to spin into more of his hysterics, so Harrumphrey begrudgingly picked up where the bombastadon left off. "Reggie's right about one thing. *They're insufferable.*" He paused for a moment to consider this. "No, they're worse than that. Much worse. We creatures were around long before you humans came on the scene. When you did, there was something of a split between us. The ghorks didn't want to share this world with anyone, while the rest of us were happy to use creature technology to stay hidden. We were content to quietly go about our business, living in our secret cities, secret enclaves. . . ." His eyes did a quick spin of the room. "And our secret mansions. The ghorks, however, would have none of it."

"They started to think they were superior to the rest of us," said Reggie. "Can you imagine? Such overweening pre*sump*tuousness!"

"Lucky for us," said Patti, "the ghorks were so disagreeable, they spent most of their time fightin' among themselves. They come in five different flavors, you see—or species, if you like. Each tribe of ghorks thinks it's better than all the others. We're happy to let 'em duke it out, but eventually, the ghork wars got bigger and bigger. They couldn't help but spill over into the rest of creaturedom. Anybody who wasn't a ghork had to head for the hills! Lately, us creatures've been scattered to the four winds." Her eyes narrowed and she looked left and right. "Believe it or not, we're hiding out *all over* the place. You'd be surprised."

"It is true," said Jean-Remy. "In fact, zere are *many* other Creature Departments, just like zis one, all around ze world."

"Those nasty images you saw," said Harrumphrey. "They just keep showing up, a collective memory of the last time any of us saw our real homes."

Everyone sat in silence, nodding solemnly after Harrumphrey's words.

"I think I've seen one," said Elliot. "A ghork."

"I have too," said Leslie. "They're big, right? Like giants?"

Harrumphrey laughed. "*Big?* Not at all. Besides, giants are peaceful as can be. But ghorks? Naw! Not peaceful, and *definitely* not giants."

Gügor agreed. "The biggest ghork that Gügor ever saw," he proclaimed, "only came up to here." He sliced one hand across the bottom of his chest (it still would have been large—at least by human standards—but not nearly as massive as whatever had been lurking in the woods).

"No," said Elliot. "What I saw was much bigger."

"I must have seen the same thing," said Leslie. "It was *huge*—and it was watching the restaurant." She looked down the table to Famous Freddy, chewing quietly. "Isn't that right, Grandpa?"

Freddy hesitated. "I'm not sure."

"But you saw it too," Leslie argued. "I know you did!"

Freddy swallowed another dumpling, his throat undulating with an audible *gulp*. "It was quite dark," he said. "I know something frightened you, but I was . . ." He shrugged bashfully. "Well, you know."

"*Drinking,*" said Leslie.

Freddy nodded sadly. "I can't say I saw anything but a few odd shadows."

Leslie was disappointed. She turned to Elliot. "You believe me, right? It had slimy green skin and it was watching me through the window."

"That's it!" said Elliot. "Exactly what followed me in the woods!"

"But if it wasn't a giant and it wasn't a ghork . . . then what *was* it?"

No one had an answer. For a moment, they all sat in silence.

"Listen, guys," said Patti. "It's quite possible you saw something out there, but if you did, it wasn't one of us in here, I'll tell you that much. And right now, we don't have time for much speculatin'. What we gotta do is keep working—especially with the professor still gone."

Leslie realized that Patti was right. Friday's shareholder meeting was fast approaching. "Have you really looked everywhere for him?" she asked. "The professor, I mean."

Gügor nodded. "We even looked in Reggie's room."

Reggie tutted. "*Without* asking, may I remind you."

"How could we?" said Harrumphrey. "You were hibernating."

"What about behind the cabinet in his office?" Elliot asked. "Did you look there?"

Everyone at the table squinted at him. Elliot, however was only looking at Leslie. "Remember? When we first came, I didn't believe he could run everything by himself. Neither could you. I joked that an old mansion like this would be full of secret passages."

"I *do* remember," said Leslie. "You went to look behind that cabinet and—"

"He kind of freaked out, didn't he?"

Leslie smiled. "Until I freaked him out more when I mentioned Grandpa Freddy."

"Maybe there really *is* a secret passage back there," said Elliot. "Maybe that's where he went!"

Elliot and Leslie didn't have to say anything else. Everyone at the table stood up. Moments later, they were all standing in the professor's office.

The cabinet was surprisingly heavy, but Gügor moved it out of the way as if it were made of straw. Just as Leslie suspected, the cabinet had been hiding something.

A safe.

Elliot looked around at the others. "Anyone happen to know the combination?

No one did.

"I'd better give it a try," said Harrumphrey, with supreme confidence. "Me and ol' Archie, we go *waaaay* back." He used his tail to spin the combination dial and then again to pull the door.

It didn't open.

Harrumphrey tried another combination. It didn't work either. When the eighth attempt failed, he stepped away from the safe.

"All right," he said looking a little dejected. "Go ahead, Gügor. It's rickum-ruckery time."

Gügor blinked at the wall. "Gügor is doubtful the professor could fit in such a tiny space."

Harrumphrey sighed. "Yes, I think we all agree that isn't actually a secret passage, but it's okay. At this point, we're just looking for clues."

"Perhaps inside it is ze professor's secret invention!"

"Gügor thinks it is private." The knucklecrumpler looked to Patti for guidance.

"Go ahead, big guy," said Patti. "If it'll help us find the doc, we gotta do it."

Gügor wrapped his massive knuckles around the handle and with the merest tug pulled the door clean off the wall.

What fell out of the safe surprised everyone.

"*Comic books?*" asked Elliot.

"Well, chop me down and call me stumped," said Patti.

Indeed it was. The safe was stuffed with old, faded, well-thumbed comic books and science-fiction magazines. They were the sorts of ancient entertainments from a time when the closest thing anyone had to the Internet would have been a radio (likely an enormous wooden one).

"*This.* This is his big secret?" Leslie crouched down with the pile of colorful, dog-eared volumes. "He's a comic book geek?"

They all leafed through the old comics, looking for something that might reveal why these old stories of superheroes and rocket ships would be so well hidden. They didn't find anything useful.

The most common comic in the heap was something called *Captain Adventure Saves the Day.* It featured a square-jawed hero in red-and-orange tights, soaring through the cosmos, planet to planet, in order to . . . well, *save the day.*

"This has to be the cheesiest comic book ever written," Leslie commented.

"I guess that's one reason to keep it in a safe," said Elliot, "but it doesn't really tell us where Uncle Archie is."

Patti put one scaly arm around his shoulders. "I'm sure he'll be back soon. Till then, we gotta keep on gallopin'."

"That's where you come in," said Harrumphrey. "You two have the most important job in the whole Creature Department."

"We do?" asked Leslie.

Harrumphrey nodded. "It's time we introduced you to the Preston Brothers."

CHAPTER 15

In which the Preston Brothers demonstrate
that some tables are bigger than others

Harrumphrey, Gügor, and Patti went to prepare the laboratory while Jean-Remy took Leslie and Elliot aboard the expectavator. Following another tug on the knottub (and another slightly sickening "AAAAHHH!" from the expectavator doors), they joined Gabe inside.

Although most of the buttons were crammed with lettering that described precisely where the expectavator might take them, this time Jean-Remy chose a button covered in nothing but tiny blue bubbles. When Gabe pressed it, the button glowed brightly, fading through a rainbow of colors as the journey began.

PING!

And ended.

"Got here faster than usual," said Gabe in his usual monotone. He looked at Elliot and Leslie. "You two must be feeling quite hopeful this morning."

Elliot and Leslie nodded; even though the safe hadn't led them to Uncle Archie, they hoped he'd be back soon.

The expectavator doors opened on a drab, creaky corridor. It looked like the rest of the mansion, with one noticeable difference.

The smell.

Unlike everywhere else they had been in the Research and Development Department, the scent here wasn't that of musty old books and moldering wood. This corridor had a clean, sharp scent, the crisp freshness of a late-November morning after the first frost.

At the far end of the hallway was a pair of ornate oak doors. As Elliot and Leslie moved toward it, the scent became more distinct. When they arrived, a silver plaque beside the entrance said:

The Abstractory

Jean-Remy stopped and hovered in front of the door. "Before we go in, I should tell you, please do not worry if ze middle one does not speak to you."

"The middle one?" asked Elliot. "What does that mean?"

"Do not worry," said Jean-Remy. "He never speaks."

They entered the Abstractory.

At first, Elliot thought they had entered a library. Beyond the foyer was a vast room with carved wooden walls and broad pillars supporting a ceiling fitted with a huge, circular stained-glass window. This huge room was packed with what appeared to be bookcases. *Many, many bookcases.*

They zigzagged and crisscrossed, went up and down stairs, and spiraled around into narrow dead ends. There were towers of bookcases; there were valleys of bookcases; there were bridges of bookcases and caves of bookcases; there were even bookcases that sprouted from other bookcases to create what looked like . . . *bookcase-trees.*

If this place were a library, it was surely the most convoluted and disorderly one ever constructed. Yet still, with only a glance, it was clear that this was *definitely not* a library.

After all, there were no books.

Instead of being packed with dusty old volumes as you might expect in a grand old room like this one, on every shelf there were glass bottles and jars of all shapes and sizes. Inside each of them was a strange substance—liquids; gases; powders; shimmering metals; chips of wood; dried tea leaves; dark, rich soil; petals from outlandish flowers. There were endless substances in a seemingly endless array of colors.

Many of the substances sat inert in their containers, while others writhed and boiled as if they were living things.

"What *is* this place?" asked Elliot.

Leslie was just as dumbfounded by the sight of the room. "And what's in all the bottles?"

"All in good time," said Jean-Remy. "First, we must have our meeting with the Preston Brothers." He fluttered to a counter (that did indeed look like the reception desk at a library) and jingled a small brass bell.

Leslie was expecting some tiny creature to pop up from behind the reception desk, but nothing appeared. Instead, she caught sight of a strange shape moving through the shelves.

It appeared to be a small crowd of people, but it was difficult to be certain because the figures were obscured by the mad jumble of shelves. In addition, what Leslie *could* see was distorted through the warped glass of all the bottles.

"Look!" said Elliot. He pointed just ahead of the figures that had caught Leslie's attention. She looked where he was pointing—and gasped.

A tentacle!

A coil of pink, rubbery skin came lolloping around one of the shelves. Its suction cups puckered and popped as it pulled itself forward.

"Uh, Jean-Remy?" asked Leslie. "Please tell me that's *supposed* to be here."

"*Mais bien sûr.* Zat . . . is ze Preston Brothers!"

"The Preston Brothers are tentacles?"

"*Non non non*!" Jean-Remy pointed to the strange figures obscured by the shelves. "Ze tentacle *belongs* to them."

They rounded the last bookcase just as Jean-Remy uttered their name. Leslie saw she had been mistaken. It wasn't *a group* of creatures moving through the shelves.

It was only one.

Or was it three?

Or was it both?

The Preston Brothers, you see, were a three-headed creature. All three heads were identical—*and identically strange.* Each one resembled that of a pug-nosed seahorse, complete with a rounded, pony-like snout and spiny protrusions instead of a mane.

The only distinguishing feature between the three heads was their mustaches.

The head on the left had a handlebar mustache, the tips spiraling up to a point. The head on the right side wore the opposite style, an aptly named horseshoe mustache, the ends growing downward and hanging off the creature's chin. Both these mustaches were thick, well groomed, and impressive.

The head in the middle, however, sported a mustache with hardly any hair at all: just the merest wisp of a pencil mustache. Topping everything off was a handsome tweed vest, specially tailored with three holes for three heads.

These were the Preston Brothers. With their three heads, two arms, and eight tentacled legs, they were surely the strangest creatures (or creature?) of them all.

"Well, if it ain't Jean-Remy Chevalier!" said the head on the left (the one with the handlebar mustache).

"We just got the memo that you were coming up for a visit," said the head on the right (the one with the horseshoe mustache).

The head in the middle (with the pencil mustache) said nothing.

"Allow me to introduce the keepers of the Abstractory," said Jean-Remy. "Lester, Nestor, and Chester Preston."

"Pleased to meet you," said the two outside heads, speaking in unison. The head between them, the one called Nestor, merely nodded.

"That's what you meant by the one in the middle," Leslie

said to Jean-Remy. She turned to Nestor. "He told us you were the quiet one."

Nestor blinked at her but was otherwise expressionless.

"What about you other two?" asked Elliot. "Which is Chester and which is Lester?"

"That's easy," said the head on the right. He pointed to his brother on the opposite shoulder. "Lester starts with *L* and he's on the left."

"*Technically,*" Lester replied, "it's a matter of perspective. I'm on their left but *our* right. Your *L* system only works if we're standing face-to-face. It's confusing. What if someone comes up behind us? Then *you'll* be on the left."

Chester raised his spiny eyebrows. "You think what *I* said was confusing?"

"Frankly, yes," said his brother.

"You're the one who's making it complicated. Left. Lester. See? Simple."

"Oh, yes, I can see the convenience; I just think we ought to strive for something more rigorous. Like our *mustaches*. Isn't that why we grew them in the first place?"

Chester reached up to stroke his bushy horseshoe mustache. "Maybe that's why you grew yours, but as for me? This 'stache is all about *style*."

"Typical," said Lester. "Mom always said you were the vain one."

"Please, please, gentlemen," Jean-Remy cut in. "We have important work to do."

"Wait," said Elliot. "How can we do this 'important work' if we don't even know what this place is or what we're supposed to do?"

"Seriously," said Leslie. "What's with all the bottles?"

Nestor, the mute middle head, furrowed his brow and nodded at them. He seemed to be saying, *Yes, a very good question.*

"These bottles?" said Chester, waving his arms at the strange shelves that surrounded them. "They contain the most important substances in all of creaturedom. We'll show you."

The Preston Brothers walked (or rather, *flopped*) behind the reception desk. They opened several different drawers with their tentacles and, taking advantage of their multiple heads, peered into several of them all at once.

"Did we lose it again?" asked Chester.

"Looks that way," said Lester.

Nestor rolled his eyes in exasperation and one of the middle tentacles fished into the drawer in front of him, coming out with a small remote control.

"Good work, brother," said Chester.

Nestor shook his head and pointed the remote at the wall. A large screen illuminated. On it was something both Elliot and Leslie recognized from science class.

"It's the periodic table of elements," said Elliot, but then he looked a bit closer. "Except that it isn't."

"There're too many elements," said Leslie.

"And number one is supposed to be hydrogen," said Elliot. "Not . . . *harmony.*"

"Is that even an element?" asked Leslie.

"Of course not," said Lester. "This isn't the periodic table of *elements*. It's the periodic table of *intangibles*, and it's the cornerstone of creature science."

"Our technology," Chester continued, "isn't based on the conventional energy sources used in the human world. Things

like gasoline and batteries and solar panels. Creature technology uses something much more powerful."

"Hope!" said Elliot, blurting it out.

"Like in the expectavator," said Leslie.

"Well done," said Lester. "You two are obviously just as sharp as we've been led to believe."

"Not many humans would make such a leap of lateral logic," said Chester. "Even if they did, they'd hardly think it was possible."

"But of course it is," said Lester. "The essences of concepts like hope or curiosity are among the most powerful substances in the world. Just so long as you know how to harness them."

"Powerful," whispered Chester, "*buuut* . . . a little unpredictable. As you can see," he said, pointing to the screen, "there are many more intangibles in the universe than simple elements. It's what makes creature science so endlessly interesting. We've got so much more to work with!"

"Indeed, we do," said Lester, in a less exuberant, more detached and scientific tone. "Just as with the table of elements, the more common intangibles are up near the top. Things like courage or infatuation, trust or despair." He pointed the remote at the screen and the table glided upward to reveal many more abstract concepts. "But if you scroll down a little farther . . ."

Elliot squinted at the screen. "Does that say 'the feeling you're being watched'?"

Chester nodded vigorously. "One of my favorites! Intangible abstract concept number 416: the feeling you're being watched."

"Scroll down even more," said Lester, "and you start to get the *really* weird ones. Or should I say the really creaturely ones, intangibles that only really exist in the realms of creaturedom."

"Like that one?" Leslie pointed to number 1,384, reading aloud from the screen. "'The shudder of revulsion upon being drooled on by a hibernating bombastadon'?"

"Precisely," said Lester.

"Gross," said Leslie.

"Wait a second," said Elliot. "Are you saying that's what's in all these bottles?"

Chester put out his arm, gesturing toward the maze of shelves. "Why don't you go and have a look? This first shelf has some of our most recognizable intangibles."

They wandered up to the nearest bookshelf, and the first bottle Leslie picked up was a tall, sleek one filled with a fast-moving, silvery-blue fluid. The label at the top of the bottle simply said:

Justice

"Seriously?" she asked. "This is a bottle of justice?"

"Be careful with that," Chester told her. "Took us *years* to collect that much."

Every bottle on the shelf contained a different unbelievable substance. Inspiration, vulnerability, egotism, patience, leniency, gravitas, nostalgia, panache, and on and on . . .

Leslie took a plump round bottle off the shelf. It was full of a bright, warm, orangey-red liquid that fizzled with tiny bubbles. She peered for a moment at the label.

"Hold on a second," she said, turning the bottle to show the Prestons. "It says here this is a bottle of *friendship*. Does that mean if I make someone drink it or pour it over their head, they'll be my friend?"

Chester and Lester laughed uproariously.

"Gentlemen, please!" Jean-Remy came to Leslie's defense. "She is new to the Abstractory. Nothing is to be gained from your laughter but ze mockery."

"Yeah," said Leslie, "what's so funny?"

"Think," said Chester. "Is it so easy to make friends?"

"I don't know," said Leslie. "I just thought because it says *friendship* on the side, it might—"

"It is the *essence* of friendship," said Lester. "Think of it like flour, for baking. It's the perfect thing for making a cake, but if you bury a sack of flour in the ground, you don't grow wheat."

"You don't grow *anything*," said Chester. "Growing wheat is hard work—just like friendship. Do you see what we mean?"

Leslie looked at Elliot for a moment. "I think I get it, but then what do you use this for?"

"Let's say we need to power some sort of machine for resolving arguments," said Lester. "In that case, I'm sure you can see how a few drops of friendship would come in handy."

To Leslie, it sounded extremely peculiar. But in an odd, creaturely sort of way, it made sense.

"What about this one?" asked Elliot, standing across the aisle from Leslie. He held up a squat glass jar about the size and shape of a can of tuna. Inside was nothing but a pile of gravel and dust. "It says here it's the essence of failure. What can you use *that* for?"

Chester smiled. "All sorts of things!"

"For instance," said Lester, "let's say we were building some sort of educational device, something to help people learn a new skill."

"Good point, my brother," said Chester. "No one learns

anything from nonstop success. In order to truly succeed, you need to make mistakes along the way."

Gently, Elliot put the failure back on the shelf. "I think I get it. Sort of."

"Speaking of inventions," said Jean-Remy. "We must get started! Already, it is Tuesday. Zere remain only three days before ze meeting!" He lowered his voice. "We *must* tell ze children what it is we are working on."

Again, Lester pressed a button on the remote control. The periodic table of intangibles vanished and was replaced by a screen that was completely blank, save for the following words:

POSSIBLE SECRET PROJECTS
THE PROFESSOR WAS WORKING
ON WHEN HE ABANDONED US

"He didn't abandon us!" Elliot protested. "He just went off to get supplies, and maybe even build his machine."

"I hope so," said Jean-Remy, "but what if he does not return?"

"I believe you," said Leslie. She put a hand on Elliot's shoulder. "He'll be back in time."

"*Ahem!*" Lester cleared his throat. "Just in case he doesn't, however, we've gone through your uncle's logbooks to determine what it was he was working on. We've narrowed it down to three."

Lester pressed another button and the screen shifted. Now it revealed the first of three unbelievable inventions. . . .

CHAPTER 16

In which Elliot and Leslie choose wisely

The screen was packed with incomprehensible equations, diagrams of cogs and gears and bits and pieces of countless arcane mechanisms. Superimposed over the images was a title:

1. TELEPORTATION DEVICE

"That's what Gügor was working on," said Elliot.

"In the Rickum Ruckem Room," said Leslie, "when we first came here."

"We have been trying to perfect zis device *for years*," said Jean-Remy.

"Years?" asked Leslie. "In that case, how can you call it a secret project?"

"Excellent point," said Chester. "But we can't rule out the possibility the professor found a way to get it working."

"It certainly might explain why he vanished all of a sudden," said Lester. "Perhaps he was testing his device."

Another press of a button and the screen shifted to a new image. Again, there were mathematical equations and inscrutable machinery. But central to this second slide was a drawing of an egg-shaped hat with elaborate chinstraps and what appeared to be a miniature radio tower on top. Superimposed across this image, it said:

2. TELEPATHY HELMET

"Aw, cool!" said Leslie. "You mean for *reading minds*?"

All three brothers nodded gravely. "Even in creaturedom," said Lester, "telepathy helmets are *veeery* tricky. As far as we know, no one has ever produced a reliable prototype."

The next slide featured more of the same mechanical and mathematical imagery, only at the center was a dotted-line silhouette of a big hairy creature with horns. Over this image, it said:

3. INVISIBILITY MACHINE

Elliot gasped. "My uncle was working on an invisibility machine?!"

"We did find certain indications," said Chester.

"That's incredible!" cried Leslie. She paused. "Hold on a sec. Teleportation. Telepathy. Invisibility. Those are some pretty big ideas, and we're just a couple of kids. What can we do?"

"More than you think," said Lester. "In fact, we've discovered many children have more in common with creatures than the average human adult. So in a way, the Creature Department is the perfect place for you."

"That's what makes your uncle so special," Chester added. "He's still got the Knack."

"The knack for what?" asked Elliot.

"For ze most important part of any invention in creature-dom," said Jean-Remy, "and it happens here, in ze Abstractory. It is here we select . . . *ze intangible essence of ze machine.*"

"Not as easy as it sounds," said Chester. "It requires not one, but a combination of intangibles. A combination of three, and we've always found it comes down to that crucial third."

"Zis is your uncle's great gift, selecting just ze right intangible essences to power ze inventions," Jean-Remy said to them. "Your gift too, we hope."

"Take the wireless breath mint, for one," said Chester. "We all knew it might require the intangible essence of freshness and information, but those alone didn't work. The flavor came out much too sharp, hit you in the teeth like a rock hammer. What we needed was the right thing to make it just a bit softer, just a bit sweeter."

"It was your uncle," Lester went on, "who realized that taste and scent trigger *memories*. Which is why our TransMints would never have worked without just a drop of this." He lifted an ornate bottle from a cart behind the counter. It was filled with what appeared to be huge flakes of snow. "Intangible abstract concept number 802: your fondest memory of winter. This is responsible for the icy coolness that goes into every mint."

For a moment, they all stared into the bottle. The snow inside sparkled faintly, each flake throbbing with light, almost like a distant memory.

"Only your uncle could have thought of zis," whispered Jean-Remy. "He is a very great man."

Elliot felt a swell of pride.

"And since you too are a von Doppler, and Leslie, as we

know from ze science competition, she is your equal, it is now up to you both to select ze intangible essence for each of our new technologies."

"*Us?*"

"Why else would we bring you here, to so hallowed a place such as zis?"

Elliot and Leslie gazed out at the maze of shelves. There must have been thousands of bottles.

"Go on," Chester encouraged them. "Give it a shot."

"Concentrate on the underlying meaning of each machine," Lester instructed them. "Then let your minds wander—along with your feet."

In between the other two brothers, Nestor seemed to agree with this advice. He nodded, just once.

"All right," Elliot said to Leslie. "Let's try."

At first they walked together, but then they split up to cover more ground. Each alone, they wandered through the winding aisles. The bookcases were so dense and twisted, while the contents (and labels) of the bottles were so strange, it felt very much like they were exploring the landscape of an alien planet.

At times, their paths crossed and they would discuss what they had seen among the bottles. Once they felt (slightly) more confident with the bizarre layout, they decided to begin with their first selection.

The teleportation device.

If you wanted to send something (or someone) to another place in a single instant, you would need something very powerful.

"Let's start with hope," Elliot suggested.

They found it in a simple clear bottle: a bright, swirling, emerald-green liquid. It shimmered behind the glass, catching light where there was none.

They also surmised that a teleportation device would need something more directly related to wanting to be somewhere else.

"I've got it!" Leslie said, with the utmost confidence. "I saw it back in one of the . . . the, um—what are we calling those?"

"Bookcase-trees?"

"Okay. In one of the bookcase-trees."

They walked back to a towering "bookcase-tree" in the middle of the Abstractory.

"That one, up there," said Leslie. She pointed to a disk-shaped bottle with an intricately pebbled surface. On the label was a word Leslie had heard from her mother many times. *Wanderlust.*

"This one," she said to Elliot. "*Definitely* this one." She climbed up a ladder to retrieve it. When she brought it down, they saw it was full of what appeared to be sand. Holding up the bottle, Leslie seemed disappointed. "I don't get it. Why sand?"

Elliot leaned close to the glass. He took out his DENKi-3000 Electric Pencil and switched from the macro- to the microscopic mode. He peered into the bottle.

"It's not sand in there," he whispered. "It's feet."

"Excuse me?"

"Millions of tiny feet—and they're all moving."

He handed Leslie the spyglass, and the moment she looked through it, she saw he was right. Every grain of sand was actually a microscopic foot. Some looked like regular human feet, while others were hairy or clawed or scaly, like the feet of animals (or creatures). Every one of them wriggled its toes and buffeted around the others as if trying to run—manically, aimlessly, in any direction at all.

"Reminds me of my mom," said Leslie.

Finally, they needed the last and most crucial part of the formula. The third essence.

In exploring the Abstractory, they had discovered that the vast room was more organized than it at first appeared. The more common essences, the ones with lower intangible abstract concept numbers, were near the entrance. The deeper you ventured into the shelves, however, the stranger and more rare the essences became. They surmised that the crucial third ingredient would come from the deepest depths of the Abstractory.

The farther they went, the stranger the essences became. There were corked bottles full of swirling smoke, bubbling slime, and foul, unnameable sludge. There were screw-top jars that trembled with tiny fingers, chattering teeth, and slithering tails. And it wasn't merely what was inside the jars that was strange; the labels were equally peculiar:

The Earsplitting Wail of a Screaming Wee Beast
The Overpowering Stench of a Bridge Troll's Feet
The Shock of Brushing Your Leg Against Something
Warm and Hairy Under the Table
The Enchantment of a Luster Bug's Light
The Dread of Meeting a Ghork in a Dark Alley

"What we need is something fast—*really fast*," said Leslie. "It's what teleportation's all about. Sending something to another place in the blink of an eye."

They wandered through the farthest aisles of the Abstractory, looking for something that fit the bill. The labels on many of the bottles were so strange, they had to guess at the contents from what they saw inside. Some bottles were bubbling rapidly, while others whipped with fast-moving noodle-like appendages. But none of them seemed fast enough.

Then Elliot saw something. "What about that one?"

At the very base of what might be called the trunk of one of the bookcase-trees was a broad jar, simple and hefty. Elliot crouched down for a closer look.

"It's a blizzard," he said. "A *really* fast one."

In fact, it was worse than a blizzard. It was a furious cyclone of snow and ice but shrunken down and contained in a glass jar.

"Looks good," said Leslie, "but what's an . . . *arachnimammoth*?" She pointed to the label, which said: **The Thrill of Your First Ride on the Back of an Arachnimammoth**.

Elliot shrugged. "Whatever it is, it must be fast. I think we should choose this one."

Leslie agreed. They brought the three jars to the front counter and returned to repeat the process for the other two inventions.

For an invisibility machine they chose the essences of obscurity (a bottle of inky gray fog) and bedazzlement (a jar of painfully flashing lights), both of which seemed like obvious choices. The crucial third ingredient, again, was trickier.

They ventured deep into the darkest, most distant corner of the Abstractory. There they passed a lopsided bottle that was turned around, facing the back of the shelf. Since they couldn't read the label and since the bottle appeared to be empty, they almost ignored it. They were just about to pass it by when Leslie screamed.

"I saw something!" she gasped. "Something inside that one! Something . . . *creepy.*"

"But it's empty." Elliot couldn't see anything at all in there.

He brought his face close to the bottle, and just as he leaned down, he saw something. It was almost as if a ghostly—*and invisible*—hand had suddenly reached out for his throat.

He stepped backward. "You're right," he said. "It looks empty, but . . ."

"Something's inside."

"We need to read the label. I'm going to turn it around, okay?" Leslie nodded.

Slowly, squinting through the fingers of one hand, Elliot twisted the neck of the bottle. On the label, it said: **The Overwhelming Suspicion Something Big and Hungry Is Hiding Under Your Bed.**

"I think we found our third essence," said Leslie.

They brought the three bottles to the counter and placed them beside the others.

Finally, they set their minds to the telepathy helmet. First, they made logical choices: the essences of intuition (a jar of cloudy, colored marbles, like tiny crystal balls). Next, they chose echoing voices (a bottle of constantly rippling water). At last, just as before, they ventured into the farthest, most creaturely depths of the Abstractory. After quite a lot of wandering, however, they were still stumped by what to select for the crucial third ingredient.

"Let's think for a moment," said Leslie. "What is *telepathy* all about?"

"Reading people's thoughts," said Elliot.

"And it could also be the opposite. Sending your ideas into someone else's mind."

"So it's about thoughts and minds and . . ."

That was when they saw the final jar.

"Brains!" they both said together.

Up in one of the highest branches (or shelves) of the bookcase-trees was a jar that appeared to be filled with exactly that. When they read the label, they saw it said: *An Insatiable Hunger for Brains.*

"Perfect," said Leslie. And so they had made their choices.

They brought the last three bottles up to the counter. Just as they were putting them down beside the others, however, the Abstractory doors burst open.

It was Reggie, rattling as always in in his absurd regalia. "Gentlemen! *Geeentlemen!*" he cried. "You must stop!"

"Gentlemen?" asked Leslie.

"Ah, yes. Indeed. And *lady.*" Reggie gave Leslie a courteous bow. *"You must all stop!"*

Before anyone could respond, the two hobmongrels, Bildorf and Pib, came rushing in. They were weighed down by the great tray of tea and biscuits.

"We're sorry," said Bildorf. "We tried to stop him, we really did!"

"But he's completely gone off tea and biscuits," Pib complained. "We can't get him to eat any!"

"Be gone, you scamps! Tempt me no more!" Reggie merely tapped them backward with the heel of one of his enormous boots, but the impact was so great, both hobmongrels clattered into the hall, a storm of fur balls, tea bags, silverware, and chocolate biscuits.

Reggie was quick to shut and lock the door behind them.

"Shouldn't you be hibernating?" asked Chester.

"How do you expect me to sleep with such *teeerible* dreams?"

Lester pointed to the door. "You could have tried the tea and biscuits."

Reggie scoffed. "*Ugh!* I'll have no more of their tea and biscuits! I come bearing news of the utmost import!"

Chester and Lester sighed in unison. "What news?"

"News of the professor's secret project!"

Jean-Remy flapped up and floated in front of the great bombastadon's face. Seeing them practically nose-to-nose made Jean-Remy seem like an insect, while it made Reggie resemble a soft, woolly mountain (with tusks).

"Can it be true?" Jean-Remy searched Reggie's enormous face. "You have information about ze professor?"

"Not about the man himself, but *his project*." Reggie lowered his voice. "I, Colonel-Admiral Reginald T. Pusslegut of Her Majesty's Royal Antarctic Brigadiers, know what the venerable professor was working on!"

"You must tell us at once."

With great solemnity, Reggie moved his eyes across every face in the room and then whispered, "*Super-galoshes.*"

"Did he just say what I think he said?" asked Leslie.

The Preston Brothers folded their arms (and several tentacles).

"Why would the professor work on something as foolish as super-galoshes?" asked Lester.

"What *are* super-galoshes?" asked Chester.

"*You cretins!*" Reggie raised his bushy eyebrows. "Super-galoshes are just that. *Super.* They are like regular galoshes, only warmer. And perhaps a bit more water resistant. One thing they are most certainly *not* is foolish!"

"You must admit, *mon ami*, it does sound just a teensy bit foolish." Jean-Remy looped away from Reggie's face and settled down on the reception counter.

"How dare you?!" boomed Reggie. "We speak of *galoshes*!" He looked down at his own enormous rubber boots. "A well-made pair of galoshes can draw the line between life and death! And more than this, they are objects of sublime beauty." Having made his case, he bent at the waist and slipped off both his boots.

Instantly, the whole Abstractory was filled with the dizzying stench of seaweed and fungus.

"No, Reggie! Please!" cried Jean-Remy. "Put ze boots back on!"

Instead, Reggie picked up the enormous galoshes and placed them on the countertop, right between Jean-Remy and the little brass bell.

"How can you deny their elegance?" Reggie stroked the galoshes lovingly. "These will take you across countless ice fields without so much as a blister. With a single boot I once held back a whole army of vicious berg biters. And nothing fits the stirrup of your trusty steed like the heel of a solid galosh! *Plus*, if you find yourself bereft of supplies, your boot becomes your teacup."

"No way," said Elliot, holding his nose. "Please don't tell

us you *drink* out of those things."

Before Reggie could answer this rather disgusting question, Chester cut in. "Hold everything. What makes you think the professor was designing 'super-galoshes'? How did you even get this information?"

"The same way I get all my information." Reggie shrugged imperiously. "It came to me in a dream."

The others sighed. Elliot and Leslie were beginning to see why all the other creatures found Reggie so annoying.

"I think we've heard enough," said Lester.

Reggie's big, jowly face sagged a little more than usual. "*But . . . but . . .*" He put out his hands imploringly, urging the others to see the same practical elegance he saw in a pair of gigantic, badly weathered galoshes. "*Look* at them! Who *wouldn't* want to work on something so . . . so . . . *gorgeous?*"

All three Preston Brothers shook their heads in pitying unison.

"*But . . . but . . .*" Reggie looked to Elliot for salvation, but Elliot simply couldn't believe his uncle was working on anything so silly as really warm galoshes.

He sighed and stepped forward, standing toe-to-enormous-hairy-toe with Reggie.

"I'm sorry," Elliot apologized, "but, speaking as a von Doppler, I just don't think this is something my uncle would be working on."

Hearing these words from Elliot had a distinct impression on the great bombastadon. A look of confusion passed over his face and his lower lip began to tremble between his tusks.

"Very well, then," he said, his voice quavering with barely restrained emotion. "I understand."

He raised one set of claws to his forehead and gave everyone a curt salute. Then he turned sharply on his heels and trudged for the exit.

"Er, *excusez-moi*, Reggie?" said Jean-Remy, hovering above the galoshes that were still standing on the counter. "I beg you, do not forget ze boots."

Without saying a word, Reggie did another about-face to collect his galoshes. He padded off with them cradled lovingly in his arms, like a pair of newborn twins.

At last, when Reggie was gone, Elliot and Leslie brought their essences up to the counter. The Preston Brothers put them in three groups of three:

Teleportation: hope, wanderlust, and the thrill of your first ride on the back of an arachnimammoth.

Invisibility: obscurity, bedazzlement, and the overwhelming suspicion something big and hungry is hiding under your bed.

Telepathy: intuition, echoing voices, and an insatiable hunger for brains.

All three of the Preston Brothers leaned over to examine the jars and bottles. They took their time nodding and squinting at their labels and contents. When they finally finished, Lester and Chester were silent because for the very first time, it was Nestor who spoke. "You have chosen wisely."

CHAPTER 17

In which Chuck Brickweather
has nothing to do with the carpet

I t was hard to believe the employees of the Research and Development Department could love such a shabby restaurant. To Chuck, it looked more like a bankrupt insurance company than somewhere you would go for a meal.

What a dump, he thought.

He checked the address on the flyer again. No, this was definitely the place. There was even a sign out front, with red arrows pointing potential customers up to the second floor.

Chuck climbed the steps and came to a curtain of dark green beads. He stooped through them and saw the waitress, an attractive, middle-aged woman whose attention was absorbed in a travel magazine. It took her a moment to notice Chuck was standing right in front of her.

"Oh, hi," she said at last. "Are you here about the carpets?"

Chuck thought this was an odd way of greeting a customer. But on the other hand, glancing at the floor, he could see the faded carpet was in dire need of a shampoo.

"Sorry," said Chuck, "I'm just here for lunch."

The woman's eyes popped wide. *"Seriously?"*

Again, Chuck was surprised by this unusual approach to customer service. "This *is* Famous Freddy's Dim Sum Emporium. Isn't it?"

"Yes, yes, of course!" The waitress searched the podium where she stood, apparently looking for a menu. When she found one, she led Chuck to the middle of the restaurant.

"Anywhere you like," she said. "Your choices are pretty open."

The woman wasn't kidding: the restaurant was empty. Chuck chose a table near what he took to be the entrance to the kitchen.

"I've heard you do a lot of takeout."

The waitress nodded. "It's most of our business. We've got a whole trailer just to lug the stuff around town."

"A trailer, you say? Those're some big orders."

"Huge!"

Chuck recalled seeing it: a great white box, towed through the DENKi-3000 compound by a rusty red Volkswagen. It looked to him like a whale—being towed by a monkfish.

"So . . . do you make the deliveries yourself?"

The woman blinked at him as if she didn't understand the question. "Maybe you'd prefer the takeout menu."

"No, no. I'm just curious."

"Anything about deliveries, you'll have to ask my father. He runs this place and does nearly all the cooking himself— although I'm starting to help out on the side, you know?"

Chuck nodded.

"Anyway, let me know when you're ready to order."

"I already am."

"But you haven't even opened the menu." She pointed to it on the table, where it still lay shut.

"I saw the sign out front, and I'd like to sample the goods. Give me two orders of your famous pork dumplings."

"Sure thing." The waitress went to the nearby doors and poked her head inside. "Hey, Pop, wake up! We just got two orders of the special. *To stay.*"

She walked back to the front of the restaurant, giving Chuck's table a wide berth (perhaps, Chuck thought, to avoid more of his questions).

Chuck looked around and tried to admire the decor, but it wasn't easy. Wobbly, dilapidated furniture and garish colors were the order of the day.

What was it about this place that so attracted the mysterious R&D workers? From the kitchen, he heard the clatters and clinks of utensils, followed by the boil and sizzle of cooking. Then came the smell.

One whiff and Chuck had his answer. It smelled *delicious.*

By the time the waitress put down her magazine and paced back to collect the food, Chuck's mouth was watering. He could hardly wait.

The woman returned to his table carrying two bamboo baskets, and at last, when he bit into his first dumpling . . .

Bliss!

When was the last time he had tasted something so wonderful? For weeks, he had consumed almost nothing except for Dr. Heppleworth's Knoo-Yoo-Juice. Perhaps his body had forgotten what real food tasted like and that was why these dumplings tasted so good.

(No, they *really* tasted this good.)

"Wow!" said the waitress, who had been watching from

across the room. "You polished those off in a hurry."

Chuck looked down at the empty dishes. "It was . . . *very good*," he whispered, with a kind of reverence.

"I guess so," said the waitress. "Maybe it's just because I grew up eating that stuff, it seems pretty ordinary to me. But it's nice to know there are people out there who go crazy for it."

Chuck laughed. "Like me."

"Don't worry," said the waitress, "you're not alone. Several times a week we get these bulk orders, always for delivery. Pop starts cooking in the middle of the night just to fill them."

"Any chance I could meet this famous Pop of yours? I'd like to offer my compliments to the chef."

"Sure, no problem. Provided he didn't dip back into the cooking wine."

Chuck wasn't quite sure what she meant by this comment.

"*Yo, Pop!* Guy wants to tell you how he liked your food!"

Chuck looked anxiously at the kitchen door. He heard a few scattered clangs and bumps, the slow shuffle of feet, and then a low creak as the kitchen door slowly opened. A stooping, wrinkly, completely bald old man came waddling out.

"You wanted to see me?" croaked Famous Freddy.

"Yes, sir," said Chuck. He rose out of his seat. "I'd like to shake your hand."

They shook, and Chuck was astonished by the firmness of the old man's grip.

"How is it," Chuck whispered, "this place is so empty?"

Freddy's answer was simple. "We mostly do takeout."

Chuck nodded. "Your daughter told me the same thing. Whole truckloads, I hear."

"Yep."

Chuck sensed a sudden chill blow through the conversation. "So, um . . . what sort of neighborhoods do you deliver to?"

"Here and there." The old man's face was impassive.

"I'm curious," said Chuck. "Do you, by any chance, get a lot of corporate orders?"

The old man said nothing.

"Well? Do you?"

"From time to time."

Chuck nodded. This was his chance to gauge how large the R&D Department really was. "Let's say, speaking hypothetically, that you got an order from that big company around the corner—think it's called DENKi-3000—let's say their R&D Department called you up; how many people would you be cooking for, give or take?"

Again, however, the old man remained silent.

Chuck waited.

After a long time, Freddy pointed at Chuck's face. "You look a little peaked."

"I—I do?"

"Is it some sort of rash?"

Chuck knew the redness in his face was a side effect of the Knoo-Yoo-Juice. "It's nothing," he told the old man.

Famous Freddy craned his face a little closer to Chuck's. "There's something odd about your eyes, too."

Chuck wasn't sure what to say. He had come into the restaurant believing his suspicions about Famous Freddy granted him the upper hand. Now he wasn't so sure.

"I think you'll agree," said the old man, gazing intently at Chuck's face, "we all struggle to become comfortable with who we really are."

"W-what?"

Famous Freddy nodded sagely to himself. "It's something we all have to come to terms with, sooner or later."

Perhaps sensing the tension between the two men, the waitress put down her magazine and hurried over to Chuck's table.

"Is there anything else I can get you?" she asked brightly. "Or just the bill?"

"The bill," Chuck muttered. "I was just leaving."

The old man who called himself "Famous" gave Chuck a curt nod. "Hope you enjoyed the meal," he said, and shuffled back to the kitchen.

Outside, the Quazicom limousine was waiting. Chuck climbed in the back and told the driver to return to DENKi-3000 headquarters.

He hadn't found out much at the restaurant, but he was absolutely certain the old chef knew more than he was letting on. In fact, Famous Freddy seemed to know even more than expected. The old man's final words repeated in Chuck's head. *We all struggle to become comfortable with who we really are. . . .*

Why would he suddenly say something like that? Could it be that, somehow, Famous Freddy knew that the only thing keeping Chuck trim and sleek and dashingly handsome was a daily regimen of Dr. Heppleworth's Knoo-Yoo-Juice?

"Traffic's awful along here," said the driver. "If you don't mind, I'm going to try a shortcut."

"Fine with me," Chuck replied.

The driver turned off the main street and eased the car into a narrow alleyway. Fastened to the walls above them was a crisscross of wrought-iron fire escapes. The afternoon sunlight came through the gaps in flashes and pops. Looking up through the window, Chuck was mesmerized by the dance of shadows and light.

Then he saw something else. High above, at the very top of one of the fire escapes, he saw what looked like . . .

A giant, jagged-toothed smile.

He saw two enormous green hands grip the edge of the fire escape.

A pair of inhumanly large eyes peeked over the edge.

Chuck pressed his face against the glass to get a better look, but there was a sudden flash of sunlight and whatever he had seen was gone.

"Did you see that?" he asked the driver.

"See what?"

"Up there, in the fire escape. It was a . . . I don't know what it was."

"Hope you don't expect me to drive while I'm looking up there."

"No, of course not."

The driver had a point. Besides, Chuck told himself, it was probably just some sort of optical illusion. Some trick of the light and shadow as they moved through the alley. Nevertheless, Chuck kept gazing up at those fire escapes.

He didn't see anything else. By the time they emerged from the alley, past the lush trees of Bickleburgh Park, Chuck had convinced himself that he hadn't seen anything at all.

CHAPTER 18

In which Leslie and Elliot brave what the creatures cannot

The day before, in the Abstractory, Elliot and Leslie had selected the intangible essences. All that remained now was to build the machines. The laboratory was divided into three sections, each one devoted to one of the three inventions: an invisibility machine, a teleportation device, and a telepathy helmet.

The same three divisions were applied to all the creatures in the department. Everyone was assigned to a team.

Patti Mudmeyer led the team at work on the invisibility machine, a task she seemed to revel in, proving herself not only as a designer but also an engineer. She used her unique scalp sludge to model both the exterior and the internal mechanics. Creatures on her team then duplicated her models on a larger scale, large enough to fit inside the machine and form the exterior.

Gügor, of course, was given another chance at the teleportation device. He proved himself to be a calm and diligent inventor, working from the principal that rickum ruckery wasn't merely for repairing something; you could rickum-ruckem from scratch, too.

He recruited many of the larger, more imposing creatures, and they threw equipment about as if they were wrestling with it, hurling cogs and gears and motors into a higher and higher heap.

Finally, Jean-Remy Chevalier was charged with creating the telepathy helmet. This made sense because, of the three inventions, this one would require the smallest working parts. As such, the fairy-bat's diminutive size was a clear asset. He worked alongside the smallest of the creatures, from the hobmongrels all the way down to mini-gryffs, creatures like tiny winged hippopotamuses, barely bigger than a grown man's thumb.

Overseeing everything was Harrumphrey Grouseman, offering advice and guidance wherever it was needed. All the while, darting in and out amid the chaos were Elliot and Leslie themselves. They ran back and forth to deliver and exchange material between the teams, or else they were sent off to other parts of the mansion to find strange bits and pieces that would help in the construction.

In this way, they discovered that many rooms in the mansion were devoted to storage. There were rooms for circuit boards and wiring, for cogs and gearboxes, for clocks, watches, and timepieces, for computer hardware and monitors, for nuts and bolts and brackets, for glue and adhesives, for plastics, for fabrics, for metals, for glass bottles, for wood and cardboard and colored paper. There was a seemingly endless array of rooms devoted to an endless array of parts and materials.

By the end of the day, the three devices were beginning to take shape.

It was Leslie who finally noticed the time.

"Elliot," she whispered. "We gotta go! If I'm not home by dinner, my mom'll flip."

Elliot sighed. "Mine too."

Patti overheard them talking. She came over, smears of oil streaking her face. "Y'all mean to say you're not gonna stay the night? 'Cuz I figure we'll be at it till morning. But don't worry." She threw a reassuring arm around Leslie's shoulders. "You can sleep in my room. We'll have ourselves a good old-fashioned slumber party. Just wait till you see my pillow in the mornin'! *Hoo-wee!*"

Leslie shuffled her feet. "I don't think I can—"

"And Elliot," Patti went on, "you can stay with Harrumphrey there."

Elliot and Harrumphrey regarded each other warily.

"Do I look like someone who has slumber parties?" Harrumphrey rasped.

"Thanks for the offer," said Leslie, "but I can't. If I'm not home for dinner, my mom'll go *crazy*. Seriously, she'll move us to a new town because she'll think I'm 'running with a bad crowd.' She's *incredibly* oversensitive about that stuff."

"The tunnels," said Gügor. "Why don't they use the tunnels?"

Every other creature there froze. Some of them even let out gasps and whimpers.

"*Gügor!*" Harrumphrey admonished. "As the professor's official Right-Hand Head, I gotta say I am sorely disappointed to hear you make such a dumb suggestion."

Patti nodded. "You know we don't go down there anymore."

"But why?" asked Gügor.

"*Because,*" Patti whispered, "*ghorks* live under the ground."

"Gügor knows this," said the knucklecrumpler. "But we have been living here for years and years, right on top of so many tunnels, and nothing bad has ever come out. Maybe there are no more ghorks."

"We can't be sure of that," said Harrumphrey.

Leslie was obviously getting impatient. She stepped forward. "How long would it take if we ran?"

"Not long at all," said Gügor. "You could get to the park in one straight line."

"There's a tunnel from here to Bickleburgh Park?" asked Elliot.

"Zere are tunnels all across this city, but surely you don't want to—"

"You haven't seen my mom when she's angry." She took Elliot's hand. "Besides, I'll have Elliot with me."

"Uh, yeah," said Elliot. He was a little apprehensive about how this plan was shaping up, but Leslie seemed determined to get home right away. He didn't want her to think he wasn't brave enough to go with her.

"You know," said Jean-Remy. "It is possible zat we have been overreacting in our fear. We must all admit, it is true what Gügor has said. Zere has not been even *a single sighting* of any ghork in a great many years—unless, of course, you count ze ones who are appearing in ze stories of ze colonel-admiral, but let us face facts: None of us truly believes his silly dreams."

Elliot and Leslie looked at each other.

"What about the thing we saw?" asked Elliot.

"The giant!"

Jean-Remy shook his head. "I don't think you

need to worry about zat. As we have told you, ze giants—
very peaceful. And besides, many of ze tunnels, zey are
much too small to fit a creature so large."

"Are you sure?" asked Leslie.

"Positive!"

"Good. Then it's settled." Leslie looked at her
watch. "We'll take the tunnel. Jean-Remy, you can show us
the way, right?"

"*Moi?!*"

"After what you just said, I thought you were volunteering."

Jean-Remy sighed. He realized he had talked himself into a
corner and was left with no choice but to guide them.

They used the hydraulic platform that had previously raised Famous Freddy's truck.

Jean-Remy flew to the wall of the tunnel, to
the same place Leslie's grandfather had stood when
he opened the secret passage to the laboratory. This
time, he opened another passage, one that led to a
staircase that went spiraling downward.

They entered, and Jean-Remy was careful to seal the door
closed behind them. As the entranceway shut, they were surprised that there was still light. In fact, the stairwell shimmered
with undulations of color.

Glass domes protruded from the walls here and there.
Inside were what appeared to be butterflies—*with glowing
wings*.

Jean-Remy noted their curiosity. "Zey are ze luster bugs.
Like ze bioluminescence of ze fireflies, only much brighter."

Elliot and Leslie stood mesmerized by the bugs. The bril-
liance of their countless colors was extraordinary, throwing a

kaleidoscope of light across the cave.

"Zis way." Jean-Remy flapped into a stairwell.

He led them down three flights of steps and then pointed them into a shadowy tunnel. "Straight through zere will take you to ze park. Very simple, a straight line, you understand?"

They nodded.

Jean-Remy turned back toward the stairwell. Already, he was eager to return. "We will send for you tomorrow, once ze machines are complete and ready for testing."

Elliot and Leslie raced down the tunnel. Rippling pools of luster-bug light shone down on them as they went.

After only a few minutes of running, they came to the end of the tunnel.

The *dead end* of the tunnel.

"There's no door." Elliot turned and looked behind them. There was another tunnel, leading down in another direction. All he could see inside was the indistinct gray of shadow, which quickly faded to an inky black. "Do you think he meant down there?"

"He couldn't have. It's in the complete opposite direction. He said it was simple. A straight line."

"What if it's another secret door?"

"*Quick!*" Leslie ran to the wall and began fiddling with every bit of rock she could find. "It's got to be one of these."

Elliot joined her, pulling, pushing and twisting every crag and crevasse, but nothing moved. After poking and prodding at most of the wall, they were beginning to lose heart.

"Should we go back?" Elliot asked.

"I'll be late." There was real panic in Leslie's voice. "You don't know my mom. A week from now, I'll be on the other side of the country."

"So what are we gonna—"

Elliot stopped. He couldn't move. Because in that other tunnel, where the gray shadows faded to black . . .

Something was there.

CHAPTER 19

In which Elliot and Leslie discover giants are neither as giant nor as peaceful as they had been led to believe

he first thing they saw was the mouth. A huge grin, full of terrible teeth. Then the eyes, enormous, wet, and unblinking. Then a crooked, pointed nose. Then a soft, oily, hair-filled ear. Finally, two enormous speckled green hands that seemed to sprout straight from a chin that was lost in shadow.

Without thinking, Elliot reached out for Leslie and grasped her hand.

"Maybe there're no ghorks down here," Leslie whispered. "But I guess nobody checked for—"

"*Giants,*" Elliot whispered. "And I don't care what Harrumphrey said. That thing *definitely* does not look peaceful."

The giant appeared to be pulling itself through the shadows with its huge, claw-like hands. They were thrown out directly in front of its face.

And what a face! It seemed to wobble and hover impossibly, as if bits of it would fall clean off at any moment. The eyes, the ears, the nose . . . none of the pieces fit. And that was when they realized: The pieces *weren't supposed* to fit together—because it wasn't a giant at all. It wasn't even a single creature.

It was five.

Each one looked like something out of an old horror movie. A gremlin or sinister troll, all slick green skin, crooked teeth, and jagged claws.

Yet still, each one was wholly distinct. Each was marked out by a single gruesomely enlarged feature, and what was most disturbing was that there seemed to be *a system* to it: Eyes. Ears. Nose. Mouth. Hands.

The five senses.

The five creatures ranged in height dramatically. The one with enormous eyes was the tallest, while the one with the enormous hands was shortest.

When they all stood together, obscured by bushes or shadows, the five creatures resembled an enormous, distorted face. Elliot and Leslie could only watch with horror as the face crumbled into these five creatures. Suddenly, they were surrounded, backs pressed against a cold stone wall.

"You're them," Elliot whispered. "The ones we saw."

"You're ghorks," said Leslie. "Aren't you?"

"That's right," replied the creature with the huge, sinister grin. "And not only did you see us, but we saw you too. Isn't that right, Iris?" He looked to the one with the enormous eyes.

"Oh, we *saw* everything," she said, batting her spidery eyelashes.

"We heard everything too," said the one with the enormous ears. To demonstrate, he twitched them. They buzzed like the wings of an enormous insect.

"The five of us," said the one with the enormous hands, holding up five incredible fingers, "we're the perfect spies."

"It's true," said the one with the huge nose, droning with a nasally voice. "We can sniff out most anything!" He threw his head back and flared his nostrils. It was like staring down a pair of bottomless pits.

"That's right," said the one with the big grin. "We know everything about you two."

"Because you've been following us," said Leslie.

"Of course we have," said the huge-eyed creature. "It's our job."

"We've been hired to make sure Quazicom gets everything it wants."

"You work for them?"

The mouth ghork grinned. "Didn't you know? Yours isn't the only Creature Department in the world."

The five creatures closed in. There was nowhere to run. For Elliot and Leslie, all they could do was press themselves against the wall, clawing at the stone behind them, hoping to find a secret latch to set them free.

The creature with the enormous hands reached out as the stench of breath from the huge-mouthed creature washed over them. "You're coming with us," he said, licking his endless lips with a soft white tongue.

"How dare you torment a pair of innocent children," boomed a voice from the darkness. "Step away from them this instant!"

All five of the strange creatures turned around, and there was Colonel-Admiral Reginald T. Pusslegut. He looked surprisingly courageous in the dim light of the tunnel, the medals of his uniform reflecting the pearlescent glow of the luster bugs.

"*You!*" said the one with the sinister smile. "We've had quite enough of you!"

Reggie drew his saber as all five of the hideous creatures leapt at him. They moved incredibly fast. Three of them instantly darted for the arm holding the golden saber aloft. Meanwhile, the creature with the enormous hands scaled up Reggie's back to sit atop his shoulders, slapping and punching at his blubbery face.

The ghork with the massive nose took a few paces backward.

"Hold him steady!" he cried.

The others did their best to restrain the great bombasta-don. The huge-nosed monster plugged one nostril, threw his head back, and exhaled sharply.

PHWOOMP! PHWOOMP! PHWOOMP!

A series of huge globs of snot flew like cannonballs out of the nose's machine-gun sniffer. They splattered all about Reggie's head and shoulders.

"*BLEGH!* You abominable creatures! Get off me!"

But of course they didn't, and in moments Reggie's whole upper body was dripping with slime.

"We need to help him," said Leslie.

She crouched down and picked up the largest rocks she could find. She flung them with all her might at the back of the nose ghork's head. He spun around and, nostril still plugged, prepared to return fire.

PHWOOMP! PHWOOMP! PHWOOMP!

Now the projectile boogers were flying thick and fast—literally. Leslie and Elliot dove for cover behind an out-crop of rocks, but not before one of the snot globs hit Elliot square in the back. It felt like he'd been hit with a hardball in an especially vindictive Little League game, one in which the balls melted into slime on impact.

He crouched down with Leslie as more snot balls exploded on the wall behind them.

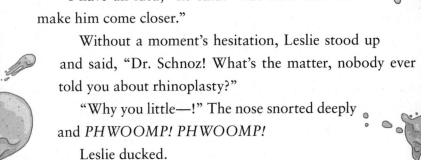

"I have an idea," he said. "But we'll have to make him come closer."

Without a moment's hesitation, Leslie stood up and said, "Dr. Schnoz! What's the matter, nobody ever told you about rhinoplasty?"

"Why you little—!" The nose snorted deeply and *PHWOOMP! PHWOOMP!*

Leslie ducked.

SPLOOSH!

SPLUSH!

"Missed again," she taunted. "I really thought you'd be able to hit me from there. Guess not."

The nose ghork growled in frustration. He lumbered toward them, snorting and snuffling and shaking his head, building up a great stockpile of snot inside his monumental sinuses.

"Now you're gonna get it," he said, standing only a few feet away and sounding more nasally than ever.

He was just about to drown Leslie in mucus when Elliot leapt up with two big rocks. He jumped over the barrier and jammed them right up the creature's nose.

The nose ghork screamed and stumbled backward, coughing and sputtering and picking frantically at his nostrils to dislodge the rocks. His heels caught on some larger stones and he fell back, bashing his head on the wall of the cave.

He slumped to the floor and just lay there, snoring through his mouth, thick green mucus leaking out around the rocks that remained jammed in tight.

Reggie, meanwhile, was still struggling to contend with the other four creatures.

"Now it's my turn," said Leslie. "Do what I do." She bent down and picked up a handful of dust and sand from the floor of the cave. "Watch this." She ran up to the ghork with the enormous eyes (who was swinging wildly from Reggie's right arm) and said, "Can you see this?" She held out her empty hand.

"See what, kid? If you hadn't noticed, I'm right in the middle of beating up a bombastadon. Hard work, you know!"

"But can you *see* this?" Leslie raised her hand higher.

"What, your hand? There's nothing there."

"Yes, there is. Guess your eyesight's not as good as you think."

Unable to resist this taunt, the bug-eyed ghork let go of Reggie's arm and leapt down for a closer look. She stooped close to Leslie's hand. "You're crazy, kid, there's nothing there."

"Sorry," said Leslie. "Wrong hand." She whipped the fistful of dust and sand into the creature's wide eyes.

"AEEEGH!" The thing shrieked like a siren and staggered away. "My eyes! My eyes! My beautiful eyes!" The eye ghork went running down the tunnel but—unable to see where she was going—ran straight into the wall, slumping down beside her partner with the gigantic nose.

With only three attackers to contend with, the odds were finally in Reggie's favor. He flung off two ghorks and sent them flying into the same heap with the others.

At last the only one left was the big-mouthed ghork, whose once-conniving grin had turned to a defeated sneer. He backed away from Reggie and tried frantically to revive his friends.

Reggie, meanwhile, picked his golden saber up off the floor and pointed it at his attacker. "You, sir, are a despicable disgrace to all of creaturedom. Gather your companions and crawl back to the shadow from whence you came!"

The beaten ghork found his sinister grin one last time. "This isn't the last you've heard from us. We'll be back—*sooner than you think*!"

He managed to rouse his friends and they hobbled, injured and whining, down into the darkness.

Reggie took a handkerchief from his pocket and wiped the dusty blade of his saber. "It's only ceremonial, of course," he admitted, sliding it smoothly back into its scabbard, "but it does the job in a pinch."

"Reggie! Thank you!" Leslie ran up to him and gave the great bombastadon a hug, or rather, she tried to. (Reggie was much too big to receive a proper hug from an average-size twelve-year-old. All Leslie could do was stand to one side, raise her arms, and gently pat his kettledrum of a belly.)

Reggie, meanwhile, was utterly bemused by this sudden show of affection. He looked down uncomfortably at Leslie, as if the very concept of a hug were foreign to him.

"Please, you don't have to—I mean, that's not at all—er, well . . . you are very welcome, madam." He waved his hands aimlessly in the air, not sure where to put them. "But truly, I was only doing my duty. Defending the home front, you see."

Leslie stepped back. "Those ghorks, they recognized you. Have you been fighting off those things all along?"

Reggie gave a curt bow. "Your uncle told me to guard the entrances to the Creature Department and so that is what

I've done."

"No wonder you have nightmares."

Reggie's mouth tightened. "On occasion."

"Why do they look like that?" Elliot asked.

Reggie shook his head, swinging his tusks in dismay. "It's absurd, but would you believe they breed themselves that way? It's the reason they spend so much time fighting among one another. It's all over nothing more important than which sense is superior."

"Kind of a dumb reason to have a war."

"There are very few good ones." Reggie tapped the medals on his chest. "And sadly, I speak from experience." He peered down into the tunnel where the ghorks had retreated. "I must say, it's rare to see five of them all working together."

"Um, sorry to cut in," said Leslie. "I *really* have to get home. Would you mind showing us the way out?"

"Certainly." From his pocket he withdrew a small hand-held device, like a mobile phone. On the screen was a map.

"What's that?" asked Elliot. "A GPS?"

Reggie seemed surprised. "How did you know that?"

"Everyone knows what a Global Positioning System is."

"*Pah!* Don't be silly. Who needs anything *global* down here? This, my dear boy, is a Ghork Positioning System. I use it on my rounds."

He displayed the map to them, a three-dimensional laby-rinth. "Ghorks are denoted by little green spots, and as you can see, the way is clear."

"Even still," said Leslie, staring at the dead-end wall. "I *really* think I'd like to get out of this tunnel, please."

"Yes, of course." He winked at her. "I'm not a bad engineer

in my own right, I'll have you know. I've rigged my GPS to open any of the secret doors down here, by remote control." Reggie pointed the device at the wall. At the press of a button, the rock face split open. Stone steps led up to an outcrop of granite in the middle of Bickleburgh Park.

"Here," said Reggie, handing the GPS to Elliot. "Use it when you return to us tomorrow."

Elliot nodded grimly. "It's our last day before the meeting."

Reggie smiled reassuringly, his jowls jostling comically with his tusks. "I'm quite certain one of the inventions the department is currently working on will be a great success! If not, we can always count on your uncle. He's a good egg, that one. He has never let us down before—and he won't now."

"I hope not."

"No need for hope, my boy. I'm *sure* of it!" He gave Elliot a sharp salute and then, as if to demonstrate his unflappable faith in Professor von Doppler, Reggie turned back toward the Creature Department, lumbering off as casually as if he were on a morning stroll.

Elliot, however, shared none of the colonel-admiral's confidence. With only one day left before the shareholders' meeting, Elliot was beginning to worry . . .

Where is Uncle Archie?

CHAPTER 20

In which the testing phase begins and ends
(with a whimper)

he following afternoon was Thursday, the last day
before the shareholders' meeting. Still there had been
no word from Professor von Doppler. When Elliot and
Leslie returned to the Creature Department, they didn't
encounter any ghorks. (Of course, Reggie's Ghork Positioning
System came in very handy.)

In the laboratory, the prototypes were complete. Three
oddly shaped structures shrouded in huge white sheets stood in
the middle of the room. They resembled a trio of lumpy ghosts.

"Welcome back," Harrumphrey greeted them. "We think
we've got these working, but we won't know until we test them.
So come on over here." It was customary, he explained, for
those who chose the essences to feed them into each new device.

They began with the invisibility machine. Patti tugged off
the sheet to reveal a tall black rectangular box. It was hollowed
out on the inside, very much like the security scanners you
walked through at an airport. However, there was one *very*
significant difference.

When it came to airport scanners, the interiors commonly featured smooth, featureless plastic. The interior of this device, however, could hardly be called featureless. That's because its surface was lined with something very strange.

"*Eyeballs!*" said Leslie.

Beside her, Patti smiled proudly. "Don't worry. They're not real; they just look that way."

It was true: Every pair of them looked disarmingly genuine. They were all different shapes and sizes, complete with eyelids and eyelashes, irises of countless colors, and even eerily expressive eyebrows.

"Super-creepy," Leslie whispered.

"Made every one of those myself. See?" Patti demonstrated by running a few fingers through her hair, collecting a glob of her scalp resin. She rolled it into a ball, molding it with such speed it was like magic. When she opened her hand, staring up from her scaly palm was an eyeball so realistic, Leslie expected it to wink.

Patti stepped up to the machine, gesturing at the many pairs of eyes. "Each one of these," she explained, "represents all the different ways you can look at someone. Suspiciously, for instance." She pointed to a pair of squinting eyelids. "Or with astonishment." She moved her hand to a pair of eyes that were popped wide open. "So the idea is, you put something in the machine, and *theoretically*, once we get all the eyes to close, whatever's in the machine will vanish."

"Will that really work?" asked Elliot. It didn't sound plausible at all.

"It's weird, but it works," said Patti. "That's creature technology for you. Anyway, it's not the design I'm worried about.

It's the *essence*. As long as you two got that right, then yes, it oughta work just fine."

"Here are the essences," said Gügor. He pointed one fat-knuckled finger at a table beside the invisibility machine.

Obscurity, bedazzlement, and the overwhelming suspicion something big and hungry is hiding under your bed: These were the three essences of invisibility (at least according to Elliot and Leslie).

Patti flipped open a tiny door on the side of the machine, revealing a tube like the place you pour gasoline into a car. "All we have to do is put a drop of all three in here, but as Harry toldja, it's gotta be y'all who do the honors."

Leslie and Elliot did as they were instructed. They took one bottle each and added a drop to the tank. The crucial final ingredient—the feeling like something is waiting underneath your bed to eat you up—they poured in together.

"Let's see if she runs." Patti stood at the control console and turned on the machine.

Every eyeball mounted in the machine's interior blinked once and began to glow. A moment later, the eyes darted every which way, searching the laboratory with intense curiosity.

"*Definitely* super-creepy," said Leslie. "I like it!"

The invention's creepiness, however, was entirely lost on Patti. She was still grinning at the thing like a proud mother. "So," she said, rubbing her hands excitedly. "Which one of y'all wants to be our first guinea pig?"

Every creature took a small step backward. A gap opened in the crowd, and through it, Elliot saw Bildorf and Pib, who were just emerging onto the laboratory floor.

"What about them?" he suggested.

Bildorf and Pib froze.

"Why is everyone staring at us?" asked Bildorf, a little worried.

"Elliot," said Harrumphrey, "I think that's a fine suggestion."

"Suggestion for *what*, exactly?" asked Pib.

"For playing an important role in the history of creature science," said Patti. "Gügor?"

The big knucklecrumpler swept up the hobmongrels, both in one hand.

"Hey, what's the big idea?!" cried Pib.

Gügor dropped them inside the machine, and before they could scamper off, a metal gate rose on either side, trapping them.

Every eyeball in the device swiveled to gaze silently at the two hobmongrels.

"Wait," said Bildorf. "Is this because of us making fun of Reggie all the time? C'mon, guys! It's Reggie!"

Pib hastily agreed. "The guy's a buffoon!" She looked around at the hundreds of glowing eyes ogling her. "Okay, I take it back! He's not a buffoon! He's a lovely guy!"

"I agree—*100 percent*," said Bildorf. "Now couldja let us out of this thing?"

"Incidentally . . . " said Pib. "What *is* this thing? We haven't really been paying attention."

Jean-Remy flew down to Bildorf's level. "Perhaps were you to do a bit more work around ze laboratory, you would know what zis is."

"To answer your question," Elliot said to Bildorf. "It's an invisibility machine."

"You mean you're gonna make us . . . *disappear*?!" asked Pib.

"Don't worry," said Patti. "It's perfectly safe."

Bildorf grinned in relief. "Oh, sure, of course. You guys've probably had this thing tested on, y'know, a grapefruit or bean-bag or whatever."

"Or a sock monkey," said Pib.

"Actually," said Patti, "this is the first time we're using it."

Instantly, the two hobmongrels pounded the metal gate with their tiny furry feet. They shouted all the obvious things. *You can't do this! Get me out of here! I'm no sock monkey! Somebody tell all these glowing eyeballs to quit staring at us!*

"Hush," Patti told them. "I need to concentrate." She fiddled with dials, and one by one, shafts of light beamed from the eyeballs. Every single one was like a spotlight, gleaming down on Bildorf and Pib.

"Now for the moment of truth." Patti pulled a lever on the side of the machine. A slow, tinkling melody, like something from an old music box, leaked from hidden speakers.

Inside the machine, a few pairs of eyes flickered, faded, and closed. They were gently succumbing to the crackling lullaby of an old music box.

"Look!" Leslie pointed.

At the center of the machine, where Bildorf and Pib stood, the light on them was going dark. As it did, the two creatures themselves became more and more indistinct.

"They're fading away," said Elliot.

"Wait, guys," Bildorf whined. "I don't wanna fade away."

"Me neither," said Pib. She held up a tiny paw in front of her face, staring in wonder as it went all hazy, an image viewed through the ripples of a pond.

"Unbelievable," said Harrumphrey. "It's actually working!"

Gügor came and stood behind Leslie and Elliot, placing his huge, warm hands on their shoulders. "I just wish the professor was here to see this."

Everyone, even the two hobmongrels, stood in silence. The interior of the machine became dimmer and dimmer and dimmer until every last pair of eyes were shut.

"Wait a second," said Leslie. "I can still see them."

"You can?" Patti pressed a button and the metal gates retreated into the machine. Leslie was right. While the bizarre process had certainly had an effect on the two hobmongrels, they hadn't been turned invisible. Instead, they had merely become . . .

Kind of blurry.

"What have you done to us?!"

"We're all foggy!"

Instead of a pair of calico-rat-like creatures, all anyone could see of the hobmongrels were two orangey-brown smudges.

"Oh, Pib!"

"Oh, Bildorf!"

The two smudges embraced, merging into a single, indistinct blob, crying like babies.

"Waaah! Waaah! Waaah!"

"Don't worry," Patti told them. "It ain't permanent. The effects oughta wear off in a matter of hours. Maybe days. Hard to say, to be honest."

"Days?!" cried the two smudges at once. *"WAAAAAH!"*

"Maybe we oughta try the next invention," said Harrumphrey.

They moved to the second device, the tallest of the three.

Gügor tugged the sheet away to reveal a plush leather recliner mounted atop a great mountain of machinery: dials, switches, gauges, cogs, gears, chains, wires, and flashing circuit boards. Unlike Patti's invisibility machine, with its elegant shape and smooth surfaces, this machine looked more like a junk heap.

"Teleportation is difficult," Gügor announced, with his usual calmness. "But Gügor is certain it will work this time. The trick, we found, is to be relaxed. Teleportation only works just before you fall asleep. You must be relaxed but still just a *little* bit awake." He slowly tapped his temple with one thick finger. "At least, that is Gügor's theory."

"Sounds doable," said Harrumphrey.

Gügor pointed to the cushy recliner atop the mountain of machinery and electronics. "That chair is the second-most-comfortable chair in the universe."

"The *second*-most?" asked Leslie.

The knucklecrumpler nodded. "Gügor had it tested."

"But why the *second*-most comfortable?"

"The most comfortable chair in the universe puts you to sleep right away. Gügor's team needed something slower."

There were grunts of agreement from the larger creatures in the group.

Gügor moved his languid eyes across the room. "So . . . who wants to be teleported?"

As if acting on group instinct, every creature there looked at the two calico smudges on the edge of the crowd.

"Oh, no," said Pib. "Not us again."

However (again), Gügor was too quick for them. Even though they were all blurry, he easily scooped them both up and held them close to his face. "Being teleported will help you," he told them. "When Gügor's machine reconstitutes you, it will put you back together exactly the way you were before."

"Are you sure?" asked the Bildorf smudge.

"Wait," said the Pib smudge. "Who said we wanted to be reconstituted in the first place?"

Gügor didn't answer these questions. Instead, he climbed up a ladder to the top of the machine and strapped the blurry smudges formerly known as Bildorf and Pib into the second-most-comfortable chair in the universe.

Elliot and Leslie poured the essences they had chosen—hope, wanderlust, and the thrill of your first ride on the back of an arachnimammoth—into the machine. Its gauges, readouts, and video screens blinked to life. On the main screen was an image of the blurrified Bildorf and Pib, struggling in the plush leather recliner.

Instead of wailing, as they had been only moments ago, the two hobmongrels now settled into a murmuring whimper that sounded like the cooing of babies.

"Just relax," Gügor told them calmly. "You're going to dematerialize and instantly rematerialize down here, right beside Gügor." He pointed to a spot adjacent to his feet, where a red X had been taped to the floor.

The readouts showed the second-most-comfortable chair in the universe was doing its job. Bildorf and Pib's crying was getting quieter. They grew calmer (and sleepier) by the moment. In no time, they were ready to nod off completely.

Gügor pulled the lever.

There was a thunderous cracking sound as a web of electric-blue lightning flashed and bolted across the great heap of machinery. It all converged on the chair above, and with one final ZZZZAP, the two blurry hobmongrels disappeared. All that remained of them were two thin coils of smoke.

Gügor looked down at the red X beside him. His faint eyebrows only rose a fraction of an inch when he saw there was nothing there.

"Oops," he said.

He fiddled with the dials, and an image of Bildorf and Pib appeared on the screen. As Gügor had predicted, they were no longer blurry. However, the test had obviously not gone as planned. They appeared to be floating in an empty white void.

"According to Gügor's readouts," the knucklecrumpler told them, "everything worked perfectly." He squinted calmly at the screen. "But I may have sent you to another dimension."

"Another dimension?!" cried Pib.

"Bring us back, already!" cried Bildorf.

"It will take Gügor a little while to figure out where you are."

"Try to look on the bright side," said Harrumphrey. "At least you're not blurry anymore."

For the hobmongrels, this was a small consolation. They huddled together, trembling, and said, *"WAAAAAAAAH!"*

"Well," Harrumphrey grumbled, "that's *two* inventions that don't work."

Jean-Remy spun in a loop and flew to land on top of the third and smallest invention, still covered with its sheet.

"Fear not, *mes amis*," he announced. "It is I, *Jean-Remy Chevalier*, who has delivered an invention that would make ze professor proud! I can assure you, beyond any shadow of a doubt, it is *absolument parfait*!"

Gripping the sheet with his hands, Jean-Remy spread his wings and flapped upward, revealing the telepathy helmet.

It looked just like the diagram in the Preston Brothers' slide show, an egg-shaped hat with an antenna that looked suspiciously like Paris's Eiffel Tower on top. On the sides, sticking out like enormous ears, were two miniature radar dishes.

"Because zis is an invention meant to be worn on ze head," said Jean-Remy, "I think it should be tested by ze one with, well . . . ze most head."

Harrumphrey sighed. "You mean me, don't you?"

Reluctantly, he allowed himself to be buckled into the telepathy helmet.

"All right, let's get this over with," he said. "How's this thing work?"

"First," said Jean-Remy, "ze essences." He opened a circular hatch in the front of the helmet, just above Harrumphrey's forehead.

For the third and final time, Elliot and Leslie poured from the Abstractory bottles: intuition, echoing voices, and an insatiable hunger for brains.

When Jean-Remy flicked the on switch at the back of the helmet, it made a sound like the distant echoing of Morse code. The miniature satellite-dish ears began twitching and spinning. The Eiffel Tower–like appendage sparkled in a way that reminded Leslie of the Christmas lights in her grandfather's restaurant.

"What you must do," Jean-Remy instructed Harrumphrey, "is focus your attention on whomsoever you choose. When you do this, ze helmet will collect ze thoughts of zat individual."

Harrumphrey looked around the room at all of his colleagues, but his eyes finally came to rest on Gügor.

"You know something, my big, reticent friend," he told the knucklecrumpler, "you may've used more words just now in explaining your teleportation device than I've heard from you in weeks."

Gügor shrugged.

"I'd like to hear what else is going on in that dopey head of yours."

Harrumphrey shuffled a bit until he was facing Gügor. All the lights on the mini–Eiffel Tower lined up, flashing in unison, while the mini–satellite dishes stopped twitching and pointed directly at Gügor's head.

"Are you getting something?" Jean-Remy asked Harrum-phrey.

"Nope. Nothing. Although I don't think we can rule out the possibility his skull's simply too thick to penetrate."

Gügor frowned.

"And you, Gügor," said Jean-Remy. "How do you feel?"

"Insulted," said Gügor.

Jean-Remy fiddled with some of the helmet's controls and told Harrumphrey to try again. Again, Harrumphrey didn't pick up any signals. This time, however, something *was* happening to Gügor.

His lips trembled. He opened his mouth and let out a deep, baritone wail, like a mournful foghorn. Tears rolled down his broad, salamander-like face and dripped from the corners of his mouth.

The unflappable knucklecrumpler was crying!

Harrumphrey turned to Jean-Remy. "Are you sure this thing works?"

Jean-Remy nodded emphatically. "*Mais oui!* Of course it works!"

When Harrumphrey turned away from Gügor, Elliot had noticed something. "Hey, look! He stopped crying."

Gügor, back to his usual impassive self, merely shrugged.

"Interesting," said Jean-Remy. He asked Harrumphrey to try again, this time with Patti. He did so, and a moment later, Patti inexplicably burst into tears.

"Well, play me twelve bars and color me *the bluuues*!" she sobbed. "I dunno why, but all of a sudden I feel lower than a river snake's belly!"

But once again, the moment Harrumphrey turned away from Patti, her despair vanished.

"It is strange," said Jean-Remy. "Harrumphrey, you must please try ze device on me. I must discover ze problem."

Harrumphrey focused his attention on the fairy-bat. Jean-Remy experienced the same sadness as Gügor and Patti, but he tried heroically to resist it. His face froze in a grim mask of determination. In the end, however, there was nothing he could do. A single tear dripped from each eye.

"*No!*" he whimpered. "Please, it is too much! In my heart I feel only ze profound melancholia of ze doomed love!"

Harrumphrey raised his tail to the back of the helmet and switched it off. "No offense, but I think there's a glitch."

"What went wrong?" Leslie asked. "All it did was make everyone sad."

Jean-Remy snapped his tiny fingers. "*Of course!*" He flew

to Leslie's face and planted two kisses on each of her cheeks (both of which blushed instantly). "Mademoiselle, you are a genius!"

"I am?"

"Of course you are! It is just as you said—it made everyone sad!" cried Jean-Remy. "Do you not see?"

"*No,*" said everyone else, all at once, "we don't!"

"What I have created, it is not a telepathic helmet. It is a *tele-pathetic helmet*!"

"Huh?" asked Elliot (which summed up precisely how everyone felt).

"Yes! It is wonderful, *non?*" cried Jean-Remy, completely ignoring the confusion around him. "It works perfectly, and it is clear proof that Elliot and Leslie have *ze Knack*—just as we suspected!"

"Hold everything," said Leslie. "What's a *tele-pathetic helmet* supposed to be?"

"Do you not know? It is a device for sending sadness directly into ze brain of another. Perhaps it is not ze invention we intended, but it is a great revolution in ze creature science!"

Elliot hung his head. "A tele-*pathetic* helmet. Who would ever want something like that?"

Jean-Remy's enthusiasm evaporated. "Ah. Yes. You make a good point."

"*Wonderful,*" Harrumphrey harrumphed. "Three inventions, but none of them work—at least not the way they're supposed to."

"Wait," said Elliot. "What about my uncle? He'll come back with something amazing, just like he said he would!"

Elliot tried to muster some of the same confidence Reggie had shown in the tunnels, but it was no use. None of the creatures were convinced.

CHAPTER 21

In which Reggie finally drifts off

Colonel-Admiral Reginald T. Pusslegut was exhausted. It was deep in the middle of the night, yet he couldn't sleep. In fact, he had hardly done any proper hibernating in days. *It's all these teeeerible dreams*, he thought.

Reggie sighed. He sat up in his enormous bed. The bedclothes tumbled down his vast flanks like a silky white mudslide. There was only one thing to do. He would head down to the laboratory and see if he could muster up some tea and biscuits.

As it was so late, the laboratory floor was deserted. Reggie noted that things looked a bit different. Many of the tables had been cleared away to open a space at the center of the warehouse-like room. In it were three new devices Reggie didn't recognize.

The first looked like an airport metal detector. The second like a very strange, egg-shaped motorcycle helmet. Rising up between them was a huge pile of machinery topped off with . . .

Something extraordinary!

Bombastadons were well known for their ability to choose suitable and, more importantly, *comfortable* places to hibernate. The chair on top of all that machinery looked wonderfully cozy. It was surely the plushest recliner he had ever seen (or possibly the second-most plush).

It looked *sooo* inviting, *sooo* ready to cradle his great, monumental corpulence! Oh, and look at that! There was even a ladder leading up to it. . . .

Reggie, however, was hardly the most elegant of climbers. Getting off the ground on his own was rarely a simple undertaking. Ascending the ladder, he scrambled and stumbled, his legs kicking wildly at the air.

More than once, his toes flung out and tapped parts of the machine. A few rungs up, his shoe hit something that might have been a control panel. But no, he thought, that was silly. Why would an extremely comfortable chair require a control panel?

The moment he sat down, he knew he was right about this chair. He felt his mind at ease. Had he ever felt so relaxed before?

No.

Never.

How extraordinary!

In just a few moments, he felt himself about ready to drift off to the land of slumber. He was so stupendously relaxed, in fact, he hardly noticed the crack of thunder that sounded as his body was suddenly *ZZZAPPED* by a great blue bolt of lightning.

CHAPTER 22

In which Monica wants a promotion and Chuck doesn't take his medicine

Chuck Brickweather was feeling stressed. Again. His palms were sweating, his temples were throbbing, and his stomach was tied in knots (although the latter was probably because already that morning he had downed four bottles of Professor Heppleworth's Knoo-Yoo-Juice).

Tomorrow was the big shareholders' meeting, and he still knew next to nothing about what went on in the company's Research and Development Department. What if the professor fulfilled his promise? What if he showed up tomorrow with a fabulous new invention and knocked everybody's socks off? It would surely be a disaster for Quazicom, and what was more, Chuck would almost certainly lose his job.

That was why, somehow, some way, he had to get into that weird old mansion. For this, Chuck had formulated *a plan.*

Having spent several days conducting his research at DENKi-3000 headquarters, he had discovered there were certain anomalies to the property. For one, the old blueprints and schematics he found in the company archives hinted at an elaborate tunnel system that connected the various buildings.

The way in, Chuck realized, *was under the ground.*

In an effort to go ahead with his plan, he had stolen the blueprints from the archives. He had come into work that day fully prepared to explore the tunnels below DENKi-3000. When he arrived in his office, however, something stopped him: an e-mail message.

It had come from the DENKi-3000 vice president Monica Burkenkrantz, and it stressed him out even more than his failure to uncover Professor von Doppler's secret. It was marked *UU!* (which stood for *Uber-Urgent!* and was pronounced "EEW!" like the sound you make when you step in something warm and mushy).

Only top-level executives at DENKi-3000 could send UU! messages, and when your computer received one, it automatically locked itself into sleep mode. The only way to wake the thing up was to read the message. In this case, it was ominously succinct:

> CHUCK. WE NEED TO TALK. MY OFFICE. 10 A.M.
> MONICA BURKENKRANTZ, VP

The first thing Chuck did when he read the message was to reach for the bottom drawer of his desk. He took out one bottle of Knoo-Yoo-Juice and gulped down its entire contents. He had a hunch he was going to need it.

When he arrived, he was somewhat annoyed to see that Monica's outer office, manned by Ralph, her administrative assistant, was even larger than the whole of the office DENKi-3000 had provided for him.

"Ah, Mr. Brickweather," Ralph greeted him when he entered, simpering from behind his desk. "Ms. Burkenkrantz has been expecting you." He glanced at his computer screen to check the time. "And I see you are a few minutes early. That's good. I know better than anyone how Ms. Burkenkrantz appreciates punctuality."

Chuck wasn't sure he liked the man's patronizing tone, but he was too stressed to voice his displeasure. Instinctively, he patted the breast pocket of his striped blazer, where he had stashed a spare bottle of Dr. Heppleworth's.

"Ms. Burkenkrantz is ready for you," Ralph said with a weak smile. "You can go right in."

The vice president's office was three times as big as Chuck's. With close to 360-degree wraparound windows, it had a better view, too—at least if you were thrilled by the drab Bickleburgh skyline and the empty farmland beyond it.

Monica was looking at her watch. "Right on time. Excellent." She motioned for Chuck to have a seat in one of the chairs opposite her desk.

"What was it you wanted to see me about?" he asked.

"I think it's time you and I had a heart-to-heart."

What did she mean by *heart-to-heart*? Chuck wondered if it was possible she had a crush on him (he wasn't quite sure if this made him *more* or *less* stressed).

With her elbows resting on the desk, Monica made a steeple with her fingers. "Did you know that before becoming vice president of DENKi-3000, I was also the *vice* president of three other companies?"

Chuck shook his head.

"It's true. I was the VP of a button factory, a toothpick manufacturer, and, most recently, a company that produced dietary supplements." She shook her head. "I hated every one of those jobs."

Chuck couldn't see what this had to do with him. Then again, when was the last time he had shared a *heart-to-heart* with someone? Maybe they were all like this.

"So you see, Chuck," Monica continued, "you and I have shared goals."

"I'm not sure I follow."

"Shared goals, Chuck! You do know what that means, don't you? We're on the same team here."

"We are?"

"Of course we are! Aren't you paying attention?"

"I am! I mean, I thought I was, but it's just that—"

"This is the *fourth time* I've been vice president of a company. It's becoming a habit. A bad habit. Which is precisely what a vice is. *A bad habit*. How would you like to go around year after year, telling people you're the president of bad habits?"

"I don't think that's what vice presi—"

"Don't interrupt me, Chuck," Monica interrupted.

"But you just asked me how I'd like to—"

"*Chuck!* Accept it. We're on the same side here. You work for Quazicom. Quazicom wants to take over this company. And I want to drop my bad habit. Get it?"

"Not at all."

"You're not as smart as you look, are you, Chuck?"

Chuck blinked at her.

"Come to think of it," said Monica, tilting her head to one side, "you don't even *look* that smart. It's your eyes. Too close together. But there's not much you can do about that, is there, Chuck? You were born that way. You gotta live with it."

"Um . . ." Chuck didn't like it when people mentioned his eyes.

"I'll put it plainly," said Monica. "When Quazicom takes

over, they're going to pick this company apart. And guess who's going to be in charge of whatever's left?"

"Sir William?" Chuck suggested.

"NO!" Monica pounded her desk with a fist. "Me!"

"You?"

"*Yes!* I'll finally drop the *vice* and become plain old president. President and CEO Monica Burkenkrantz! It's all been arranged."

At last Chuck understood.

"I've even spoken to your boss," said Monica, beaming with confidence. "He knows all about it."

Chuck gulped. "The Chief?"

"Once Quazicom takes the reins, this is going to be a *very different* company. But in order for that to happen, I need you to file your report—*before* the shareholders' meeting tomorrow." She pursed her lips, her expression turning sour. "If your report gets to the Chief before the meeting, he'll go ahead with the takeover regardless of what the shareholders want. That way, Archie von Doppler won't have any chance to present whatever it is he's working on. Do you see what I mean?"

"I think so," said Chuck, "but how can I file my report if I haven't seen the inside of the R&D Department?"

Monica slapped her desk. "You're a spy, Chuck! You're supposed to be spying!"

"A spy? I thought you hated spies."

"Only when they're not on my side."

"I see."

Monica rose from her chair and padded over to the windowed wall of her office. The DENKi-3000 courtyard spread out below. "I can tell you this, Chuck: Your boss isn't very pleased with your progress."

"He's not?"

Monica pointed down below. "He was hoping that by now you'd have found out what goes on in that weird old mansion down there."

"I will," said Chuck. "I have a plan."

"I'm afraid the Chief doesn't have faith in your plan."

"How would you know?" Now Chuck was getting angry (not good for stress). "I just thought of my plan this morning!"

Monica returned to her desk and pressed a button on the surface. A section of the glass brightened to reveal a hidden control panel. "The Chief thinks you might need a little help."

Chuck narrowed his eyes. "From you?"

"Not from me directly, no. Rather from some of the Chief's associates. You might call them *real* spies."

"What?!"

Monica held up her hands. "Sorry, Chuck, his words, not mine."

"*Real spies?* He said that?"

Monica nodded casually. "Why don't I introduce you?" She pressed the button on the glowing control panel. "You can come in now," she said, speaking into a hidden microphone embedded somewhere in the surface of her desk.

"I must warn you," she said, turning back to Chuck. "They do have a somewhat unusual appearance."

Chuck turned toward the door, not sure what to expect.

"Not that door," Monica told him. "Over here."

Chuck turned back again and saw that Monica was pointing at the bare wall behind her desk. It split open and in walked five . . .

M-m-m-monsters!

"A somewhat unusual appearance" didn't even *begin* to describe them. There were five in all: speckled, sinewy, green-skinned ogres (or trolls, or gremlins, or . . . *things*). Each of them had one grotesquely enlarged feature: an enormous mouth, an enormous nose, two enormous ears, two enormous eyes, a pair of enormous hands!

"Mr. Brickweather," said Monica, "I'd like you to meet Grinner, Adenoid Jack, Wingnut, Iris, and Digits. Or, as they like to call themselves, the Five Ghorks."

Chuck nearly fainted. If his face was red before, now it was utterly flushed—*with fear.*

"G-g-g-ghorks," he whispered.

"Don't worry," said Monica. "They're here to help."

Chuck tried to stand up. His only instinct was to run away as quickly as possible.

"What's the matter?" asked the one called Grinner, speaking through what looked like a hundred clenched teeth. "You got a problem with ghorks?"

"N-n-no!" Chuck waved his arms emphatically. "Of course not! It's j-j-just that—"

"Hey!" Monica put her hands on her hips, glaring at the ghorks. "What happened to you?" She pointed at the bandages that each one of them was wearing. Chuck had been too shocked to notice them at first, but now he saw that all the ghorks were covered with bumps and scrapes and ratty bandages.

Perhaps worst of all was Adenoid Jack, the one with the big nose. Two huge wads of cotton were jammed up his massive nostrils.

"Nothing," said Grinner petulantly. "Just fell down some stairs."

"*All* of you?" asked Monica.

"You callin' us liars?" Iris narrowed her enormous eyes and took a menacing step toward the woman (Chuck was pleased to see Monica finally blanche with fear).

"N-no," said Monica hastily. "Those must have been some steep stairs!"

"They were," sulked Digits, waving a foot-long finger at her.

"Must've been a million of them!" said the one called Wingnut. He shook his head gloomily, causing a rush of wind from his enormous ears.

"But don't worry," said Adenoid Jack, prodding gingerly at the swollen bridge of his massive schnoz. "We'll get revenge on those stairs soon enough."

"Um, okay," said Monica, who seemed eager to change the subject. "I think that's enough about the stairs. I wanted you to meet Mr. Brickweather. You can call him Chuck."

All the attention turned to Chuck . . . and he froze. Every fiber of his being still wanted to run away, but he was too stunned to move.

"He's also a spy," Monica went on, smiling insincerely at Chuck. "Just not a very good one. Like yourselves, he was sent here to gather information before the siege—I mean, *takeover*."

Did she say siege? Chuck wondered. But he didn't wonder for long because the Five Ghorks surrounded him, looking him up and down. None of them seemed impressed.

"I thought it might be advantageous," said Monica, "if all of you worked together."

"M-M-Ms. Burkenkrantz," stammered Chuck, struggling to his feet. "I'd really prefer to work alone."

"Why the rush?" asked Grinner. "I thought you just said you didn't have a problem with ghorks."

"No, no! It's not that at all! Of course I like . . . g-g-g-*ghorks*!"

"Is that so? 'Cuz it sure sounds to me like you're lying." Wingnut flicked the tip of one enormous ear. "I can *hear* it in your voice."

Chuck laughed nervously. "Oh, I would never lie. I'm just a bit on edge, that's all."

"It's true," said Iris. "You do look a bit stressed."

Chuck gasped. "S-s-stressed? Do I?!"

Grinner sucked suspiciously on his innumerable teeth. "It's 'cuz of your face," he said. "It's all red."

Instantly, Chuck spun into a panic. This was too much! This woman was in cahoots with the Chief! *And* these abominable creatures! He could feel his sleek, trim body sliding out of his control. He could no longer resist the bottle hidden in his breast pocket. *I need my Dr. Heppleworth's!*

He reached into his jacket, unscrewed the bottle, and—

"*Stop!*"

Chuck had the bottle almost to his lips.

"Give that to me," said Monica.

Chuck shook his head. "I—I can't."

"NOW!"

Instead of handing over the bottle, Chuck made a lunge for the door. The ghorks, however, were too quick for him. Chuck was immediately overpowered. The bottle was wrenched from his grip, and Digits shoved him back into the chair.

Iris brought the bottle to Monica, who turned it over in her hands. "Well, well, well. I never would have guessed."

All Chuck could mutter was, "I-i-it's medicinal." He reached weakly for the bottle. "I need it."

"I'm sure you do." Monica sniffed the bottle and pulled it away quickly, making a thoroughly disgusted face. "In fact, *I know* you do."

"What?" Something about the way the woman said *I know* sent a chill down Chuck's spine.

"Remember I told you I was once vice president of a company that made dietary supplements? Can you guess what the name of that company was?"

Chuck was speechless. He moved his lips, but no sound came out.

"Dr. Heppleworth's Knootri-Vitamins Incorporated."

"You worked there?"

"I told you, I was the *vice* president." Monica winced as she said the word.

Chuck's body sagged in the chair. "So you know what Knoo-Yoo-Juice does, don't you?"

"Actually, I don't."

"You don't?" Chuck's face brightened (a pinkish glow).

"Nope," said Monica, "but I'm about to find out."

Again, Chuck was rendered mute.

"You see, the reason I quit at Dr. Heppleworth's is the same reason I've always had trouble working here at DENKi-3000." She leaned forward, looming over Chuck, who sat glued to his seat by Digits and his enormous hands. "Too many secrets. In fact, Dr. Heppleworth had one area of the company that was a lot like the mansion down there. No one was allowed in except for old Heppleworth himself. I always wondered what went on in there, but no matter how many times I asked, he never told me anything. Do you have any idea how frustrating that was?!"

All five ghorks nodded in sympathy with Monica.

"Well, one day, just before I quit for good, I started digging around in old Heppleworth's computers. I didn't find much about that secret wing of his company, but you know what *I* did find? A memo that referred to a secret product they were working on." She raised Chuck's precious bottle of purplish-red liquid. "It was something called Knoo-You-Juice."

"N-now, wait," Chuck stammered. "Y-you have to give that back to me. I n-n-need it for—"

"*For what*, Chuck? Maybe if you tell me, I'll give it back."

Chuck bit his lip. How could he ever hope to explain? It was impossible, especially surrounded by a gang of ghorks!

"Don't worry, Chuck. You don't have to say a word. We'll just wait." Monica rounded her desk and locked the bottle of Dr. Heppleworth's Knoo-Yoo-Juice in one of her drawers. "I'm sure it won't be long before we all see what happens to Mr. Chuck Brickweather when he *doesn't* take his medicine."

EAR PLUNGER

3000

CHAPTER 23

In which Reggie talks some sense

When Colonel-Admiral Reginald T. Pusslegut opened his eyes, all he saw was white. *Where am I?* he wondered. He had no answer to the question, but he was certain of one thing: For the first time in a long time, he felt well rested. *Absurdly* well rested. It felt *extraordinary*!

A bracing breeze whistled over his body. To anyone else, the wind would have been numbing, but it didn't bother Reggie at all. He was a bombastadon. He was built for the cold.

He rolled his head to either side. White. Everything was white. *Could it be?*

He sat up. A blizzard of fluffiness fell from his epaulettes.

"Snow!" he cried aloud. "Extraordinary!"

Groaning to his feet, he saw he was inside an icy cave. He walked to its mouth and peered out.

Instantly, he recognized his home, the barren wilds of Antarctica. He was near the foot of Mount Codrington in Enderby Land (a lovely vacation spot this time of winter).

But how had he arrived here? He vaguely recalled nodding off in a wondrously comfortable chair. Perhaps he was still sleeping. Yet if this was a dream, it felt more real than any of the others.

Just to be certain, he raised his arm and pinched the loose, blubbery skin above his elbow.

"Ouch! Indubitably *not* a dream."

Perhaps if he could locate some of his old comrades, they could explain what he was doing here. He was about to set off across the vast ice field before him when he stopped.

There was a sound from behind him, a faint noise like the chipping of ice. He turned around, but the cave appeared to be empty. Then he spotted something: a block of blue ice in the back corner. It appeared to be trembling.

Reggie braced himself for an earthquake or a glacial collapse, but he realized it wasn't *the ground* that was shaking; it was merely that single block of ice.

"How curious," he muttered.

He wandered into the cave, and after only a few steps, he saw why the ice was palpitating in such an odd fashion. There was something frozen inside it. When Reggie bent down to see what it was, he couldn't believe his eyes.

It was Bildorf and Pib, those two insufferable hobmongrels. Somehow, they had gotten themselves stuck inside a cloudy block of ice.

"What are you two doing in there?"

Frozen in a block of ice the way they were, they couldn't answer Reggie's question. All they could manage was to judder the ice block back and forth.

"I suppose you'd like me to cut you out of there, is that it?"

This question provoked a good deal of juddering.

"Very well, you silly things." Reggie drew his ceremonial saber and, with a growling roar, swiped it clean through the middle of the ice, narrowly missing the two hobmongrels within. They emerged howling and blue with cold, icicles dripping from their whiskers.

"Oh! Thank-you-thank-you-thank-you-thank-you-thank-you-thank-you!" cried Bildorf.

"What he said," added Pib.

Reggie returned their farcical gratitude with a curt bow. "You're very welcome—I suppose. Now please, stop hopping about like that, quivering like a pair of fools. You'll cause an avalanche."

"How can we stop?" cried the pair of practically hypothermic creatures. *"WE'RE FREEZING!"*

"Are you? Feels quite nice to me."

"That's because you're a . . . you're a . . ." Pib pointed a shivering finger at Reggie's face. "A whatever you are!"

"A bombastadon, madam."

"Yeah, one of those."

"*Pah!* I would have hoped you two could at least identify *my species* by now, in light of all your incessant belittling of me, but evidently that was too much to ask."

"Listen," said Bildorf, "you didn't happen to bring any tea and biscuits with you, by any chance?"

"I regret I came bearing no such comestibles. In fact, I was on my way to fetch some tea and biscuits myself when I spotted that wonderful chair."

Pib sighed. "Can't you tell the difference between a chair and a teleportation device?"

"Ah, I see. So that's what it was."

"Only it doesn't work very well," said Bildorf. "Everything you put in it gets sent to Antarctica. See?" He pointed to a pile of sock monkeys in the corner of the cave. "They've been testing it all week."

"Sent to Antarctica, you say?" Reggie tapped one of his tusks thoughtfully. "Is that a problem?"

"Yes!" said the hobmongrels. "*IT'S FREEZING!*"

"Oh, stop whining. Perhaps this will help." Reggie picked Bildorf and Pib up by the scruffs of their necks and stuffed them both down the front of his uniform. "There. Hopefully that will keep you warm—*and quiet.*"

"Actually, yeah," said Pib. She wound herself into the woolly hair on Reggie's chest. "It's quite nice in here."

Bildorf agreed. "Though I could do without the smell of pickled herring."

"Sorry," said Reggie. "I may have spilled some of my dinner."

"So now what?" Bildorf asked. "How are we supposed to get home?"

"Simple," said Reggie. He exited the cave and set off across the ice field. "We'll just have to find ourselves an arachnimammoth."

"*Please,*" said Pib. "Could you talk sense for once?"

"Madam, as a soldier and a gentleman, I make a point of *only* speaking sense. It is my duty."

"Oh, brother."

"Which is precisely why I suggest an arachnimammoth."

"What is that even supposed to be?" asked Bildorf.

"A big, woolly, eight-legged pachyderm, of course."

"A hairy elephant with eight legs?"

"Indeed. *Frightfully fast!* They can cross a whole continent in a matter of hours! Terrific swimmers too, make no mistake! Riding one of those, we'd be back in no time."

The two hobmongrels stuck their heads out through the neck of Reggie's uniform.

"You honestly expect us," said Pib, "to believe such a creature exists?"

"Of course I do!" Reggie continued doggedly lumbering across the ice. "They're quite common in these parts. We ought to stumble upon one at any moment."

Pib scoffed. "Sounds about as ridiculous as 'bringing peace to the vast wastelands of Antarctica.'"

"Which I did," said Reggie. "The proof is all around us. Look how peaceful it is."

"There's *nobody here*," said Bildorf. "You might as well tell people you brought peace to the moon."

"No, that was someone else."

"Once," said Pib. "*Just once*, I would love to hear you admit that it's all hot air, that 99 percent of everything you say is complete—"

She stopped.

She couldn't speak because of something she saw. Something coming across the ice field toward them. Something big and very fast.

It was exactly as Reggie described it: a huge, eight-legged woolly mammoth with a spider's abdomen, clomping elephant's feet, and not one but *two* blubbery trunks!

"Ah, here's one now." Reggie spit on his paws and rubbed them together in anticipation. "You'd better hang on tight. Could be a tad bumpy at first."

The two hobmongrels gripped tight to Reggie's lapels. They watched in terror as the arachnimammoth came storming straight for them, trumpeting through its woolly trunk.

BAROOOOOOO!

Just when it seemed about to trample them to death, Reggie leapt to one side and grasped hold of one of the beast's coiling tusks, swinging up to its back in a single elegant arc.

"*Wooaaaah!* Whoa there, my tremendous friend!" Reggie whispered a series of clicks and clucks into the arachnimammoth's ear and the creature was instantly soothed.

"I don't believe it," said Pib.

"Me neither," said Bildorf. "But it's happening."

"Now then," said Reggie. He deftly steered the great beast in a slow circle. "Which way is north?"

Before Reggie could regain his bearings, a whole stampede of arachnimammoths came thundering across the ice field. On the back of every one were bombastadons, all dressed in the same military regalia as Reggie, complete with medals, polished buttons, and ceremonial sabers.

They were such a fearsome and imposing sight that both hobmongrels dove back into Reggie's uniform to hide.

When the army of bombastadons saw Reggie standing in their path, they all came to a crashing halt, kicking up a squall of snow and ice. When it settled, a young bombastadon cantered forward on his arachnimammoth.

"Colonel-Admiral Pusslegut? Is it really you?"

Reggie snorted. "Who else would you expect to find in a place like this?"

"We all heard you'd been killed in the battle of Elephant Island."

"*Pah!* Takes more than the melting of a few ice caps to do away with old Reggie!"

"Evidently, sir." The young soldier's eyes moved down to Reggie's chest. "Though I must say, it seems perhaps you've . . . changed."

It took Reggie a moment to realize that with the two hob-mongrels stuffed inside his uniform, it looked like he had grown a pair of lumpy breasts.

"Ah, yes—I mean, *no!* I mean . . . these aren't what you think they are. These are merely my, uh . . . er . . ."

Bildorf and Pib popped out of Reggie's collar.

"We're his friends," they said.

"Friends?" asked Reggie.

"Any friends of the colonel-admiral," said the young bombastadon soldier, "are friends of ours. Isn't that right, gentlemen?"

There was a booming roar of appreciation that echoed for miles across the ice. When the cheering finally subsided, the young soldier up front led all the rest in a solemn salute.

"Sir," he said. "It is a great honor and privilege to finally meet you."

Seeing this—a whole army of Antarctic bombastadons, their rigid paws pressed to their foreheads in a profound show of respect—Bildorf and Pib were overcome with emotion. They couldn't help but do something they thought they would never do, not in a million years.

They looked up at Colonel-Admiral Reginald T. Pusslegut and they saluted him too.

FIREWIRE

3000

CHAPTER 24

In which Elliot and Leslie attend the
wrong shareholder's meeting and the Chief muses
on alternate means of production

It was casual Friday at DENKi-3000. The creatures had tinkered with the machines all through the night, but none of them worked properly. The final shareholders' meeting was later that afternoon, and the creatures had nothing to present. Worse, no one had heard anything from Elliot's uncle.

Leslie and Elliot decided they would return to the Abstractory. Perhaps if they selected fresh new essences, the devices would work properly. They met in the forest of Bickleburgh Park and used Reggie's GPS to open the entrance. Just as they turned toward the Creature Department, however, Elliot stopped.

He was gazing into the other tunnel, the one into which the ghorks had fled. Facing it, with daylight streaming in from the entranceway, Elliot saw a glint of light on the floor of the cave.

"What is it?" Leslie asked him.

Elliot didn't answer. He took out his electric pencil, peering into the shadows through its telescopic lens.

"We shouldn't go that way," Leslie warned.

"I know, but . . ." Elliot took a few steps into the tunnel. "It's okay. There're no ghorks. See?" He held up the GPS to show her.

Leslie followed him into the tunnel and saw he was right. There *was* something there: a DENKi-3000 ID badge on the ground. Elliot recognized the photograph instantly.

"Uncle Archie!" Elliot started down into the cave. "What if the ghorks have taken him? We've got to bring him back somehow."

"Shouldn't we get the others?"

"They won't come. They're too scared to come down here."

"What about Reggie?"

"It'll be okay," said Elliot. He held up the GPS. "As long as we have this."

"I don't know. . . ."

"It's my uncle. I *have* to find him, and we've got to bring him back in time for the meeting."

The tunnels under DENKi-3000 were a maze of shadow and stone, illuminated by the fluttering phosphorescence of luster bugs.

They moved deeper, and the little green dots that represented ghorks on the screen became more and more numerous. Soon, they had to duck into alcoves or tiptoe into dead-end caves to avoid roving groups of ghorks. They kept expecting— and hoping—to see Reggie, but there was no sign of him.

A quiver of brightness began to glow around the next bend. The luster-bug light hit the wall in ripples, casting shadows that washed over the stone like gentle ocean waves.

Leslie stopped.

"What's that?" She pointed to a pool of darkness on the

wall: a solid, moving shadow. "There's something else in the tunnel."

Elliot checked the GPS. "Definitely not a ghork," he said.

It certainly wasn't. This thing was much bigger. Its bulky shadow rose up on the wall facing them.

"If it's not a ghork, then it must be Reggie." Elliot was just about to take a step forward when Leslie grabbed his arm.

"No," she whispered. "Look at the shape of it."

Leslie was right. The shadow was all wrong. Reggie stood with an imperiously straight back; this creature, however, had the posture of a gorilla. There was also the matter of its tail. Reggie didn't have one. The beast casting the shadow, on the other hand, had a long, thick tail that swished and slithered like a python.

They hid themselves behind an outcrop of rock and waited for the creature to pass. Only it didn't. It turned down another tunnel and the shadow faded.

"I'm beginning to understand," Elliot whispered, "why nobody wants to come down here."

Again, they moved toward the wavering light, and it wasn't long before they found themselves on a ledge overlooking a truly vast cavern.

It was as big as a football stadium. Hanging from the roof was a great glass dome so full of luster bugs, the huge space was nearly as bright as day.

The floor of the cave was laid out with prim rows of chairs. Seated in every one was a ghork. There were *hundreds* of them. They all sat facing a stage at the far end of the cavern (the scene bore an eerie resemblance to the DENKi-3000 share-holders' meeting).

Elliot shuddered. There was something particularly chilling about creatures as nasty and thuggish as ghorks being organized in such a regimented way.

The five ghorks they had already met lumbered onstage and were greeted with cheers from the crowd. At last, they were followed by none other than . . . *Monica Burkenkrantz!*

They took seats behind the long table onstage, sitting in silence. Everyone seemed to be waiting for something.

Suddenly, an image appeared on a massive screen behind the stage. It was the silhouette of a man's head and shoulders. His face was lost in shadow, and even though it was impossible to tell who he was, every last ghork erupted in wild cheers.

"Quazicom forever!" cried one of the ghorks.

"Hail to the Chief!" cried another.

The Chief.

Whoever he was, he held up a hand to silence the crowd.

"Thank you," he said. "No need for applause." He had a dry, loose, gravelly voice, but his words came with honeyed warmth that made it pleasant and almost seductive. "I'd like to start by welcoming the soon-to-be president of DENKi-3000, Ms. Monica Burkenkrantz, as well as some more familiar faces. The heads of the five tribes: Grinner, Iris, Wingnut, Adenoid Jack, and Digits. And of course, welcome to all of you—the loyal shareholders of Quazicom International."

A thunderous roar rose from the crowd as the ghorks let out a cheer for themselves.

"*Shareholders,*" whispered Leslie.

Elliot could hardly believe it. "The ghorks are behind

Quazicom."

The Chief cleared his throat. "*Ahem!* For some time now, we at Quazicom have been expanding our operations with the acquisition of firms from around the world. We targeted these companies because they all share the same unusual traits. First, they created products unlike anything else out there. And second, the origin of these products was always a closely guarded secret."

On the stage, Monica Burkenkrantz was nodding to herself.

"Of course," the Chief went on, "we know the secret, don't we?"

There were boos, hisses, and jeers from the ghorks.

"Yes," said the Chief. "*Creature Departments.*" He held up what looked like a speckled blue robin's egg. It was a wireless breath mint. "Products as good as this ought to be Quazicom products—and they will be, *very soon.*" He popped the mint into his mouth.

More angry cheering from the ghorks.

"This is why a collaboration between Quazicom and the ghorks is such a fruitful partnership. We at Quazicom will take over DENKi-3000's technology and you ghorks—well, you'll be running all our new Creature Departments."

The crowd clamored with shouts and claps and fists drubbing at the air.

"They'll be working for us!" one of them shouted.

"We'll make 'em our *slaves*!" screamed another.

On the screen, the Chief sighed. "You know, I'm almost jealous. Among us human folk, slave labor went out of fashion many years ago." He sighed wistfully. "Those were the days. . . ."

High in the darkness of the cave, Leslie and Elliot backed away from the ledge.

"Creature slaves," whispered Elliot. "That's what'll happen when Quazicom takes over."

"We've got to stop them!"

"How? Look how many there are."

"First," said Leslie, "we have to go back. We can't let the creatures ignore what's happening right under their—"

Elliot slapped his hand over Leslie's mouth. Something was coming toward them.

Silently, he took out the GPS. There were no green dots nearby. It wasn't a ghork coming up the tunnel toward them; it was the same thing they had seen before, the same hunched creature with the lizard-like tail.

"It's coming this way," Leslie whispered.

Elliot looked down over the ledge where they stood. He saw only a precipitous, overhanging cliff. "Where can we go?"

As he whispered the question, an odd thing happened. The light from the luster-bug domes shifted and twinkled (it was always shifting and twinkling, of course, but something about this time was different). They looked up at the dome of glass protruding from the wall above them. The luster bugs inside were suddenly fluttering in unison.

"What are they doing?" Leslie whispered.

The luster bugs arranged themselves into a tapered tube of light. One end broadened to create a triangular shape.

"It's an arrow!"

The radiant insects flashed like the signs on a highway, the ones that guide the way to safety.

"But it's pointing straight over the ledge." Elliot looked in that direction and only saw open air. "Is that where they want us to go?"

Every luster bug in the dome went dark.

"I guess not," said Leslie.

A low, gurgling growl echoed down the tunnel. The creature was getting closer.

The luster bugs brightened once again, but this time the arrow was curved, looping backward on itself.

"Maybe they want us to go around the side," said Elliot.

The luster bugs twinkled excitedly.

"Yep, I think that's it." Leslie tiptoed out to the overhang, leaning forward to peer around the wall of the cave. "Look! There's another ledge out here."

Another growl echoed down the tunnel. The creature was very close now. Hiding out on the second ledge was their only hope. Out there, however, the ghorks might see them; they would only have to look up. But what choice did they have? There was nowhere else to go.

"Thank you," Elliot whispered to the miraculous luster bugs. They blinked once in the dome and dispersed, going back to their random flutter.

Holding hands, their backs pressed against the wall of the cavern, Leslie and Elliot carefully stepped around the wall to the other ledge. Just as they reached the other side, they heard the slow, lumpish footfalls and ragged breath of whatever had been following them. It came right out on the ledge where they had just been standing.

Leslie had gone first, so she was too far from the other ledge to see anything, but Elliot, who was still close, could make out a small patch of the creature's skin. All he saw were shimmering red scales. *What could it be?* he wondered. A small part of him was curious, but a much larger part simply wanted to get as far away as possible. Elliot nudged Leslie farther along and suddenly, *she vanished.*

It was another tunnel. She had backed into it and pulled Elliot in after her.

"Where are we?" Elliot whispered.

"Check the GPS thing. Can we get back this way?"

According to the Ghork Positioning System, however, the tunnel didn't exist. It simply wasn't on the map. But since there was no going back (not with a big scaly monster waiting for them), they followed it.

The tunnel ended at a heavy iron door. It was rounded at the top and windowless, made from slats of metal studded with countless rivets.

"Now what?" asked Elliot.

"Aren't we going to try the door?" asked Leslie.

"It's gotta be locked." Elliot put one hand on the enormous latch. "Doors like this are never—"

It opened.

Inside was a large room that looked like a shabby imitation of the Creature Department laboratory. Crumbling desks featured dusty computer equipment and smashed chemistry sets. There were tables and shelves strewn with broken components and wrinkly, old books, as if each one had been dropped in the bath and left to dry.

Despite the cluttered, ramshackle state of the room, it was the heavy table in the middle that caught Elliot's attention. Or rather, what was lying on top of it.

"Uncle Archie!"

CHAPTER 25

In which the professor coos like a baby
and Elliot reads the fine print

lliot's uncle lay unconscious on the table. His head was strapped into a makeshift cerebellows. Its poorly made canopy opened and closed in time with the rise and fall of the professor's chest.

"They're stealing his ideas!" Elliot cried. He ran to his uncle. "Uncle Archie! Wake up! We're here to rescue you!"

But the professor only responded with a stream of cooing nonsense.

"Bworble-bworble-quackle-mickle-zumpty-zizz-suuuwahmbah-bah-bah-baaah . . ."

"Elliot, look at this."

There was a computer on a cluttered table against the wall. The rubber tube on top of the cerebellows was connected to it.

"What're these supposed to be?" Leslie pointed at the screen.

At first it was just a stream of words, symbols, and equations, but as Elliot watched, they melted away to reveal what appeared to be a large pair of bright red metallic ski boots. The peculiar footwear bristled with pipes and gauges and coiling wires, and they were decorated with red and orange flames, blazing upward from the soles.

On the one hand, they looked super-cheesy, but at the same time, they were . . . *kind of cool,* like something a robotic biker gang might wear in a science-fiction future.

Once again, the image shimmered and vanished, returning to scrolls of schematics and data.

"I guess this is what my uncle has inside his head."

"But what are they?" Leslie asked.

Again, the words and figures disappeared and the garish ski boots were back.

"What if Reggie was right?" Elliot whispered.

"About what?"

"Super-galoshes."

Leslie screwed up her face. "Is that going to impress the shareholders?"

Elliot was a little disappointed too. "C'mon," he said. "Let's try to wake up my uncle."

They returned to the professor and shook his arms, shouting into both his ears. They jostled him so hard the flap of his white lab coat fell open. Slipping from an inner pocket was a single sheet of paper.

"What's that?"

Elliot stooped to pick it up. Even before he touched it, he could see what it was.

"It's a page from a Captain Adventure comic."

"What does it say?" Leslie leaned across the table.

Elliot unfolded the paper. "Looks like the end of a comic book story." He held it up to show Leslie, who squinted at the page.

"Why would he carry it around? It's just a random page from an old comic."

"*No,*" said Elliot. He was looking at the opposite side of the page. "That's not what it is at all." He stepped past Leslie and stood beside the computer. "These aren't super-galoshes. They're *rocket boots.*"

Elliot raised the comic page, showing Leslie the other side. It was an advertisement with a picture of Captain Adventure soaring through the cosmos. Printed below him was a drawing of boots just like the ones on the computer screen. In bold, daredevil lettering, it said:

This Halloween, get your very own
CAPTAIN ADVENTURE
ROCKET BOOTS!*
(only $19.95 plus shipping & handling)

Elliot knew what the little star beside *Rocket Boots!* meant. He moved his eyes to the fine print at the bottom of the page. Typed in tiny, almost illegible lettering, it said: **Rocket boots are not real.*

"What's going on? Where am I?"

Behind them, Professor von Doppler was sitting up, removing the cerebellows from his head.

"Hello, you two." He blinked at them, obviously dazed. "What's going on? I remember picking up supplies, tinkering with the boots, and then . . . and then . . ." He shook his head. "Nothing."

"*And then,*" said Leslie, "you were kidnapped by ghorks,

who are actually working for Quazicom and helping them to take over DENKi-3000!"

The professor raised his eyebrows.

"We came down to rescue you," Elliot told him.

His uncle gazed at them with a grogginess that showed he wasn't quite fully awake. His eyes tracked from Leslie to the computer monitor to Elliot and the comic book page in his hand. He reached into his lab coat, feeling in the now-empty pocket.

"It fell out when we were trying to wake you up." Elliot folded the page and gave it back to his uncle.

The professor gazed at the advertisement. "I'm beginning to remember," he said. "I came down here because some of these passages lead to Creature Depots."

"Depots?"

"Shops, really, ones that sell the strangest things you can imagine." He swung his legs over the side of the table and rose unsteadily to his feet. "I had gathered everything I thought I might need, but on my way back to the laboratory, I was attacked."

"By ghorks," said Leslie.

"Five of them."

Elliot shuddered. "I think we know the ones."

"They took me down here and forced me to begin work on my secret invention. I did as they said, but only because I thought it would help me escape. But as you can see, I was barely conscious much of the time." He glanced at the table and the ghorks' flimsy imitation of a cerebellows. "They kept me in that thing for hours at a time. Whenever I was awake, I was under close guard. I suppose the only reason you found me is because every one of those beastly things is in that meeting with—"

"*The Chief*," said Leslie.

The professor nodded. "Quazicom and the ghorks, working together. It's abominable!"

"Well, you're free now," said Leslie. "So let's get moving before any of them come back."

"Wait," said Elliot. "You said the ghorks forced you to make your invention." He looked around at the room's ramshackle equipment. "Where is it?"

The professor's jaw tightened and his face took on an expression of steely resolve. Even though he was still dizzy, he stumbled across the room to a wooden cabinet in the corner. When he opened the doors, all three of them looked in on something amazing.

Rocket boots.

They were identical to the ones on the monitor and on the page of the comic book, but they weren't drawings.

"They're real," Elliot whispered.

His uncle reached in and picked up one of the boots. "When I was a kid, I worshipped Captain Adventure. When I saw the ad in the back of his comic, I really believed it. I saved up for months and sent off for what I thought were genuine rocket boots." He chuckled to himself. "Imagine how disappointed I was when they arrived. As soon as I opened the box, I knew they were only toys." He brought the boot up close to his face, his eyes poring over every detail. "It's the reason I became an inventor. I wanted to make them real." He put the boot back beside its mate and hung his head.

"Uncle Archie? What's wrong?"

"They don't work. I've never been able to figure out the essence to power them."

"Yeah, we found out the hard way," said Leslie. "Picking essences—that's the tricky part."

"The ghorks want the boots for themselves," said the professor, "but they need the all-important final ingredients. *The essences.* That was why they kept me in the cerebellows. They thought they could pick the answer straight out of my brain, but I didn't have it. There was no answer to find." He sighed again, sounding even more hopeless than before. "I guess it's true what they say in the fine print. Rocket boots aren't real."

Elliot didn't like seeing his uncle so upset. "We're breaking you out of here and taking the boots up to the Creature Department," he said. "If we all work together, we'll figure it out."

Professor von Doppler was still a bit dizzy. Leslie and Elliot took one boot each and stood on either side, helping him toward the door. When they opened it, however, all three of them screamed.

DAPPER BUG ZAPPER

CHAPTER 26

In which a new creature is discovered

O n the other side of the door was a chubby, bright
red, one-eyed dinosaur. It screamed too.

"*BLEEEEEEEEAAARGH!*"

After that, however, likely seeing it easily weighed more
than all three of them put together, it stopped. "Sorry," it said,
regaining a kind of portly composure. "You startled me."

"*We* . . . startled *you?*" asked Elliot.

The dinosaur nodded.

"What about you startling us?!" asked Leslie.

"I know," said the dinosaur, sighing deeply. "I'm *horrible*
to look at. Anyway, I'm really sorry if I frightened you, but
maybe you can help me. I'm a bit lost."

"Why do I recognize your voice?" Leslie asked.

"That's because we've already met. Well, sort of."

"No offense, but if we *had* met, I think I would remember."

"Earlier this week," said the dinosaur, "at the shareholders'
meeting. You're those two kids who live in the ventilation
shaft."

"We don't *live* there," Leslie corrected him. "We just happened to be there at the time."

"How do you know about that?" asked Elliot.

The professor was equally puzzled. "I was up onstage for that entire meeting, and I can assure you, there were *no* one-eyed dinosaurs present."

"The official term is *cycloptosaurus*."

"I should have known," muttered the professor. "Well, I didn't see any of *them* either."

The dinosaur lowered his voice. "I was *in disguise*," he whispered. "You see, my name's Charlton. Just Charlton, that's all, but when you three met me, I was called—"

"*Chuck Brickweather!*" Leslie snapped her fingers. "*That's* how I know your voice!"

"You're telling us you're the guy from Quazicom?" Elliot leaned a bit closer and whispered, "Don't take this the wrong way, but you don't look anything like him."

"How is this possible?" asked the professor.

Charlton shrugged. "I told you, I was in disguise."

"Some disguise!" said Leslie.

"Actually, it's more of a . . . *treatment* than a disguise. For weeks I've been drinking a concoction that makes creatures look like human beings, at least temporarily. It's called Dr. Heppleworth's Knoo-Yoo-Juice." Charlton looked down at himself, his mouth frowning in disappointment. "I'm sure you can see why I take it."

They couldn't, however.

"Change your appearance?" asked Elliot. "Why would you want to do that?"

"I'm a fat, scaly cycloptosaurus when all I really want to

be is sleek, trim, and handsome. But look at me! I'm the kind of creature that makes people *scream* whenever they see me coming. You three are proof of that."

"Only because we weren't expecting you," said the professor.

"I think you look cool," said Leslie.

"You do?"

"Me too," said Elliot. "Who *wouldn't* want to be an eight-foot thunder lizard with shiny red scales?"

Charlton looked left and right, as if to make sure no one was listening. "Let me tell you a secret," he whispered. "I'm *scared* of creatures. They're all so . . . *weird looking*. They give me the creeps!"

"You do realize," said the professor, "you are one yourself. I'm sure among other, uh . . . *cycloptosauri*, you're everything you dream of. Sleek, handsome . . ."

"Trim?"

"Well, maybe not trim, no, but what self-respecting dinosaur—sorry, *cycloptosaurus*—wants to be 'trim'?"

"*Me!*" Charlton pointed to his snout. "I never asked to be part of *creaturedom*. All I ever wanted to be was sleek and handsome. And maybe get a job in finance. I wanted it so badly I was willing to gulp down nothing but Dr. Heppleworth's for months! That was why I took this position with Quazicom. I had a hunch they were buying up creature departments. So I knew the job would eventually lead me to one that specialized in new inventions—and that would lead me to you."

"Me?" asked the professor. "But why?"

"You and your department are the only ones who can make *my invention*."

"You're an inventor?"

Charlton shrugged. "Not really." He had a leather satchel slung across his body, from one shoulder down to the opposite hip. He flipped it open and took out a large scroll, tied with red ribbon. Unraveling the paper, he revealed the thin parchment of a technical blueprint, which he pressed flat on the tabletop.

On the left-hand side of the page, scrawled in childish crayon, was a stick-figure drawing of a creature, complete with horns, fangs and tentacles. An arrow pointed from the creature's body toward a large black square dominating the center of the page. Emerging from the opposite edge of the square was a second arrow, this one pointing to a human stick figure.

"Pretty brilliant, huh?"

Professor von Doppler tilted his head, squinting at the page.

"It's not a very detailed schematic."

"That's where you come in," said Charlton. He nodded confidently. "I'm more of an idea man."

"You mean idea *cycloptosaurus*," said Elliot.

"Sorry, I'm still adjusting. . . ."

The professor sighed, spreading his arms over the poorly drawn blueprint. "So *what is* this thing?"

"It means no one will ever again have to drink Dr. Heppleworth's Knoo-Yoo-Juice!" Charlton grinned, teeth sparkling all around his formidable snout. "I call it *the Humanizer!* It turns creatures into human beings. *Permanently.*"

They all stared at drawing, which suddenly took on a rather more sinister appearance.

Professor von Doppler frowned. "It's a terrible idea! What on earth made you think the creatures in my department would want to build something so . . . so . . . *appalling?*"

Charlton paused. A look of confusion passed over his big, one-eyed face. "Doesn't everyone want to be trim and sleek and . . ." Charlton trailed off, not knowing what to say next.

"Seriously," said Leslie, stepping forward. She put one hand on the side of Charlton's distended potbelly. "I agree with Elliot. You look *way* cooler as a cycloptosaurus."

"I do?"

Leslie nodded.

"Maybe," said Charlton, unconvinced. "Anyway, it doesn't matter anymore. All my Knoo-Yoo-Juice is gone." He explained how Monica Burkenkrantz had discovered the truth about him and how the Five Ghorks had smashed all his bottles of the precious liquid that had kept him in the form of Chuck Brickweather for so long.

"This is all I have left now." He took out a single bottle of Dr. Heppleworth's Knoo-Yoo-Juice. It was barely filled halfway. "Monica and the ghorks were so surprised when I turned back into my old self, I had just enough time to escape. The only place I could think of to run was down here to these tunnels, but now I'm completely lost."

The professor reached up and patted Charlton's arm reassuringly. "I know you don't feel like you're worth much in your natural form, but I have a feeling you'd be a good hand at rickum ruckery."

"Rickum *what*-ery?"

Professor von Doppler smiled. "Come work for me and I'll show you."

"You mean in the Creature Department?"

The professor nodded. "But you'll have to stop drinking that stuff." He put out his hand, as if to take the bottle from Charlton.

The cycloptosaurus, however, wasn't ready to give it up. "Thanks for the offer," he said, "but I'll need some time to think about it." He slipped his one last bottle of the potion back into his bag.

"Fair enough," said the professor. "But at least come up to the department and have a look around. Once you get to know a few creatures, I'm sure you'll find there's a lot to like."

Charlton agreed. He would join the Creature Department (at least for the afternoon).

"Great!" said Leslie, clapping her hands. "Now that we're all friends, can we please leave the secret underground dungeon?"

"She's right," said Elliot. "There's only one hour before we have to present at the shareholders' meeting. But don't worry." He held up the one rocket boot he was carrying. "When we get these working, we'll knock their socks off!"

"*If* we get them working," said the professor.

CHAPTER 27

In which the professor gets a hug and Elliot and Leslie
make an unconventional choice

hen they returned, the four of them were greeted
with resounding cheers from everyone in the
Creature Department. They were overjoyed to
see the professor again. The celebration was short-lived, however, because the intangible essence to power the rocket boots
was missing. There was only one way to find it.

In the Abstractory, the Preston Brothers set the rocket boots
on the countertop (right beside the little bell, just as Reggie had
done before with his smelly old galoshes).

"Y'all designed these puppies yourself, didn't you, Professor?"
asked Patti Mudmeyer. She didn't quite approve of the boots'
inelegant pipes and gauges, to say nothing of the flaming red-
and-orange paint job. "Looks like something Gügor would
crumple together."

"What do you mean by that?" asked Gügor.

"I think she means it looks like a rickum-ruckem job," said
Harrumphrey.

"Please, my friends!" Jean-Remy descended from the air,
alighting on the rim of the left rocket boot. "Ze meeting with

ze shareholders, it begins very soon. And yet, we have nothing to show them!"

"The essences!" Elliot called out to everyone. "We have to find the intangible essence of *rocket boots*!"

Every creature dashed through the forest of bookcase-trees, snatching up any essence they thought might get the boots working.

Logically, many thought the essence of rocket boot technology would have something to do with flight, or with simply going *up*. They tried elation (a jar of feathers, hovering magically inside), buoyancy (an ethereal fog that gathered near the mouth of its tinted flask), high spirits (a thick jug of something that smelled very much like rum), and triumph (a hot, bubbling, orange liquid, fizzing with a noise that sounded like applause). They combined these with many of the creaturely intangibles from the back of the Abstractory, but nothing they tried had any effect on the rocket boots.

Next, they wondered if the crucial essence would have something to do with fire. They tried the essences of combustion (a beaker full of flames), electricity (a glass cylinder leaping with blue sparks), and radiance (a jar that glimmered with galaxies of tiny stars). These, too, failed to get even a splutter from the rocket boot engines.

Finally, they thought they had solved it. The rocket boots were the professor's childhood dream, something he had read about in a Captain Adventure comic book. Perhaps the character's *heroism* was the key. They tried the essences of valor (a jar packed with rods of dense metal), pluck (a sticky, molasses-like syrup), kindness (a jar of warm, colorful yarn), and daring (a fizzy, carbonated soda). Sadly, none of these worked either.

Every creature—from the Preston Brothers all the way down to the smallest pixie—was dismally disappointed. The professor slumped at the end of the counter, gazing gloomily at the beloved invention he had always dreamed of. His rocket boots just sat there, cold and inert.

"They're as useless as the toys that came in the mail all those years ago."

Gügor lumbered over to the professor. He put one arm around the man's shoulders. "Gügor thinks you should be proud," said the knucklecrumpler. "Even if they can't fly, Gügor thinks they look very pretty."

"You *would*," said Patti.

The professor groaned and gritted his teeth. "Gügor! Not so tight!"

Gügor released the man from his well-intentioned embrace. "Sorry, Professor. You have to forgive Gügor. He is a knucklecrumpler, after all."

"I understand, and you're right. I *should* be proud. Thanks to Leslie and Elliot, we can present all kinds of interesting things to the shareholders."

"Can we?" asked Harrumphrey.

"I know they don't work properly," the professor explained, "but an *almost-*invisibility machine, a willfully unpredictable teleportation device, and a tele-pathetic helmet are still incredible achievements. I'm sure if we present them all together, we can—"

"*That's it!*" Elliot cried. "That's the answer!"

"What is?" asked the professor.

Everyone turned to Elliot, but their faces were blank. Even Elliot's uncle was confused.

The only one who understood was Leslie. "Just like the professor said: *Put them all together.*"

"We're on the right track," said Elliot. "The essences of flight, flames, and heroism seem like just the things to power a pair of rocket boots, but maybe what we need is more power."

"He's right," said Leslie. "Maybe rocket boots are so incredible, only the most creaturely essences will do."

Elliot turned to the Preston Brothers. "Has anyone ever tried using *three creaturely essences*, all in one invention?"

The brothers looked at one another.

"Risky," warned Lester.

"Never been done," said Chester.

Nestor merely narrowed his eyes.

"The meeting starts in ten minutes," said Elliot. "This is our last chance."

So Leslie and Elliot went for one last race through the forest of bookcases, searching for the three most creaturely essences they could find, one to represent each aspect of the professor's invention.

First was flight. It took several circuits through the narrowest aisles, but they knew they had found it as soon as they saw it: a plump bottle that wobbled strangely on its shelf.

Inside was a kind of slow-motion storm. Fluffy clouds lazily buffeted one another. When their edges met, instead of thunder and lightning, the clouds glowed softly from within. Red and green and yellow. Elliot and Leslie stood for a moment, staring at the bottle and wondering what caused it to wobble.

"There's why," said Leslie. "It's not *on* the shelf at all!"

She was right: The bottle was *hovering* above it. The only thing that kept the round glass container from floating away was a thin length of twine. It was wound around the jar and tied to an eyelet screwed into the wood of the shelf. The label said: **The Joy of Discovering Creatures Are Real.**

"It's perfect," said Elliot.

For a creaturely essence relating to fire, they chose one they had seen before but hadn't fully understood at the time: **The Enchantment of a Luster Bug's Light.** Inside the jar, ghostly blobs and colorful splashes of light whirled and fluttered like the creatures themselves.

The final selection was the most difficult of all. How was *heroism* represented in the world of creatures? They wandered back and forth for several minutes as their time ticked away. At last, Elliot and Leslie noticed something slightly different about the very tallest of the bookcase-trees.

"Does that one seem brighter to you?" Elliot asked.

"It is. But why?"

They circled the tree several times before they traced the source of the brightness.

"There are *cupboards* in this one," Leslie observed. She cleared one of the lower shelves to reveal hidden compartments. When they opened them, a glow of light seeped out. "It's all coming from in here."

When they opened the third in a series of inner compartments, they found it: a darkly tinted bottled that nevertheless
glowed with the light of *a tiny sun*. It burned with such bril-
liance they had to cover the bottle with all four of their hands
just to read the label. It said: **The Desire for Creatures to
Live in Harmony with Human Beings.**

"This is the one," Elliot whispered.
Leslie knew he was right.

When they brought
these three to the
counter at the front
of the Abstractory, the
Preston Brothers remained
skeptical.

"These are three of the rarest
essences of all," said Lester, reading the
labels. He looked tensely at the other brothers. "Combining them could be dangerous."

"Anything could happen," said Chester.

At last, just as before, Nestor waited until the very last
moment to speak. "I think you've done it again," he said.
"You've chosen wisely."

"And we have no other choice but to proceed," said Jean-
Remy. "Ze meeting, it begins any minute now!"

So Elliot and Leslie, having selected the essences, once
again did the honors. They poured a few drops (or vapors, or
glimmers) of each substance into the rocket boot engines, and
this time, when the professor switched them on, the gauges
glowed and the lights flickered.

"They're working!"

Patti Mudmeyer clapped. "Love me tender and color me Elvis! We did it!" She beamed at the professor. "So what're you waitin' for, Doc? I'd say it's about time you took your invention for a test run."

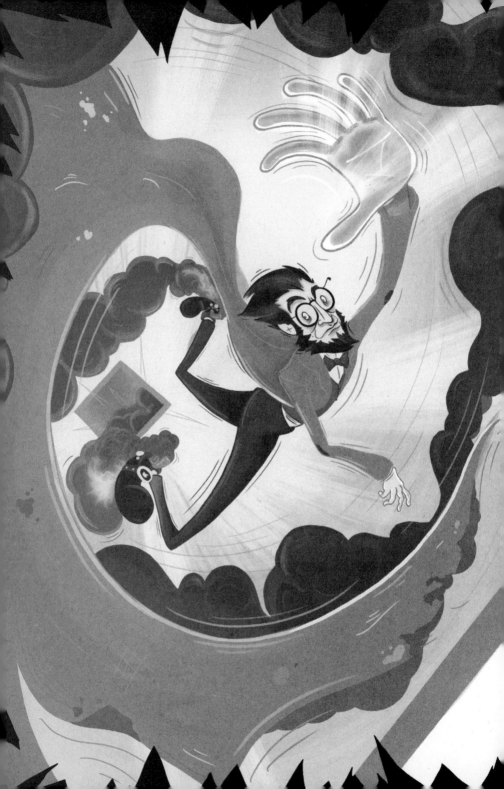

CHAPTER 28

In which Monica does a jig, Carl wears a rubber ninja suit, and Sir William finally remembers that thing he forgot

ir William Sniffledon took his seat before the DENKi-3000 shareholders. It was casual Friday, so three or four of them weren't wearing ties. The rest, however, remained in staid blue and gray suits.

Sir William, on the other hand, embraced casual Friday wholeheartedly. He wore faded jeans and a wool sweater embroidered with the head of a moose.

The eyes of the shareholders darted nervously toward the end of the stage, where the chair usually occupied by Professor von Doppler was empty.

Sir William knew exactly what they were thinking. Wasn't the very point of this meeting to have the professor demonstrate his fabulous new invention? Wasn't that invention supposed to save the company from ruin and defend it from Quazicom's hostile takeover?

Where could he be?

"Welcome, ladies and gentlemen of the executive shareholders' committee," said Monica Burkenkrantz, rising from her seat beside Sir William. "I'd like to thank you all for coming today. Some of you may note that our guest of honor appears to be missing." She looked down the table to the empty seat on the end. "Don't worry, I have a perfectly reasonable explanation for the professor's absence. In fact, I have here an e-mail he sent me only this morning."

Sir William furrowed his brow. Why hadn't *he* received an e-mail?

Monica took out her phone, reading from the screen. "'Dear Monica, please tell Sir William I'm very sorry.'" She glanced down at him, puffing her lips in a pout. "'But unfortunately I wasn't able to complete work on that new invention I promised. I suppose you'll just have to sell everything to Quazicom. Your friend, Archie.'"

A wet blanket of silence fell over the room.

The shareholder spokesman rose from the front row. "Well, that seals it," he said. "Without anything new from the R&D Department, we the shareholders have no choice but to recommend proceeding with the sale of DENKi-3000 to Qua—"

"No! Wait!"

Suddenly (just like in the *last* shareholders' meeting, thought Sir William), the grating over the ventilation shaft cracked off the wall. Those same two children came tumbling out, the girl who looked like a gothic ballerina and the boy in that rather dapper fishing vest. What were their names again? Oh, yes— Elliot and Leslie. Wasn't the boy related to the professor in some way?

"How did you get in here?" snapped Monica Burkenkrantz. "The security bots were supposed to turn you away!"

"*You're* the one who should be turned away," said Elliot. "Why don't you tell Sir William what you're really up to."

Monica narrowed her eyes at the children. "I'm not up to anything."

"Oh, yeah?" said Leslie. "You've been working for Quazicom this whole time!"

"Because you want *his job*!" said Elliot.

Sir William was astonished to see the boy pointing at him. Could it be? His own vice president working for a rival, trying to usurp his position at the head of the company? Surely, *this* was the important thing he was meant to remember.

Or was it?

He turned to Monica. "Is this true?"

She laughed loudly. "Don't be ridiculous! How can you believe a couple of trespassing kids who live in the ventilation system?"

"I must admit, their entrances tend to be a bit unorthodox, but if they're willing to crawl around in there—*twice*—just to come talk to me, perhaps I ought to listen."

"Don't tell me you believe a couple of—"

"Now then," said Sir William, "what is it you want to tell us?"

"Basically," said Elliot, "that your VP's a liar."

"It's a serious accusation, young man. What proof do you have?"

"That e-mail she read was a fake," said Leslie.

"My uncle would never want you to sell the company to Quazicom."

"If that's true," said Monica slyly, "why didn't he come here and tell us himself?"

"He did," said Leslie.

Elliot nodded. "He's right behind us."

The two children stepped aside. Everyone peered into the darkness of the ventilation shaft. Slowly, the darkness brightened and—

SWOOOSH!

There was an explosion of light and the professor came flying out of the wall.

Literally.

Flying.

On his feet were a pair of garish red-and-yellow boots. They spit blue-and-green flames from their soles, propelling him through the air like a—well, like a superhero from an old comic book (his lab coat even flopped out behind him, a bit like a cape).

Finally, he hovered down, standing on the stage in front of the executives' table.

"Ladies and gentlemen," he announced. "I give you my secret invention: honest-to-goodness rocket boots!"

Sir William was stunned. He was speechless. So were the shareholders.

"Wait a minute! Hold everything!" Monica Burkenkrantz pointed to the boots. "Those aren't supposed to work!"

"How, pray tell," said Sir William, "would you know that?"

"Because she stole them," said Elliot.

"But we got them back," said Leslie.

"Is *this* true?" asked Sir William.

"N-no, of course not," Monica spluttered. "I would never . . . why would I . . ." Her stammers trailed off and finally she said, "They *can't* work. Rocket boots are impossible!"

Professor von Doppler smiled at her. "Don't look at me," he said. "It's all thanks to those two trespassing kids from the ventilation shaft."

Monica stomped her foot on the stage. "But how can a couple of kids get them to work? We tried *everything* when we had you locked up down in the caves, hooked up to the . . . to the . . . uh . . ." She realized she had said too much.

Sir William was beginning to believe the two children. "When you had the professor hooked up to what?"

"The cerebellows," answered the boy in the fishing vest. "They were trying to steal his ideas."

"Who's this '*they*' you're talking about?" asked Sir William.

"Her and the boss of Quazicom," said Leslie.

"*You mean me?*" said a loose, gravelly voice from behind the stage. It had come from the screen, which suddenly flickered to life.

"That's him," said Elliot, pointing to the huge, shadowy face. "It's the Chief!"

"I hope you realize," said Sir William, "that is a private screen. Only DENKi-3000 employees can use that!"

"Correct," said the Chief. "And as of today, I'm not only an employee, I'm the boss. Or rather, *the Chief.*"

Sir William felt his wrinkly old skin getting hot. "What do you mean, *the boss*? This is still my company, you thief!"

"He's right," said the shareholder spokesman, raising his voice to address the shadowy face looming over the room. "You can't take any action until the shareholders have voted!"

"I wish it didn't have to be this way, I really do," said the Chief (unconvincingly). "But, you see, I've grown impatient. I'm afraid I've decided to go ahead with a *hostile* takeover. And when I say hostile, *I mean it.*"

He did.

Right on cue, a whole army of Quazicom security robots came whirring out from behind the stage. They surrounded the executives, the shareholders, even Leslie and Elliot.

"We are awfully sorry for any inconvenience that may arise as a result of your unemployment," a robot announced to the room, "but effective immediately, all current DENKi-3000 employees are fired."

"*Ha ha!*" laughed Monica Burkenkrantz, dancing a little jig on the stage. "That means you, Sniffledon! And guess who's *finally* up for promotion! *Me, me, me!*"

"Actually," said the Chief. "I've decided to fire you too."

"*WHAT?!*" Monica froze mid-jig, one leg sticking out and her hands waving fruitlessly in the air.

Sir William snickered. *She looks ri*jig*ulous!* he thought.

"We would like to ask all the DENKi-3000 employees," said one of the robots, "to kindly accompany us in vacating the premises."

"I'm not going anywhere," said Sir William.

"We haven't even voted yet," moaned one of the shareholders. "What's the point of being a shareholder if you don't get to vote on anything?"

"Please," said a robot, "we would appreciate it if you didn't make a fuss. We have been programmed to zap anyone who doesn't comply and we would hate to have to—"

ZZZAP!

"*Ow!*" cried a shareholder at the back. It was the same old woman who had showed off her original DENKi-3000 electric pencil in the previous meeting. She leapt to her feet and kicked one of the robots in the face (although it didn't really have one). "What'd you do that for?!"

"Awfully sorry," said the offending robot. "Just a quick test of my zapper."

Sir William was outraged. First, hijacking a private screen and now zapping an unsuspecting shareholder (not to mention firing the whole company). He shook his fist at the Chief's shadowy face. "You'll never get away with this, you villain!"

When Sir William said this, Professor von Doppler switched on his rocket boots. "This is it!" he cried. "It's really happening!" He pointed excitedly to the screen. "A menacing arch-villain!" He pointed to the robots. "His insidious henchmen!" He pointed to the shareholder who had just been zapped. "A damsel in distress!" He pointed to Sir William. "There's even a kindly old man shaking his fist and saying, 'You'll never get away with this!' *It's all absolutely perfect!*"

Monica Burkenkrantz folded her arms. "We have very different measures of perfection," she grumbled.

"I mean it's *just like a comic book*, and since I'm wearing rocket boots and a cape—well, sort of a cape since it's really just my lab coat—then that makes me *the hero!*" He stood up a little taller. "*Ahem!* Good citizens of DENKi-3000, *fear not!* It is clear that it has come down to me, *the Amazing Captain von Venture*, to save the—"

ZZZZZAP!

Several robots shot him with their fizzling blue rays, and he fell flat on his back.

"*Uncle Archie!*" Elliot ran and knelt beside him, cradling the professor's head. Luckily, his uncle was only stunned unconscious, but Elliot was still so angry he was ready to fight every last Quazicom robot single-handed.

However, he didn't have to because the back door of the

conference room flew open and Carl, the friendly security guard, dashed in (looking rather odd). The man was wearing some sort of scuba-diving wet suit. Except this one wasn't made of neoprene; it was made from bicycle inner tubes. Carl had mummified himself in them!

Several robots penned him in. "We are awfully sorry, but we will have to ask you to halt."

"Sorry," said Carl. "No can do." He stepped over the robots even as they *zap-zap-zapp*ed him. But the zapping had no effect. He was protected by his homemade rubber ninja suit.

"I don't wanna alarm anyone," he said, "but I just came to say that the company is under attack."

"Uh, yeah," said Leslie. She rolled her eyes from the giant shadowy head to the multitude of robots to the unconscious Professor von Doppler. "We kinda noticed."

"Be reasonable," said the Chief. "It's not an 'attack.' It's simply Quazicom's aggressive approach to business."

"Not an attack?" asked Carl. "Then what do you call that?" He pointed out the window.

In the courtyard below, the old mansion was beset on all sides—on *five* sides, in fact—one for each tribe of Ghorkolians. They were swarming up to it, armed with nets and nasty-looking weapons.

"What *are* those things?!" cried one of the shareholders.

"Ghorks," said Elliot.

"Whatever they are," said Carl, "they're attacking the R&D Department. And if we're going to keep this company, then we're going to have to *fight* for it!"

A couple of robots tried zapping him again, but they trundled off sadly when the electricity had no effect.

"One question," said the shareholder spokesman. "What's a ghork?"

"Isn't it obvious?" asked Leslie.

"It's a creature," said Elliot. "A bad one."

"That's it!" cried Sir William. "*That's* the thing I forgot! This whole company was started by *the Creature Department!*"

"They might have started it," said the Chief, "but now it's about to end—*with me.*" With this dire warning, his mysterious silhouette vanished from the screen.

"We'd better get down to the Creature Department," said Sir William. He looked out at the mansion under siege below. "Those are our employees down there, and we have to protect them."

Carl, along with the other rubber-suited security guards, was able to protect the shareholders from the Quazicom robots. Everyone was ferried down to the Creature Department via the expectavator.

Some of the shareholders fainted when they came face-to-face with Gabe, but they soon calmed down when they saw how harmless (and depressed) he was. Eventually, everyone had congregated in the broad corridor outside the laboratory.

The shareholder spokesman looked around at the patterned wallpaper, the ornately carved woodwork, and the filigreed light fixtures. "Looks like some kind of haunted old mansion!"

"Don't worry," Elliot told him. "This building is definitely *not* haunted."

Unfortunately, that was when Jean-Remy, Patti Mudmeyer, Gügor, Charlton the cycloptosaurus, and Harrumphrey Grouseman came out from the laboratory.

"AAAIIEEEGH!"

Every one of the shareholders screamed, en masse. The scream was so loud, it awoke the professor.

"Did I save the day?" he asked.

"Not quite," Leslie informed him, "but it was a nice try."

"I—I—I thought you said this p-place *w-w-wasn't* haunted," said the shareholder spokesman.

Sir William rapped the man's knee with his cane. "Buck up, you coward! Those aren't ghosts; *they're creatures.*"

The professor rose groggily to his feet. "How are the defenses holding up?"

"Ze ghorks have not yet found a way in," Jean-Remy told him, "but we fear it is only ze matter of—"

CRASH!

Behind the shareholders, Gabe quietly exited the expectavator. Inside, ghorks had broken through the ceiling and a number of mottled green arms flailed down from above. Gabe reached in and shut the doors.

"I doubt that will hold them for very long," he droned.

Indeed, the doors began to rattle and large, fist-shaped impressions appeared from the other side of the metal.

"Everyone into the laboratory!" called the professor, clunking off in his rocket boots.

It was a historic moment: the first time so many non-creatures had ever set foot in the Creature Department. Sadly,

there was no time to commemorate the occasion.

"We need a plan," the professor announced.

"Maybe I could talk to them," suggested Monica Burken-krantz. "I think they respect me."

"Is that why the Chief fired you?" asked Elliot.

"Good point." She looked to the professor. "So what's the plan?"

Elliot's uncle believed the best means of fighting back was to use whatever inventions they had on hand. Unfortunately, most of them were broken, unfinished, or entirely ineffective as defensive weaponry.

"I have two other pairs of rocket boots," the professor announced, "but they're only testing models that—well, never got off the ground."

He had them in a dusty box from his office, and when he took them out, there were sighs of disappointment.

"Why are they so small?" asked Harrumphrey.

"I told you, they're testing models."

"Definitely won't fit me," said Gügor.

"I know," said the professor, "but they *will* fit a couple of kids."

"*Us?*" asked Elliot.

"Of course! What good is a rocket-propelled superhero like me without a couple of trusty sidekicks?"

The boots fit perfectly, and as soon as they were fueled with essences, they rumbled to life.

PHWWOOSH!

Elliot and Leslie took to the air. The rocket boots made flying seem easy, as if it were the most natural, most beautiful thing in the world—and perhaps it was.

Next, they sent shareholders and creatures, one by one, through the sort-of-invisibility machine (as it was now being called). It was thought that if everyone was a little bit blurry, they might evade capture.

"You really need to work on the name," said the shareholder spokesman after being turned into a hazy blob. "What about the translucinator or the haze-a-tron? Something catchy like that. We'll never sell anything called a sort-of-invisibility machine."

"I don't wanna get touchy," said Patti, "but this *really* ain't the time for nomenclature."

It certainly wasn't! At that moment, the laboratory doors splintered to pieces and a great terrifying pother of ghorks came roaring and snarling into the Creature Department.

CHAPTER 29

In which the professor recommends adult supervision
and Leslie and Elliot boost the signal

t would go down in the history of creaturedom as the
Battle of Bickleburgh. Sadly, the ghorks were the overwhelming favorites to win. Certainly, they were clumsy,
boorish creatures, incapable of helping one another (even in
a united cause), but none of that mattered. They made up for
their gracelessness with sheer numbers.

It also should be stressed that corporate executives and
company shareholders aren't known to be very good in a fight.
Almost instantly, nearly every one of them was caught in a
Ghorkolian net and hoisted up like a fisherman's catch.

Harrumphrey, on the other hand, surprised everyone with
his fighting prowess. With his tail, his horns, and his low center of gravity, he was not only agile but quite adept at tripping
the ghorks, causing comical domino effects that felled many of
the creatures at once.

Patti Mudmeyer, meanwhile, was an expert marksman
with her scalp clay.

"Me and my sisters used to ping river nymphs back in the
day," she told the others, slinging a headful of resin into the

eyes of an eye ghork and right up the nose of another (a nasal ghork, of course).

By far, the finest fighter among them was Gügor. He gave every ghork he met a thorough crash course in rickum ruckery (with emphasis on the word *crash*). With the horrid creatures clinging to his arms, his legs, and even to his face, he stumbled backward and *crashed* straight through the wall.

Daylight streamed in through the huge Gügor-shaped hole, revealing yet another battle in the courtyard beyond, this one between the robotic security of Quazicom and the human security of DENKi-3000 (in rubber ninja suits).

Meanwhile, back in the laboratory, the creatures who had been blurrified by the sort-of-invisibility machine were able to sneak up on *some* of the ghorks. Unfortunately, their haziness was useless against the eye ghorks, whose sensitive peepers could see them coming in spite of their vagueness. Soon, they too were rounded up into an indistinct mass of fuzziness, wriggling and jostling in the Ghorkolian nets.

Elliot, whizzing above the bedlam in his rocket boots, saw that at the end of the room, the Five Ghorks—Grinner, Adenoid Jack, Iris, Digits, and Wingnut—were directing the action like petulant generals.

They had their former employer, Monica Burkenkrantz, tangled tightly in a net at their smelly feet. It was clear she had been very wrong: The ghorks *didn't* respect her. Now and again, one of them would poke her with a toe, making her yelp indignantly (much to their delight). Elliot was surprised to find himself feeling sorry for her.

We have to stop this, he thought. *We can't let them win.*

But the creatures of the Creature Department were losing the battle. Nearly all the smaller creatures had been captured, and without their help the larger ones were running out of steam. Only Jean-Remy and the others who could take to the air remained capable of defending the laboratory.

"Look!" cried Leslie, pointing to the top of the teleportation device and the second-most-comfortable chair in the universe. Sir William and Harrumphrey were standing on its plush leather arms, batting away ghorks as best they could.

"Maybe," said Leslie, "we can teleport everyone out of here."

"How?" asked Elliot. "You gotta relax for it to work, remember? How're you gonna do that when you're surrounded by ghorks?"

"There's also the fact that we have no idea where it'll send us."

"Plus," Elliot added, "if we leave the Creature Department now, we'll never get it back!"

"Take *that*, you monster!" Sir William bravely brandished his cane and rapped a large ear ghork square on its forehead. The creature tumbled off the machine, thumped on its butt, and cried like a baby.

"*I've got it!*" said Elliot. He swooped down and collected the tele-pathetic helmet, rising again to the scaffolding above the laboratory floor.

Leslie rocketed up to join him. "Of course! They're a bunch of *crybabies*! Remember in the tunnels? How they ran off wailing and moaning? I'll bet they'd be super-sensitive to the tele-pathetic helmet."

"That's what I'm hoping." Elliot donned the helmet and beamed pure sadness at them—*and it worked*! (Well, at least a little.) The hoard paused, in a slightly melancholic way, but then went right on fighting.

Elliot tried again. Same result.

"There are too many of them," said Leslie. "We need to boost the signal."

"But how?" Elliot asked.

Leslie snapped her fingers. "The roof of the North Tower! There's that big antenna."

"Good idea, but we'd better get up there fast—we've got company."

A group of ghorks was coming along the scaffolds, while on the other side was a group of Quazicom security robots.

"Wait for us!" said the professor. He soared up to join them, followed by Jean-Remy. "If you intend to hook up a tele-pathetic helmet to a giant transmitter on the roof of a tall building, it's always advisable to have adult supervision." He thunked down on the scaffolds, hands on his hips. "But fear not! The Amazing Captain von Venture is sure to put the *super* in *supervis*—"

ZZZZAP!

Professor von Doppler collapsed unconscious (again).

"Uncle Archie!"

Jean-Remy sighed. "He is a brilliant inventor, but he is not very good at saving ze day."

"Awfully sorry," said the robot responsible for this latest zapping, "but I'm afraid we'll have to ask you to climb into the nets of our associates."

"*No way!*" said Leslie, blasting off. She spun around to where Elliot knelt with his uncle. "We have to go! We have to get to the roof!"

Jean-Remy flapped out over the railing, "Leslie is right! We must—"

A huge butterfly net swooped up and caught Jean-Remy like an insect.

"*Go on!*" he urged them, even as the ghorks were tugging him out of the air. "Plug ze transmitter into ze back of ze helmet. Good luck!"

Elliot knew he had no choice but to leave his uncle, at least for now. He dove off the platform amid swipes from Ghorkolian fists and wild arcs of blue electricity. Joining Leslie in the air, he soared with her across the laboratory and saw that nearly everyone—Patti, the Preston Brothers, Harrumphrey, and even Gügor and Sir William himself—had been captured.

The two of them swooped out through the hole Gügor had made in the wall. Outside, Carl and the other security guards were losing the upper hand, their protective rubber suits coming to pieces. Without their help, Charlton the cycloptosaurus could hardly fight on all by himself. Already, his bulky red form was ensnared in countless layers of netting.

Leslie and Elliot were the only ones left.

Rising higher, they saw the citizens of Bickleburgh gathering outside the company gates, staring in horror and fascination at the commotion within. When they saw Elliot and Leslie, the people cheered. Every finger pointed up in amazement at the two children, ascending skyward on nothing but *honest-to-goodness rocket boots.*

Setting down on the roof of the building, they saw the antenna was much larger up close than it appeared from the ground. At the bottom they found an enormous control box full of fuses and wires. It took a long time to find something that fit the plug in the back of the helmet.

Elliot leaned over the edge of the building. He could see all of Bickleburgh.

"What if we make the whole city sad?"

"Concentrate straight down," Leslie suggested. "Just on the ghorks."

"I'll try." But Elliot was worried. The antenna was *huge.*

Elliot stared down at the courtyard, where the ghorks were rounding up their prisoners. He focused all his attention on them.

He felt a strange wave of energy, like an intense case of pins and needles. The feeling began at the back of his neck and swept down to his feet and up again. It washed out through an invisible hole in his forehead, and he could almost see a funnel of sadness spreading out to the courtyard below.

All of a sudden, the chaos on the ground eased. The ghorks stopped taunting their prisoners and bickering among themselves. Even the crowd out by the gates stopped shouting. Then, all at once, everyone down there began to cry.

The ghorks gave up tightening their nets, and several prisoners were able to slip free.

Leslie jumped up and down. "It's working!"

It *was* working! Unable to figure out what was making them so sad, some of the ghorks were even running away.

SPLOOSH!

Something wet, warm, and slimy hit Elliot on the back of his head. A sizzle of orange sparks erupted from the helmet. Elliot just managed to pull it off and throw it to the ground before it short-circuited and burst into flames.

He felt a dollop of the slime drip down the back of his neck, and when he wiped it away, he knew what it was. A massive glob of snot.

QUACK HAMMER

5000

CHAPTER 30

In which the Five Ghorks compare recipes
and Elliot revises his to-do list

W e've got a nose to pick with you," said a nasally voice from behind them.

Leslie and Elliot looked up from the ruins of the tele-pathetic helmet and saw they were surrounded by the Five Ghorks.

SPLOOSH-SPLISH-SPLOSH-SPLASH!

Adenoid Jack, the ghork with the enormous nose, shot four more snot globs aimed perfectly at Leslie and Elliot's feet. When they tried to take off, nothing happened. Like the helmet, the rocket boots were ruined.

"He means a *bone* to pick, by the way," said Iris, rolling her enormous eyes. "He always gets that mixed up."

"Are you sure?" Adenoid Jack wiggled a finger inside one cavernous nostril. "Doesn't *a nose* to pick make more sense?"

"Speak for yourself," said Wingnut. "If it were up to me, I'd say, 'I've got an *ear* to pick with you.'"

"You would," said Iris.

"At least you can." Digits put down his net and held up his enormous hands. "If I wanna pick my nose *or* my ear, I gotta use little spoons. My fingers don't fit."

Meanwhile, Adenoid Jack was still thinking. "So which is it? Nose or bone?"

"Or ear?" asked Wingnut.

"That's enough!" said Grinner, gnashing his countless teeth. "We're not here to discuss the etymology of certain idioms that may or may not be applicable to our present situation!"

"Huh?" asked Wingnut.

"I mean, we're not here to talk," Grinner clarified. "We're here *for revenge.*"

"Exactly," said Adenoid Jack. "Revenge. It's like I said: We got *a nose to pick* with these guys."

"Or an ear," said Wingnut.

Grinner stomped his foot. *"Quit it!* Just get 'em already!"

On the roof of a building, with no way down and only slimy, defunct rocket boots on their feet, there was no escape. Even if there was somewhere to run, they couldn't, because Adenoid Jack's snot globs had hardened.

"Disgusting!" cried Leslie. "It's booger glue!"

A moment later, Digits was throwing a net over each of them.

"You know," said Grinner, smiling malevolently, "in the varied and multitudinous realms of creaturedom, we ghorks fall somewhere in between trolls and ogres." His grin widened. "But we're way worse than either of them."

"We are?" asked Wingnut.

Grinner nodded. "See, even in creaturedom, these are enlightened times. Those trolls and ogres? Naw, they gave up eating children a *long* time ago. But we ghorks, especially ones like me, if we get *reeeally* hungry . . ." He opened his mouth so wide it seemed like his whole head was hinged at the back of his neck. His breath smelled of sewage and sulfur and he had *teeth growing upon teeth*. There were rows of them, puncturing the soft flesh of his gullet all the way down into the darkness of his throat. "So the only real question," he said, "is which one of you do we eat first?"

"Ooh, ooh!" cried Wingnut. "The boy. They're salty! Save the girl for dessert."

"I've always preferred girls as an appetizer myself," said Iris.

Adenoid Jack flared his nostrils. "If you wanna do it right, you gotta break them *into pieces*. That's the only way to really bring out the scent."

"*Ugh!*" Grinner scoffed. "I swear, I'm surrounded by philistines. I'll tell you what we're gonna do. We're gonna drag 'em back to the lair and slather 'em in ketchup. That's how you do it in style!"

Digits clapped his huge hands. "Ketchup, yeah! We'll deep-fry 'em! Then we'll have *finger food*!"

Elliot couldn't believe what he was hearing. It was the worst coincidence he could possibly imagine! After so many years of lying in bed each morning, listening to his parents tell him he would soon be cooked and eaten, that was exactly what was going to happen!

To make the unthinkable prospect all the more terrifying, the ghorks' argument over how to properly roast (or braise, or poach, or curry) a child went on and on. It might have been a good opportunity for Leslie and Elliot to escape, but how could they? Making a run for it wasn't exactly a viable option when they were tangled up in nets and super-booger-glued to the roof of a building. Meanwhile, down below them, they could see that the ghorks had regained their advantage. All the creatures and staff of DENKi-3000 were prisoners once again.

If Elliot had felt merely hopeless before, now he felt right on the verge of despair. He thought about all the things he would never get to do, all the goals he had set for himself. To grow up and be an inventor like his uncle, for instance. To drive a car. To travel the world. To vote. He would have liked to have tried fishing. Just once. He certainly had the wardrobe for it. Now, however, none of those things would happen. It just didn't seem fair.

"Hey," he whispered to Leslie. "I guess this isn't going the way we planned, huh?"

"Not really, no." She smiled sadly at him. "But I'm still glad my mom moved us to Bickleburgh. I'm glad I met you, and your uncle, and everyone else too. I'm glad I got to find out all these weird creatures were real before . . ." She stole a quick glance at the quarreling ghorks. "Before *you-know-what*."

"We're eaten by ghorks?"

"Yeah."

"I was just thinking about that myself." Elliot paused. He wasn't quite sure how to say what he was thinking. "Anyway, I thought maybe . . . well, maybe we should kiss."

"*WHAT?!*"

The ghorks looked over at them.

"Pipe down," said Grinner. "We're still trying to decide how to cook you."

Leslie was looking at Elliot as if he was crazy (and Elliot was inclined to believe her).

"Trust me," he said, "it's not like 'kissing a girl' is at the top of my list of things to do before I die. In fact, I'm pretty sure it never made the list. But since it looks like I might never get to do the things that *are* on the list, and since you're a girl and you're right here, I just thought we might try it."

Leslie thought about this for a moment. "Well, since we're gonna get eaten by ghorks anyway . . ."

They leaned closer together, but it was difficult for them to reach each other without moving their feet. Their lips, puckering awkwardly through the mesh of the net, were just about to touch when they heard something. It sounded like thunder, but the sky was completely clear.

"You guys hear something?" Wingnut asked the other ghorks.

"What *is* that?" asked Digits, looking up at the empty sky.

"Over there, look!" Iris pointed to the buildings of Bickleburgh. A brownish-gray cloud of dust was rumbling through the streets. The crowd at the gates heard it too. They parted just in time to avoid being trampled because that was when—

BAROOOOOOOOOOOOOOO!!!

A deep baritone trumpeting sound split the air as an army of bombastadons riding high on the backs of countless arachnimammoths came galloping through the gates of DENKi-3000.

Leading the charge (of course) was Colonel-Admiral Reginald T. Pusslegut, and for the people of Bickleburgh, it was a deeply surprisingly turn of events. For the creatures of the Creature Department, however, the most astonishing thing of all was the fact that seated triumphantly on Reggie's magnificent epaulettes was a pair of hobmongrels!

CHAPTER 31

In which Elliot's parents have a change of heart,
Leslie's mother proves she's been paying attention,
and Leslie can't believe what she smells

With a battalion of bombastadons on your side, it's difficult to lose in a fight, but the sheer number of ghorks did a good job of bucking the trend. Their ropes and nets were surprisingly handy against the arachnimammoths, whose many appendages (trunks, tusks, and eight thunderous legs) made for easy targets. Plus, the great woolly creatures were slower in the summer heat of Bickleburgh, far from the cold of their native land.

The Quazicom security bots were equally adept (though much more polite) in their fight alongside the ghorks. Bursts of blue light dazzled and flared across the courtyard. The flashes froze the scene into moments of bizarre, split-second tableaus: strange creatures locked in strange battles, their strange faces twisted into strange expressions (needless to say, it was all quite strange).

In the end, however, even struggling together, the ghorks and the Quazicom robots were no match for the Creature Department—not when supported by Her Royal Majesty's

Antarctic Brigadiers. Most of all, the disorganized ghorks were hopeless against the tactical shrewdness of Colonel-Admiral Reginald T. Pusslegut, who conducted his forces with all the pluck and daring of a true hero.

Eventually, the ghorks were repelled, hounded back into the tunnels whence they came. A phalanx of mounted bombastadons pursued them deep under the ground, where the arachnimammoths hefted huge boulders over the entrance to their lair, sealing them inside.

On the surface, the robots were reduced to cracked moldings and disembodied circuit boards. Their shattered remains hissed with static, occasionally belching up distorted (but polite) phrases like, "AH-FuLL-eEEeee sOR-EEEeeeeee . . ."

The bombastadons returned to the surface, where Reggie's puffy, pontifical manner suddenly seemed entirely appropriate as he rode a snuffling, eight-legged, elephantine steed. The creatures even cheered when at last he swung gallantly down to the ground.

The first thing he did was wander over to the topiary rocket ship. The professor lay beneath it in the shade, still zonked out from his second zapping of the day. Reggie stooped to examine the poor man's feet.

"Just as I suspected. Super-galoshes."

Next, he strode up to Gügor and the others. "My dear friends," he said, shaking their hands enthusiastically. "That chair you designed is *extraordinary*! I've never slept better in all my life! There is that rather unfortunate teleportation problem, of course, but I'm sure we can iron that out."

Now that the gates were smashed, Bickleburgh's citizens wandered, utterly gobsmacked, into the courtyard. They ogled the creatures with a mixture of curiosity and trepidation. A similar response was elicited from DENKi-3000's human employees, who had had no idea the creatures existed.

When they saw Elliot and Leslie, however, freshly rescued from the roof of the North Tower and obviously friends of these peculiar beings, they relaxed. The manager of DENKi-3000's Human (and only human!) Resources Department was heard to say, "I always knew there was something fishy about this place, but I never would've guessed it was *this* fishy!"

"You talkin' about me?" asked Patti Mudmeyer, a bit miffed.

"I'm talking about the whole lot of you," the manager replied.

"Get over it," Harrumphrey harrumphed. "We're an odd bunch. That's creaturedom for you."

Sir William (after being untangled from his net) predicted that a workable model of the rocket boots would easily fend off the Quazicom takeover. "But only," he said, looking to the shareholders, "if all of you vote against it."

"You can count on it," said the shareholder spokesman, dusting off the sleeves of his suit. "We want nothing to do with Quazicom and that creepy chief of theirs. Anyway, hiring ogres—or whatever those things were—"

"Ghorks," said the professor.

"Yes, well, hiring them to kidnap an entire company is *definitely* a violation of corporate responsibility guidelines."

"Elliot! Elliot, what's going on?! Look at this mess!" It was Elliot's mother. His parents were pushing through the crowd.

"Where's your uncle Archie?" asked his father sternly. "I'd like to give that man a piece of my mind."

Elliot pointed to the professor's feet, jutting out from under the topiary rocket ship.

"Oh, I see," said Elliot's father, a little disappointed. "What are *those shoes* he's wearing?"

"Not shoes," said Elliot. "*Rocket boots.*"

"Of course they are," said Elliot's mother, shaking her head. "Sounds quite dangerous to me."

"What is *going on* here?" asked his father. He leaned down to his son. "And what are all these . . . these . . ."

"Creatures," said Elliot.

His mother frowned. "That's what I thought they were. I hope you realize that if you insist on fraternizing with creatures like this, they'll never let you into Foodie School. They'll assume you're contaminated!"

"Actually," said Leslie, stepping forward in Elliot's defense, "these creatures have impeccable taste in food."

"They do?" Elliot's parents didn't look convinced.

"Besides," said Sir William. He placed two hands protectively on Elliot's shoulders. "If Elliot wishes, I'd say the boy has a bright future here at DENKi-3000."

"Really?" asked Elliot.

"If your parents see fit to permit it."

Elliot's mother and father, however, had nothing to say on

the subject. They were too busy glowering at the creatures, at the wreckage of the courtyard, at the unconscious form of Elliot's uncle.

"And speaking of a bright future at DENKi-3000 . . ." Sir William hobbled over to the big red cycloptosaurus in the midst of the creatures. "I could really use an experienced corporate creature with insider knowledge of Quazicom."

"Really?" asked Charlton.

"I think it's time we got you creatures involved in other areas of the company, and besides—I'm definitely going to need a new VP."

"Hey!" cried Monica Burkenkrantz. She lay on the ground beside Elliot's uncle because no one had bothered to untangle her. "Does this mean I'm fired?"

"If you were in my shoes," asked Sir William, "what would you do?"

Monica sighed. "I'd fire me."

"Precisely."

Monica looked ready to complain, but she was interrupted by a loud *BANG!* It was the sound of a car backfiring. A rusty red Volkswagen bounced erratically into the courtyard and Leslie's mother leapt out, still dressed in her black-and-white uniform.

"Leslie! What's going on?! Someone told me the whole city was under attack from—" She stopped suddenly because she saw she was standing in the midst of a bunch of: *"CREATURES!"*

"Don't worry," said Leslie. "These are the nice ones."

"Are you sure?"

"They're my new friends."

"These things?!"

"And the one behind your head."

Leslie's mother spun around and came face-to-face with Jean-Remy Chevalier.

"*Enchanté, madam.*" He floated down to the woman and, just as he had done when he first met Leslie, kissed the tip of her finger. "What a pleasure to meet ze mother of so remarkable a child."

Leslie's mother, however, was immune to Jean-Remy's charm. She pulled her hand away, turning back to her daughter. "Just because your friend is a handsome little man with wings, it doesn't mean he can sweet-talk me into forgetting you've been hanging around with . . . with . . ."

"*Creatures,*" said Leslie. She took a deep breath. "I guess this means you wanna move somewhere new, huh?"

"Why would you think that?"

"'Cuz that's what you *always* wanna do."

Leslie's mother nodded. "I'm sorry. It's just my—"

"*Wanderlust.* I know. It's powerful stuff."

"But you don't have to worry," said her mother. "In spite of all this . . ." She scanned her eyes across the courtyard. "I've decided to stick it out."

"You have?"

"Yep. We're staying in Bickleburgh."

"*Seriously?*"

Leslie's mother nodded again. "I decided that maybe you're right. Maybe the reason nothing seems to work out the way I plan is because I never give it enough time. But there's also another reason we're gonna stay."

"What is it?"

"Your grandfather. He had to go away for a while and he wants me to take over the restaurant."

"He went away? He didn't even say goodbye."

"Whatever it was, it sounded quite urgent. He left in a terrible rush."

"But wait, how're you gonna run the restaurant? Do you know anything about cooking?"

"Sure I do!" Leslie's mother put her hands on her hips. "Believe it or not, I learned a thing or two from Famous Freddy. In fact, I'll bet my pork dumplings are every bit as good as his."

At the mention of pork dumplings, all the creatures crowded around them.

"Now, them's fightin' words," said Patti. "Y'all really think your cooking's as good as Freddy's?'

"Perhaps," said Jean-Remy. "But you should really let us be ze judges of zat."

Elliot's parents couldn't help overhearing.

"This is that restaurant Elliot's been telling us about, isn't it?" asked his father.

Elliot's mother seemed impressed by the number of creatures clamoring (and slobbering) to eat at this odd little place. She looked at her husband. "What do you think, honey? Shall we give it a try?"

Leslie was worried. "Mom, are you sure you know what you're doing?"

"Let's all go down to the restaurant," she answered confidently. "I'll show you what I know!"

As she said this, Professor von Doppler finally awoke. He sat bolt upright and shouted, "It's up to us to save the—oh. I missed it again, didn't I?"

"Kind of," said Elliot. "But look on the bright side. You're just in time for Famous Freddy's."

They all went together—creatures, executives, shareholders,

inventors, regimental bombastadons, and the regular people of Bickleburgh—all marching through the streets to Famous Freddy's Dim Sum Emporium. The closer they came to the restaurant, the larger the crowd grew. Word was spreading that a great secret, once hidden at the center of the city, had finally been revealed: *Creatures were real*, and they were right here in Bickleburgh!

By the time they reached the restaurant, the crowd was so big it spilled out into the street. It was impossible for Leslie's mother to do all the work by herself, so she enlisted help.

The kitchen became a kind of mini–Creature Department, everyone helping out with preparing the food.

"Thank you for including me," said Charlton, his bulky red form suddenly hovering over the counter where Elliot and Leslie were folding pastries. "I've spent much of my life in one disguise or another." He looked around the kitchen, crowded with every manner of outlandish creature. "But for the first time, I feel like I belong."

"You do," Leslie told him.

"So I was thinking . . ." Charlton flipped open his satchel. As he did so, the scroll he had shown the professor earlier tumbled to the floor.

"What's this?" asked Harrumphrey. His tail snaked around the scroll and lifted it to his face. "Some kind of blueprint?"

"Oh!" said Charlton, suddenly flustered. "N-no, it's nothing!" He snatched it away from Harrumphrey and hastily tore it up.

Harrumphrey squinted up at him suspiciously.

"It wasn't a very good idea," said Charlton. "Just garbage, really! And so is this." He took his last bottle of Knoo-Yoo-Juice out of his satchel and turned back to Leslie. "As I was saying, I won't be needing this anymore. You can pour it straight down the sink."

Leslie took the bottle from him, but when she got to the sink and unscrewed the lid, she froze.

"What is it?" asked Elliot, noticing something was wrong.

"It's the smell."

"Of the Knoo-Yoo-Juice?" Elliot stopped folding dumplings and joined Leslie at the sink. "What does it smell like?"

Leslie didn't know what to say. She sniffed once more from the bottle. It was a chemical sent, sharp and acidic, but beneath that was something she recognized: the smell of honey and vinegar, overripe fruit, and just a hint of Worcestershire sauce. "It smells like my grandfather's cooking wine."

"Then it's a good thing he never cooked with it," said her mother, glancing at the medicine in the bottle.

"No," said Leslie, thoroughly bewildered. "He only ever . . . *drank it*." She shook her head. "It can't be."

"Are you really sure?" asked Elliot.

"There's one way to find out." She led Elliot to the large cupboard where Famous Freddy kept his countless bottles of cooking wine. "He keeps it all in—oh!" The cupboard was empty.

Leslie's mother laughed. "Did you really think he'd leave behind his precious cooking wine? He packed it all up and took it with him."

"It's probably just a coincidence," said Elliot.

"It must be," said Leslie, nodding emphatically to herself. "It's the only explanation. Because if Famous Freddy's cooking wine is the same as what's in this bottle, it would mean my very own grandfather . . ."

"*Is a creature,*" Elliot whispered.

"No," said Leslie. "That's impossible." She hurried to the sink and poured every drop of the Knoo-Yoo-Juice down the drain, making sure to rinse the bottle when she was done.

Elliot followed her back to the table. "What if it's not?" he asked.

Leslie shook her head. "It *is* impossible. I was just being silly."

Before Elliot could ask any more questions, the scent of the first steamed dumplings filled the room. It was a smell so rich and delicious it instantly reminded them that a celebration was at hand.

They soon discovered Leslie's mother really *had* learned something from Famous Freddy.

Even Elliot's parents were impressed.

"Amazing!" cried his father.

"This establishment," said Elliot's mother, "might get the most glowing review we've ever written!"

"Mom!" Leslie gave her mother an enormous hug. "I'm so proud of you!"

"This calls for a toast," said Sir William, leading everyone in raising a glass. "To wonderful food, to Professor Archimedes von Doppler and his Creature Department, to the wonder of invention and the rigors of science, and *especially* to two children who saved the day!"

Everyone cheered. Leslie put on one of her favorite Boris Minor and the Karloffs albums and they all danced to the bounding rhythm of "Monster Gnash": Leslie, Elliot, Professor von Doppler, Gügor, Harrumphrey, Patti Mudmeyer, Colonel-Admiral Reginald T. Pusslegut, Jean-Remy Chevalier, Charlton the cycloptosaurus, and even the two hobmongrels, Bildorf and

Pib. Everyone joined in, and the celebration went late into the night.

Yet it wasn't merely the deliciousness of the food, the rhythm of the music, or the crowds of friendly faces that made the night special. It was something else. It was something intangible, something like a strange otherworldly substance you might only find hidden in the Abstractory. It was *a feeling*.

Not just one feeling, but many. Neither Elliot nor Leslie could describe them all, but there was certainly one that stood out, stronger than all the rest: the feeling of friendship. For the very first time they both felt that they had found a true friend.

They smiled at each other. In fact, everyone was smiling. That was because of another feeling that filled the room: the feeling of change. It was the sense that from that moment forward, the odd little city of Bickleburgh was going to be very, *very* different.

Acknowledgments

Without the support of the following people, *The Creature Department* would have never emerged from its secret underground cave. Enormous thanks to my very savvy agent, Jackie Kaiser, to whom I owe so much; to my editor, Rebecca Kilman, whose kindness and insight made the manuscript eminently better; to Nick Hooker at Framestore New York and Zack Lydon, whose eye-popping artwork was an inspiration to me as I wrote; to Simon Whalley, who generously peeled back the curtain at Framestore London; and to the incredible Ben Schrank, who got this odd ball rolling in the first place.

Finally, my deepest thanks to my wife, without whom nothing would happen—especially this book. Your calmness, patience, and support are the essences that power me.